UNDONE

REBECCA SHEA

DEDICATION

Ava,
Follow your dreams and never take *no* for an answer.

EPILOGUE

LANDON

Sifting through the clothes that are strewn about my darkened bedroom, I find my boxer briefs and slide them on. Collecting her bra, panties, shorts, and shirt, I reflect that this is never the fun part of my evening, yet I feel no guilt in asking her to leave. She fell asleep shortly after I fucked her senseless and, for the last hour, I've been contemplating how long I should let her sleep before I kick her out.

Sidling up to the edge of the bed, I nudge her shoulder gently. "Hey, Maria." I keep nudging her until she shifts slightly. "Time to go." I drop the pile of her clothes on top of her. Giving her some privacy to get dressed, I walk to the bathroom connected to my master suite and close the door behind me.

I turn on the cold water, lean down, and splash my face with it. Grabbing the hand towel from the hanging towel rack, I dry my face and look at the man staring back at me in the mirror. I hear her moving around my room, so I toss my towel onto my bathroom counter and open the bathroom door. The light from the bathroom illuminates the dark bedroom. She is sitting on the

1

end of my bed, leaning down to fasten the straps on her sandals.

Leaning against the doorframe while she finishes up and collects her purse, I can't help but feel nothing for her. This is not unusual for me; I don't connect emotionally with most women. I let a woman "in" once—to a place in my heart I really didn't know existed, but I let her go, knowing she needed something I could never be. I don't do romance, I don't do relationships, and I definitely don't do love.

"Ah, thanks for coming by," I offer as I walk towards my bedroom door to usher her out of my house and out of my life. I never sleep with the same woman twice; it complicates things. Walking her down the hallway and through the dark, yet modern living room, I open the front door for her, holding it open so she can leave.

Planting herself in front of me, she leans up to kiss me, but I turn my head and successfully dodge her lips—I rarely kiss women either, just not something I like to do unless I care about them, and there's only been one I've cared enough about to kiss.

"Bye, Maria." I nudge her towards the open door.

"Maria?" She laughs a bitter laugh. "It's Mariana, asshole." Just as she says that, a hand connects with my face. I deserved it; I usually do.

"Mariana… Maria, same thing," I say, closing the door behind her. For a brief moment, a flash of guilt washes through me before it all but vanishes and I feel nothing—again.

CHAPTER 1

LANDON

"So this one slapped you too?" he bellows. Matt Kennedy is my partner; we ride patrol together for the Wilmington, North Carolina Police Department and have for the last four years. In a sense, Matt is family. He is my "brother", my partner, but he is also my closest friend. There are very few people that know the *real* me—Matt is one of them.

"Yeah, you know they tend to get a little pissy when I don't want to snuggle and I ask them to leave," I snicker.

"What were you thinking, bringing her to your house?"

"I wasn't," I admit.

"Dude, when she gets all *Fatal Attraction* on your ass, I'll be the first one to remind you that you brought *her* to your house."

Sighing in frustration, I rake my hands over my face. "Yeah, yeah. As always, thanks for your support, man."

Shaking his head at me, he continues to laugh quietly to himself. Matty, as I call him, is easily entertained. He claims to enjoy living vicariously through my fucked up life. Matt grew up just outside Wilmington, North Carolina, in the seemingly perfect family—mom, dad, and a younger brother. I love listening to stories of his perfect life, how his dad would take him and his brother fishing, or coach their little league teams, and how his mom made dinner every night. My life was a far cry from little league and home-cooked meals, so I revel in his stories, as much as he revels in the stories of my non-parental upbringing and currently non-committal sex life.

Pulling into the drive-thru at the Starbucks that we frequent every shift, Matt places our order. Working the swing shift, we never know what to expect, but we are *always* busy, so fueling up on caffeine is always our first line of business. Handing me my *venti* dark roast—black, I laugh and give Matt hell for drinking an iced Frappuccino.

"You always going to drink those pussy drinks?" He has a temper and if I push him just far enough, I can see the vein in his neck start to bulge. It's how I can tell just how much I've pissed him off.

"Fuck off," he fires back, pulling out of the drive-thru. "I'll stop drinking pussy drinks when you finally settle on one pussy instead of a different one every other night." I can't help but laugh.

"Looks like you'll be drinking pussy drinks for the rest of your life, Matty." He sets his Frappuccino in the cup holder and flips me off.

Spending the last thirty minutes of our shift filling out paperwork in the empty parking lot of a strip mall isn't my idea of "fun" for a Friday night, but at least it's been a fairly quiet evening. As we sign the last few papers, dispatch announces, "Unit 142, disturbance at 500 East Franklin."

"That's us," Matt announces, and responds to dispatch, "Code three, Unit 142 en route from 800 Main Street." Tossing his cell phone into the center console, he flips on the lights and siren on our cruiser. Pulling up to the small brick building with "Mac's Bar" illuminated on the side, Matt shuts off the siren and lights, and double parks behind two pick-up trucks. Matt radios our arrival while I take in the surroundings as I always do. I notice the parking lot is quiet and there doesn't seem to be any disturbance outside of the building.

Matt enters the bar first through the main door, and I follow closely behind. The bar is packed and, from the front entrance, I don't see any signs of a disturbance. Matt walks up to the bar, gaining the attention of an older gentleman who is filling mugs of draft beer.

I stay near the entrance, monitoring the crowd. This place is standing room only with every pub table, booth, and barstool taken. A band is playing country music on a small stage in the far corner of the bar, with a parquet wooden dance floor full of people, young and old, dancing to the sounds of the live music. I maintain my position at the front entrance and continuously scan the crowd, looking for any signs of a disturbance, when I see her. Dark wavy hair lies just past her shoulders and she's wearing a tight pair of blue jeans and a black tank top.

Carrying two pitchers of beer in each hand, she maneuvers through the crowd with ease. Smiling and greeting each person she passes, she owns the room. I follow her every move, watching her weave through the sea of bodies from table to table and booth to booth. The crowded bar is hot and stuffy, and I can see a small sheen of sweat across her chest as she sets a pitcher of beer on the table directly in front of me.

"Here you go, boys." She smiles at the four older men sitting at the high-top table. "Sorry it took so long; it's crazy in here tonight." She picks up some empty beer bottles that had been discarded in the center of the table.

"Thanks, darlin'." One of the men hands her a crisp twenty-dollar bill. Shoving the bill in her back pocket, she picks up two more empty bottles and starts toward the bar.

"Reagan!" the older man hollers, stopping her as she turns back to look at him. "It's good to have you back! Keep the change, darlin'." She smiles and nods at him as she begins weaving through the crowd. Matt makes his way back to the front entrance and stands next to me, scanning the crowd.

"Something catch your eye?" He smirks as he follows my eyes, which are fixed on the dark-haired beauty.

"When doesn't someone catch my eye?" I smile as I watch "Reagan."

"Good point. Clearly, there is nothing going on here. Let's go; we have to clear this call and finish up this damn paperwork."

I nod and Matt heads out the door behind me. I stay put, leaning against the doorframe, watching Reagan for a bit longer. An older man at the bar hops off his barstool and takes her hand, spinning her around to the music. She throws her head back and laughs as he pulls her to him, giving her a quick hug before releasing her. Something inside me stirs, a hunger from within as I watch her smiling, laughing, and talking. There is something about her, something different from most of the women I'm attracted to. I'm intrigued.

"Coming, bro?" Matt hollers from outside the door.

"Yeah, I'm coming," I yell over my shoulder to him as I turn to leave. Stepping out into the cool night air, I slide into the passenger seat and glance at Matt, who has already started working on the paperwork.

"I think we should swing by here tomorrow night for a couple of beers," I toss out to see what Matt will say. He fights a smile, but continues filling out paperwork, never stopping to acknowledge what I've said. I keep my eyes fixed on the entrance to the bar, wondering as people filter in and out if maybe I'll catch one last sight of her.

Tossing his paperwork between the front seats, Matt starts the car and drives slowly through the parking lot.

"Never took you for the country music kind of guy." His tone is snarky and a giant smile is spread across his face.

"As of tonight, I fucking love country music." I laugh.

"All right, we'll come back tomorrow night. Just promise me something." Matt's tone is serious.

"I don't make promises, you know that."

Matt sighs and thinks about what he's going to say. "Okay then, just try something for me, will ya?"

"I'll try lots of them for ya, but I prefer brunettes." I glance sideways and see him grimace.

"Fuck, Landon. Be serious for a just a goddamn minute, please." He turns his head and fixes his eyes on me.

"Sure, whatever," I respond coldly. I know I'm about to get one of Matt's famous lectures on how unhealthy my casual sex life is, and that a fulfilling relationship is what I need. But damn if the fucker doesn't love my stories. I know he does.

"Just..." He pauses, again choosing his words wisely. "Just, I've seen this look on your face before. It's different." He pauses. "Don't try to sleep with her on the first night. Or hell, maybe even the second night..."

I actually bust out laughing. "Okay, that's pushing it."

"Trust me."

"You know there are only a handful of people I trust, and you're one of those people. I'll try my best." The drive back to the station is quiet as I consider his suggestion.

Unlocking the door, I step inside the quiet house. The living room light is on and I can see my sister Lindsay sitting on the couch with her back toward me.

"Hey, Linds," I announce, letting her know I'm home. It's almost one in the morning and honestly, I'm surprised to see her here on a Friday night. Tossing my keys on the kitchen counter, I kick off my shoes and step into the living room.

"Hey, Linds," I say again. Again, she doesn't reply. I finally notice the ear buds stuck in her ears. She's leaning forward with her feet propped on the coffee table and she's painting her toenails. I sneak up behind her and pull the ear bud out of her right ear just as I yell, "boo!" She jumps and I notice she smears nail polish all over her big toe.

"Goddammit, do you always have to be a dick?" I can't help but laugh at her reaction.

"What are you doing home? I thought you'd be out with your new boyfriend," I say sarcastically.

"He's not my boyfriend," she says, wiping the dark polish off the side of her toe. "Plus, I kind of wanted to just lay low tonight." I throw myself down on the couch next to her and stretch my legs out onto the coffee table as well.

"Take off your socks. I'll paint your nails 'Midnight in Moscow' to match mine." She laughs and lifts her toes, wiggling them in my face.

"Fuck off, Lindsay." I push her leg away, causing her to laugh even harder. We are so much alike, it's comical.

"You totally deserve it after scaring me like that. I was just about to watch a movie. Want to join me? I have *Pitch Perfect*. It's your favorite," she says sarcastically and laughs again. She's really busting my balls tonight.

"How about *Fight Club*?"

"I hate blood and hitting, plus, you love Fat Amy," she laughs, and I roll my eyes.

Knowing that we will never agree on a movie, I let Lindsay have her way. "*Pitch Perfect* it is, but if you tell anyone I watched this movie, you're going to have to move out," I joke with her, jumping up to go make some popcorn.

"Yes," Lindsay says with a little fist pump. She starts sorting through the pile of DVDs on the coffee table, until she finds the one she's looking for as I bring back a large bowl of popcorn. I made sure to sprinkle Milk Duds and Mike and Ikes in the popcorn, just like Lindsay used to love when she was little. I'm actually glad she's home tonight. It always takes me a few hours to unwind after work, and normally I do it with a woman, a stranger—but movies with my sister is a nice change.

I set the bowl of popcorn down on the couch between us and she reaches for a handful. Pulling out a half melted Milk Dud, she mutes the TV and turns her body towards me. "You always did this for me when we were little." She swallows hard. Her voice falters and her face loses color as she brings up painful memories. We've gone for years dancing around the topic of our shitty and chaotic childhood, and I'm really hoping to avoid this conversation tonight.

"You always liked candy in your popcorn," I remind her.

"It was the only way you could calm me down after..."

"Linds, let it go," I cut her off. "I didn't mean to bring up bad memories by tossing some candy into your popcorn bowl, okay? I just knew you liked it. That's all this was." I realize I'm gripping the bowl rather aggressively. She nods her head, and turns back to the TV. Before she unmutes the movie, she turns to me one last time.

"Lan, you know I would have done anything to help you, right?"

"Linds," I warn her again.

"Thank you for always protecting me," she whispers. I can still see the fear in her eyes, just like when we were young.

"I would do it all over again if I needed to. Plus, I kind of like you, kiddo." I reach out and tousle her hair.

She smiles and turns back to the TV, unmuting it. My stomach drops in remembrance of the shit we went through as kids. I'm finding it hard to concentrate on the movie, so I lay my head back on the cushion and try to push the bad memories out. The visions of those days and nights so clear, so ingrained in my memory, it's as if it happened last week. I feel the sting on my skin from the belt, and I still see the red marks and bruises from his fists. There are times that I believe I can actually still feel the pain he inflicted to this day.

I feel my heart rate increase as those buried memories resurface. Trying to shake them from my thoughts, I close my eyes and, with three deep breaths, I focus on the vision of Reagan floating around that little bar tonight. I think about her bright smile and the sway of her hips. I catch myself smiling when I think about what she'll feel like lying beneath me. She *will* be lying beneath me.

CHAPTER 2

LANDON

Knock, knock.

"Aca-Landon, are you up?" I hear her giggle as my door squeaks open.

"Are you going to aca-everything for the next fucking week, Linds? Because I'm not sure I can handle it." I groan and roll over onto my back. I fling my arm over my eyes to block out the bright morning sun that is making its way through the French patio doors in my room. Lindsay is standing in my doorway, wearing a bikini top and a pair of denim shorts. I glance at the clock on my nightstand and notice it's almost eleven in the morning.

"You know I only do it to annoy you," she says, taking a few steps inside my room.

"What do you want, Linds? I was trying to sleep."

"I've been waiting for you to get up. I made breakfast this morning," she announces with a giant smile on her face.

"My baby sister who can't make macaroni and cheese made breakfast? What did you do, pour Frosted Flakes into a bowl?" I muster up a hoarse laugh.

"Don't be an asshole," she snaps at me and tosses a throw pillow at me. "I actually made pancakes." She smiles proudly. "Now get your sorry ass out of bed. I'm going to go float in the pool and read some smut." With a tight sarcastic smile, she quickly turns and leaves my room. I shake my head slightly and laugh at her, pushing myself up and out of bed.

I change into a pair of black board shorts and decide that sitting by the pool sounds like a great way to spend the morning. Making my way to the kitchen, I notice the plate of pancakes sitting on the kitchen island, next to a bowl of chopped fresh fruit and a bottle of syrup. After I spoon some fresh berries on top of the pancakes, I cover all of it with maple syrup. Hesitantly, I take a bite, and find that they actually taste decent. Lindsay's cooking has damn near killed me before, so I always approach anything she cooks with caution.

Opening the door that leads from the kitchen to the back patio, I find my sister floating on an oversized raft in the middle of the large pool, her face stuck in a book.

"They're good," I announce as I sit down on one of the poolside lounge chairs that line one entire side of the pool.

"Really? You like them?"

"Yeah, I actually do." I shove another forkful of pancakes in my mouth and set the plate on the small side table that sits next to the lounger. Lowering the back of the chair, I lie down and stretch out, feeling the warm sun sting my unprotected skin. It's humid this time of year, and the moist North Carolina air hangs heavily around the lush backyard.

I can feel the sweat starting to bead across my forehead and along my hairline. Most people hate the humidity, but I love it. I inhale deeply and feel the warm air burn my lungs. With my arms raised and behind my head, I close my eyes and let the sun seep through me. I find the silence and the warmth relaxing, and feel myself nodding off to sleep. The spray of ice-cold water startles me and causes me to jump.

"Godammit, Lindsay," I bark at her. She giggles and cups her hand, splashing me again with water. I lunge from my lounger and dive in, tipping the raft and dumping her into the pool. She screams as she sinks into the icy water.

She emerges laughing as she brushes her long blonde hair off of her face. "You deserved that," I say, pushing the oversized raft out of the pool. Swimming to the edge, I lean against the pool's cool tiles, tipping my head back with my face directed toward the sun.

It's quiet again, but I can feel the water shift slightly as Lindsay swims closer to me. She mimics my position on my left side and sighs loudly as I peek at her through one eye. I can tell there is something on her mind because she always scrunches her nose when she's thinking deeply.

"What'cha thinking about?"

"Lots of things." She sighs deeply again.

"Like?"

"Things you don't like to talk about."

I take a deep breath and lower myself entirely into the cool, crisp water. Fully submerged, I count to fifteen slowly, feeling the burn start building in my lungs around the number ten. I burst through the surface and inhale sharply. As I wipe the water from my face, I see Lindsay standing and watching me.

"Let's talk," I offer. I know I'm going to fucking regret this, but if it's what she needs to do, I'll try—for her.

With a small, sad half-smile, Lindsay pushes herself away from the wall and walks to the large sun shelf in the pool. She sits down on it and runs her hands through the water in front of her. I walk over and stand in front of her.

"Did you ever tell anyone about what Dad did to you?" she asks quietly, and I know what she's referring to.

"No."

"Why?"

"Because, Lindsay, it was different times then. No one would have done anything because of who *he* was."

I sigh; I know she still struggles with this shit. I've fucking let it go—at least I think I have, until she wants to talk about it and I get angry all over again. "Lindsay, I know you loved him, but he was an asshole. Everything that was ever fucked up in our lives was because of him."

"Landon," she tries to stop me.

"Don't. Don't defend him. He didn't touch you because I wouldn't fucking let him. I would have killed him. Even at eight years old, I would have killed him before I let him lay a hand on you. The night that Mom left was just the beginning of our hell, so please let's try to find hints of good memories where there are none."

"I'm sorry," she whispers. I meet her eyes and see they're stained pink. "I'm so sorry you had to take care of me."

I take a few steps in the water to where she sits cross-legged now on the sun shelf. I rest both of my hands on her shoulders.

"Don't ever be sorry for that. I'd do it all over again, a hundred times if I had to. You are all I have, Lindsay. We are all each other has." She nods her head and a tear rolls down her face.

"You know I remember that night, right?"

I inhale sharply, hoping it's not the night that is burned into my memory, a recurring nightmare that haunts me to this day.

She was only four years old, and we've never discussed this night in particular. Before I can stop her, she starts sharing her memories with her voice shaking and her hands trembling in her lap.

"I remember you getting a bowl of water and that little scrub brush that Mom kept under the kitchen sink." I watch Lindsay twist and pull at her fingers as she retells the nightmare of that night—detail for detail. "You scrubbed down the wall and the wood floor with that little brush and cleaned up all the blood." She says it so matter-of-factly. I'm numb, listening to her revisit the worst night of my life. "I remember you being worried about the mess, and him coming home to see it." She pauses. "And I remember her throwing clothes into a suitcase while you scrubbed and scrubbed. You didn't even know she was packing. I stood in the corner of the bedroom, watching her pack up her belongings while you were worried about cleaning up her blood."

I nod my head at her recollection of that night. She remembers the details just like I do.

"You stood in the corner in your purple nightgown, holding your teddy bear. I remember looking up from scrubbing the floor and you were huddled in the corner, watching me. I hated that you had to see... to watch..."

"I remember her leaving," she whispers, cutting me off. "She didn't even say goodbye to us. She stood next to the bed with her suitcase in her hands and her last words to us were, 'Get that cleaned up before your father gets back,' and she walked out of that room and never looked back, like we were nothing to her."

She remembers it exactly as it was, every last fucking detail. I hadn't realized she remembered so much, being as young as she was.

"That's exactly how it happened, Linds. You remember everything I do," I confirm her memories.

"Did she ever call, write, try to contact us?" she asks, her voice breaking.

"No." My tone is cold, harsh... bitter.

"Do you ever think about her? Or wonder where she's at? Or have you ever thought about looking for her?"

"No!" It's a definitive answer. "She left us to fend for ourselves with an out-of-control, abusive, alcoholic father. We were eight and four years old, Lindsay. What kind of mother does that? Leaves her kids with an animal like that? She left and never came back for us."

"Do you think she had to?"

"Had to? Had to leave her kids? No. Who the fuck leaves their kids in that situation with that kind of person? She didn't even say goodbye to us. She never apologized to us as she was packing her suitcase; there was no remorse when she walked out on us, Lindsay. She didn't say 'I love you,' as she floated out the door and left us with him. She told me to fucking clean up the blood on the floor and walked out. Walked the fuck out of our lives and never looked back."

I realize both of my fists are clenched and I can feel the anger, the hatred simmering just below the surface. I lean my head back, aiming my face to the sky as I let the sun scorch my skin some more. Breathing deep, calming breaths, I push the memories down again, burying them.

"Landon, do you think this is why you can't commit to a woman? Do you hate women because of what Mom did?"

"Are you trying to psychoanalyze the situation?" I actually laugh at her suggestion.

"I don't know. You've built these walls around you, and you've only let one person even remotely close to those walls, then you let her go. Gave her up without a fight…"

"She didn't love me, Linds. You know that. We were both so fucking damaged that nothing good could have come of that."

"Do you really believe that?"

"Yes."

"You're more fucked up than I originally thought," she sighs.

"Jesus, thanks, Linds. Let's talk about you and your issues, should we?"

She glares at me with narrow eyes and I see her breathing catch slightly.

"I don't have issues."

I actually laugh at her response.

"Sure, Linds. You cling to men, like I push women away. You fall in love with anyone that will give you the time of day."

"Not true," she scowls.

"True. Where should we start? Jeff? Brandon? Cam? Those are just three off the top of my head."

"So are we comparing notes now?" she fires at me. "You've been with more women in one month than I've been with men in my entire life."

"Between you and Matt and your lectures…"

"Well, someone needs to get through to you before your dick falls off." She actually starts laughing, and so do I.

"My dick is not going to fall off, and can you not talk about my dick? It's weird. You're my sister."

"Yeah—whatever." She looks away, and I can see that I've upset her.

"Look, I'm sorry. I didn't mean to get you upset, okay? I

guess we each are fucked up in our own little way. There is nothing you could do that would make me not love you, Linds. Even when you cling to fucking douchebags."

"Jeez, thanks." She splashes me with water and I laugh. "I know talking about Mom and Dad is hard to talk about, but I have more questions that I need you to answer for me at another time, okay?" she asks me hesitantly.

"Sure, Linds," I say as I splash the cool chlorinated water on my face and shoulders. I walk over to the steps that lead out of the pool and step out onto the hot concrete. Grabbing a towel from the stack I keep sitting on the flagstone bar, I wrap it tightly around my waist.

"You going out with the boyfriend tonight?" I ask.

"I don't have a boyfriend, so no. For the first time in, well, almost ever, I don't have plans tonight." She smiles almost proudly.

"Matt and I are headed to Mac's Bar over on Franklin Street. You're welcome to join us if you want; it might be fun."

"Mac's, the country bar? I love that place. You sure you don't mind me tagging along?"

"Not at all."

"Wait, why are you and Matt going to a country bar?" She tilts her head and narrows her eyes at me. Her mouth curls into a sly little grin. "What's her name?"

"I have no idea what you're talking about." I shrug and continue to dry myself off.

"Bullshit."

"I like country music," I say with a laugh. I can't even keep a straight face when I say that.

"Okay, Blake Shelton." She shakes her head at me.

"Be ready by nine o'clock." I hang the towel on the towel

rack and follow the paved walkway to the French doors that lead to my room.

"This should be interesting," I hear Lindsay mumble from behind me. I can't help but smile, because she has no idea how interesting this night could get.

CHAPTER 3

LANDON

"You are not wearing that," I bark at Lindsay. "There's nothing there." I motion my hand up and down from her head to her feet.

"All the important parts are covered," she smirks. "Plus, it's modern country."

"What the fuck is 'modern country'?"

"This." She points to her outfit, which consists of an extra-small denim skirt that barely covers her ass, a cream-colored too tight tank top, and a pair of brown cowboy boots. Matt is sitting on the couch, watching us go back and forth.

"She looks nice. Leave her alone," he pipes in.

"She's not *your* little sister," I remind him.

"I'm not little anymore, Landon. You don't always have to look out for me," she says quietly, tugging at the hem of her skirt.

Sighing, I remind myself that she's damn near twenty-five years old, and she's right; I have to trust that she can take care of herself.

"You're right. I'm sorry. Just... I don't know, just... don't..."

"Landon," Matt cuts me off. "Let it go. Let's go have a good time." He smiles at Lindsay and motions toward the door for us to leave. Matt guides Lindsay out the door to his car as I lock up. Lindsay slides into the back seat and I ride shotgun.

It's quiet as we drive the few short miles to Mac's. Pulling into the parking lot, I notice there are fewer cars here tonight than last night. We park and I see a group of men standing outside the doors of the main entrance, smoking and laughing. The door is propped open and the sounds of the cover band are spilling into the parking lot. Lindsay is about five paces ahead of us, walking fast with almost a skip to her step.

"C'mon guys." She prods us to move faster.

"We're coming," Matt says, shaking his head at her.

Stepping inside the small bar, Lindsay leads us to a high-top table near the small wooden dance floor. As we settle in, a guy who looks to be around my age approaches us and sets down three coasters.

"Welcome to Mac's. I'm Sam. What can I get you all to drink?" he asks, smiling at Lindsay. He's a decent enough looking guy; he's built like a UFC fighter, all muscle, tall and lean, and I notice both of his arms are covered in full sleeve tattoos. Lindsay stares at Sam, caught up in all that is the enormous man standing in front of us.

"What do you have on tap?" Matt asks, interrupting the little love-fest going on between Lindsay and Sam.

"You name it, we got it," he replies, turning his attention back to Lindsay.

"We'll take a pitcher of Fat Tire, please," I say, noting the extra attention Sam is displaying towards Lindsay.

"Eww... bring the beer for *them*. I'll take a Grey Goose and cranberry," Lindsay says with a giant smile.

"You got it," he responds, backing away slowly. Lindsay's eyes follow him all the way back to the bar.

"Good lord, I have never seen him here before," she says with a giant smile as she takes in the small country bar. It's not nearly as crowded in here tonight, yet there are large groups gathered in the far corner, surrounding two pool tables. "How did you two decide that this was where we were going out tonight?" She laughs and keeps her eyes firmly set on Sam, who is at the bar.

"We had a call here last night," Matt answers as I recall every detail from last night. "It looked like a cool little dive bar, so we thought we'd come back and check it out." He raises his eyebrows and shrugs hesitantly. I know this is not his element— hell, this isn't where I'd normally hang out—but I need to see *her*.

I scan the bar as nonchalantly as I possibly can. I take notice of Sam behind the bar, pouring our pitcher of beer, and the bartender from last night serving customers seated at the large wooden bar that runs almost the entire length of the wall. People are slowly filtering into the small space, filling up the once empty pub tables and booths.

Sam finds his way back to us, holding two frosted mugs and the pitcher of beer in one hand, and in the other he has Lindsay's Grey Goose and cranberry. Handing Lindsay her drink first, he then pours Matt and me our beer.

Lindsay takes a long sip of her drink and starts coughing. "Jesus, that's strong." She coughs again and begins laughing. Wiping the corners of her eyes, she looks at Sam.

"Are you trying to get me drunk?" She clears her throat and raises her eyebrows, waiting for him to respond. Matt chuckles and sips his beer. Sam has no idea what Lindsay is about to unleash on him.

"No." He laughs. "Mac made your drink." He nods toward the bar. "He's old and has a tendency to get a little carried away with his pour. Most people don't complain, though. It's like getting a double for the price of a single," he smirks.

"I'm not complaining," Lindsay fires back.

"It sure didn't sound like you were happy."

"A heads up would have been nice." She tilts her head and narrows her eyes at Sam.

"Look, I'll go make you a new drink..."

"No. I want this drink."

"Has anyone ever told you you're difficult?"

I actually choke on my beer and Matt starts laughing.

"You have no idea, man. No fucking idea," I say. Matt raises his glass to me and we toast Sam's revelation.

"Very funny, assholes." Lindsay takes another sip of her drink and Matt high fives Sam.

"Are you going to help us out, or socialize all night with the guests?" a female voice asks.

"Reagan," Sam announces, wrapping her into a giant bear hug and lifting her off the ground.

"Sammy! How in the world have you been?"

"Thank God you're here. I am not meant to wait tables." I notice Matt catch Lindsay's eye and nod his head slightly toward me. Lindsay's eyes brighten with the knowledge that Reagan is why we're here. Sticking her hand out to Reagan, Lindsay, the social butterfly that she is, introduces herself.

"Hi, I'm Lindsay. Your boy Sam here is either trying to get me drunk or kill me." Reagan laughs and pats Sam's back.

"Hey, hey... in my defense, I just told her about Mac."

"I'll make sure the next one isn't so bad." She winks at Lindsay. Our eyes meet, but I just sip my beer and look away, casually. *Play it cool.* Matt stands up immediately, and reaches over the tall pub table to shake her hand.

"I'm Matt; nice to meet you," he offers.

"Nice to meet you too," she responds, glancing at me again. "I don't think I've ever seen you in here before."

"We were here last night," Matt corrects her.

"You were?"

"Yep." Matt smiles and shrugs at her. "Thought we'd come back and check it out again." Sam has since quietly disappeared now that Reagan is here, and I notice Lindsay scanning the bar, looking for him.

"Landon." I nod and offer my hand to her. Hesitantly, she reaches out and takes it in hers.

"Reagan." She smiles.

"Nice to meet you, Reagan." I hold her hand firmly in place. It's soft, yet her grip is firm. She makes no effort to pull away and I make no effort to let her go.

"Likewise," she answers quietly with a tight swallow.

The band that has been taking a break since we walked in finally starts playing a song. Lindsay jumps up from the table and grabs Matt's hand, dragging him up.

"Dance with me!"

"I don't dance," he grumbles.

"It's easy. Just take my lead." She drags him to the dance floor. I finally release Reagan's hand and she raises it to her chest, then to her neck, holding it as if she was checking her pulse. I notice a flush spread across her neck and I can't help but grin as I finish off my beer. When I set down my mug, Reagan refills it from the pitcher.

"I should probably go check on the other tables before Sam scares everyone off." She smiles. "I'll be back in a bit to check on you."

"Sounds good," I say, trying to appear unaffected by her. But I am. There's something sweet and innocent about her. Physically, she reminds me a lot of Jess, the only girl I think I have ever cared for—but let go.

Reagan is tall with long, dark hair, just like Jess. She carries herself with a softness in her demeanor and a little insecurity, just like Jess. Although she appears to be a little older, most likely in her mid-twenties, that seems to be the only noticeable difference between the two women.

Sliding into their chairs Matt and Lindsay both stare at me, waiting for me to say something.

"What?" I ask.

"Is *she* why we're here?" Lindsay asks coyly. I smirk and take a drink of beer.

"Maybe."

"Jesus, Lan, I did a double take there for a second, she reminds me so much of…"

"Linds," Matt cuts her off. He's tired of my sorry ass still moping around because of Jess. It's been a year since she's moved back to California and she's now engaged. While I know I did the right thing in letting her go, I can't help but wonder what if I could have been the man she needed? What if I could have changed for her? But I know I couldn't, or wouldn't. I would have hurt her. I would have drawn her in and pushed her away, because that's what I do. But more importantly, I knew I never had her heart. It had always belonged to someone else.

"It's okay. I thought the same thing when I saw her last night. The similarities are uncanny."

"No shit," Lindsay snorts, taking a long pull of her drink through the skinny straw.

"Jesus, Lindsay, you're so fucking blunt," Matt says, finishing off the beer in his mug. I laugh because I'm used to it—it's Lindsay.

"So what, I've got a thing for tall, leggy brunettes." I shrug.

"You don't have to say that twice," Matt interjects. Lindsay smacks Matt's shoulder and shakes her head. "And this is why we find ourselves at Mac's bar on a Saturday night." Matt motions with his head toward Reagan, who is squeezing through the groups of people standing around the tables.

"She seems really nice," Lindsay says, finishing her drink. She shakes the tall empty glass and the ice cubes rattle together. "Well, would you look at that," she says sarcastically. "Looks like I need another drink." She cranes her neck, looking for Reagan. As she gets her attention and waves her over to our table, Lindsay smirks at me.

"Reagan, can I get another Grey Goose and cranberry? And as much as I love them, I'd like to be able to walk out of here in a few hours, so maybe ask Mac to take it easy on the vodka pour." Reagan laughs.

"Of course." Examining our half-full pitcher of beer, Reagan looks between Matt and me. "Is there anything else you two need?"

"I'll take a glass of ice water. I'm driving tonight," Matt explains. Reagan looks at me, waiting for me to answer.

"No thanks, I'm good—*for now*. I'm sure I'll want something *later*." The remark is laced with undertones and Lindsay kicks me under the table while Matt lowers his head and laughs. Regan gives me a little smirk and shakes her head while clearing the glasses off the table. Leaning into me, she whispers, "Then maybe I'll be back later." I catch my breath as her long hair sweeps across my cheek and her arm brushes against mine. But as she turns to leave, she smirks and says over her shoulder, "Or maybe I won't."

The rest of the evening, Reagan stays busy helping the tables and standing-room-only guests at Mac's. Lindsay drags poor Matt to the dance floor numerous times, trying to teach him to two-step, and the poor guy looks miserable. But being the stand-up guy that he is, he won't tell Lindsay no.

Last call was announced fifteen minutes ago, and Matt, Lindsay, and I finish off our waters. The bar started emptying when the band stopped playing about half an hour ago.

"So are you going to ask her for her number?" Lindsay asks, noticing Reagan clearing beer bottles off a nearby table.

"I don't normally ask for phone numbers; they usually find their way to me," I remark, trying to remember the last time I actually asked a woman for her phone number.

"Well, if you don't go ask for this one, I have a feeling you're leaving empty handed." Lindsay giggles, then hiccups.

Matt stands up and reaches for Lindsay's arm to steady her as she slides off the barstool. "We'll wait for you outside. Take your time," he says, guiding Lindsay toward the door.

"Bye, Reagan." Lindsay waves as they pass her. Reagan smiles at Lindsay and turns back to look at our table, where I'm still seated. She smiles at me and cocks her head to the side in confusion as she walks toward me. She's juggling a handful of empty beer bottles in each hand.

"They gonna leave you here?" She laughs.

"No, they're just waiting for me outside." She watches me intently as I sit, running my finger around the rim of the beer mug. Setting the beer bottles down on the table, she runs her long fingers across the pockets of her jeans, wiping her hands.

"Well, it was nice meeting you, Landon. Maybe I'll see you here again sometime." She smiles at me and picks up the beer bottles, and turns to walk away.

"Wait," I blurt out. Fuck, why is this making me nervous? She stops and turns around, yet she's still a good four paces away—too far away. I want her closer.

"I was hoping I could get your number. Maybe I can call you sometime." Her eyes flit nervously to the floor, then back to mine.

"I don't give my phone number out at work, but it was really nice to meet you." She backs away slowly and offers me a small smile. I can't remember the last time someone told me no. I shake my head and laugh quietly at the rejection. Taking the last swallow of my beer, I stand to leave.

Walking toward the door, I stop and look at Reagan, standing behind the bar. Her long hair hangs down the middle of her back, and she stands with her hands on her hips. Talking to Sam and Mac, her head falls back slightly as she laughs at something one of them has said. She stands barely a head shorter than Sam, and at eye to eye with Mac, putting her easily at close to five-foot-nine. Her cheeks are rosy pink, presumably from the warmth inside the bar. She's stunning. Looking up, she catches me looking at her and smiles at me. I smile back and step outside to the nearly empty parking lot.

Matt and Lindsay are sitting on the hood of Matt's Tahoe, waiting for me. Lindsay is leaning on Matt and resting her head on his shoulder.

"What the hell is going on?" I ask. Matt shrugs and lifts his finger over his mouth to shush me.

"She leaned on me and passed out."

"She wasn't that drunk," I mention, trying to recall how many drinks she had.

"I didn't think so either, but she made a couple of comments about how strong they were. Here, open the back door; I'll get her in the car." Matt lifts Lindsay's head and slides down off the hood of the truck. In one motion, he's carrying her to the back seat. Setting her in the truck, she mumbles something as Matt buckles her in.

"So did you get her number?" he asks me with a grin.

"Uh no, actually."

"What? You struck out?"

"Hardly, brother. She's just going to be a little more difficult than I thought."

"Difficult, huh?" He laughs at me as he shuts the door after securing Lindsay. "So what did she say?"

Grunting and rubbing my hands over my face, I look at Matt and sigh loudly.

"I asked her for her number, and she said she didn't give her number out at work. I assume she doesn't date customers."

"So what's your plan? What are you going to do?"

"I'll ask her again."

"And if she says no again?"

"Then I'll ask her again, and again, and again until she finally says yes."

"What if she never says yes?"

"She will."

I'm confident that she will. I saw the way she looked at me. I felt the connection when we shook hands, when we talked, when her arms brushed mine. Something was holding her back, but I know that she will come around eventually. Matt and I both turn to see where the sounds of voices and laughing that fill the quiet parking lot are coming from.

Sam, Reagan, Mac, and a couple of other people stand in a small circle, laughing and talking. Mac locks up the front door to the bar while Sam and Reagan stand waiting for him, saying their goodbyes to the others. Reagan glances in the direction of Matt and me, turning back to look at us when we've caught her attention.

Even though it's dark, and we're standing across the parking lot, I notice the smile cross her face. She leans into Sam and whispers something in his ear. Nodding his head, he turns to look at Matt and me and, with the nod of his head, acknowledges our presence. Reagan leans in and places a quick kiss to his cheek and a rush of something that resembles jealousy washes over me.

Carrying a small purse in one hand, and her car keys in the other, Reagan moves toward Matt and me. With her long legs, it takes her just a few seconds before she's standing in front of us.

"What are you still doing here?" she asks, tilting her head as she looks between Matt and me.

"We were… just… uh, I'll be in the car," Matt says, making a hasty retreat to the comfort of his Tahoe.

For seconds, Reagan and I stand staring at each other. The dim light in the parking lot casts a glow behind her. Her long hair falls over her shoulders and brushes the top of her breasts. Perfect breasts. Her eyes shift between mine as we stand in silence. I take two steps toward her, placing myself directly in front of her, inches from her.

"I'm going to ask you again, can I have your number, Reagan?" She swallows hard and I notice her eyes shift from my eyes to my lips several times. She shakes her head slowly, and retreats back by a small step.

"Why?" I whisper.

"I don't give my number out at work," she stutters.

"You're not working right now," I point out, taking a step forward and closing the distance between us once again.

"I'm still at work." She smiles.

"Technicalities."

She laughs lightly at my response. Her eyes drop and she kicks at the loose gravel on the blacktop. "Look, I'm just really private. I don't just hand my number out to people I don't know, okay?"

"Then go out with me. Get to know me. You can give me your number after you're comfortable with me," I compromise.

Letting out a deep sigh, she looks back at me. "You don't take no for an answer, do you?"

"Nope."

"I don't have a lot of free time—I work really odd hours, and help out here," she motions towards Mac's with her arm, "when I can."

"Tomorrow morning, then. Meet me for breakfast at the Beachside Café on Franklin at eleven."

She thinks about it while working her bottom lip between her teeth. I see her trying to fight the small smile tugging at the corners of her mouth when she finally agrees.

"Fine. I'll meet you for breakfast at eleven at the Beachside Café."

"It's a date," I say, backing away from her slowly.

"It's breakfast," she corrects me.

"It's a date over breakfast."

"Technicalities," she says, smirking and shaking her head as she walks backward towards her car.

I retreat to the passenger side of Matt's truck, but before I get there, I glance back to Reagan, who is still watching me as she continues to walk backward slowly.

"Goodnight, Reagan."

"Goodnight, Landon," she whispers as the smile she's been fighting finally spreads across her face.

CHAPTER 4

LANDON

I choose a small bistro table outside on the patio that overlooks Wrightsville Beach, and make myself comfortable as I wait for Reagan to arrive. I got here early to make sure there would be a table ready and we wouldn't have to wait to be seated.

It's a perfect morning—overcast, yet warm and mildly humid. There is a slight breeze off the Atlantic that makes sitting outside pleasant. I purposely chose an outside table, as most everyone else wants to be seated inside this time of year and I knew this would give us more privacy.

The waitress delivers tall glasses of ice water that she sets on the table next to the small vase with two large, multi-colored, fragrant flowers. Plucking one of the flowers from its small vase, I lift it and smell its light fragrance.

"Peonies," a voice says from behind me. "They're my favorite."

Turning around, I find that Reagan is standing just behind me. She's wearing a black strapless dress that stops well above her knees, bringing attention to her long, slender legs. When I stand up to greet her, she smiles nervously.

I pull the chair that sits across from me out, and motion for her to sit. As she slides into the chair, I find myself leaning in close to her, slowly taking in the scent of her floral perfume.

"Peonies, huh? I took you more for the rose kind of girl," I say as I find my way back to my seat.

"My mom has peony bushes all over our yard. I used to cut them and place them in vases or jars all over my bedroom when I was young."

"Where are you from?" I ask curiously, taking a sip of ice water. "You're not from around here—your accent is different."

"Accent?" She laughs.

"Yeah, you have a little accent, and I can't place it."

"Very observant." She raises her eyebrows, acting impressed. "Minnesota. I'm from Minnesota. A little town near the North Dakota border." She folds the corners of the small paper napkin that the water glass is sitting on. She's fidgeting, which means she's nervous.

"How the hell did you end up here?"

"A job." She smiles.

"You moved here to work at Mac's? There has to be a country dive bar in Minnesota. You surely could have found a job." She laughs, and her smile is genuine. Her eyes crinkle a little at the corner when she smiles, but I can't help but notice how blue they are against her light skin and nearly black hair.

"No, I didn't move here to work at Mac's. I'm actually a doctor." I am truly stunned silent. "What? You look surprised," she says with a small laugh. She pulls out the lemon that is floating in her water and gives it a squeeze, releasing the juice into her water.

"A doctor, but then why are you working at Mac's?"

"Mac is my uncle. I help out once in a while— which is rarely ever, considering how busy I am, but if he needs help and I can do it, I will. This weekend, he just happened to be short staffed, so I helped him out."

"So you're a doctor... huh?" I say, still genuinely in shock. "So you're not only beautiful, but smart too." She blushes at the compliment, but it's the truth.

"You seem surprised."

"I don't know what I expected, but I think it's great. What do you practice?"

"I'm an OB/GYN. Women's health—and delivering babies," she says with a little laugh.

"Babies." I say the word and a chill runs through me. I want nothing to do with babies or kids. I will do everything in my power to help and protect them, but I don't want any of my own—ever. Shaking that thought from my head, I almost feel intimidated by her career.

"So this is a private practice, right? You don't work for the hospital?"

"Correct. It's just me and three other doctors; we're a relatively small practice." She shrugs. "What do you do? For a career?" she asks just as our server approaches us, saving me from having to tell her. I hate telling people what I do. Not because I'm not proud, but because people have preconceived notions of this job. They either love us or hate us. There is always some remark or joke about being a cop.

"Could we have a couple of minutes to look at the menu?" I ask our server, sending her away again.

"What's good here?" Reagan asks as she flips through the pages of the menu.

"Everything. Seriously." I can't seem to pry my eyes away

from her. She plays with the large turquoise stones on her bracelet and chews on her bottom lip as she intently scans the menu, eventually closing it. Something in the pit of my stomach is telling me this girl is dangerous—she's beautiful, confident, *and* smart—a dangerous combination.

"So you never answered me. What do you do—for a career?" She sips her water and leans forward, resting her arms on the edge of the bistro table.

I pause, staring at her, watching her movements, her mannerisms, her eyes. Clearing my throat, I contemplate my answer. I have no intention of lying to her, but I hardly imagine she'll be impressed. She works with men who make a hell of a lot of more money than I do and are fucking geniuses. I fucking clean the streets of drug peddlers and occasionally write a fucking speeding ticket.

"I'm a police officer." Her face lights up when I tell her. Still twisting the stones of her bracelet, she smiles at me again, a simple small smile.

"Do you like your job?" she asks.

"Fucking love it," I admit. And I do.

"How long have you been a police officer?"

"Five, going on six years. I actually just applied and am testing for a detective position in narcotics."

"Drugs," she says quietly.

"It was either that or gangs, and there really isn't much going on around here but a bunch of young gang-banger wannabes and I want to be where the action is at—so narcs it is."

"You're a thrill-seeker," she says as a statement, not a question.

"Aren't we all, to some degree?"

"No," she says, tapping her short, manicured nails on the glass tabletop. "Some people play it safe their whole lives. They never take chances or risk anything."

"Well, that's not me." I shrug. "I like the thrill... the hunt... the chase." God, if she only knew what I was *really* talking about.

"I suppose. But what happens when the thrill, the hunt, and the chase are over?" she asks. I chuckle as I meet her gaze, her blue eyes fixed on me.

"I'll find another thrill, another hunt, another chase."

With a smirk, she sits back in her chair, crossing her arms in front of her. "Interesting. Well, congratulations. When do you find out if you've got the position?"

"Hopefully, soon. We just lost a detective who left and moved to take a position in Charlotte, so I know they'd like to bring someone on board quickly."

Our server is back and sets a small pot of coffee and the accompaniments on our table. Reagan orders first, Eggs Benedict and a side of yogurt, and I order whole-wheat banana nut pancakes.

"So what made you decide you wanted to be a police officer?" she asks, her head tilted to the side. She studies me almost as intently as I've been studying her.

"I like to help people." It's my "go-to" answer, but it's the honest-to-God truth.

"Me too," she whispers and smiles at me. I love that she smiles so much. There is a genuine kindness about her.

"So why did you move to North Carolina? Why Wilmington?" I ask, turning the questions back to her as she stirs creamer into her coffee.

"I love the beach." She shrugs a little. Turning her head, she casts her eyes out on the water. The light breeze gently lifts the bottom of her hair, moving it around slightly. She keeps her eyes trained on the water as she finishes, "I grew up in the Midwest, went to college and medical school in the Midwest. It was just time for a change. Mac is really the only relative I'm close to, and he lives here, so it just made sense to come here." She turns back to me and our eyes meet.

"Where are you from?" she asks, sipping at her coffee.

"Born and raised right here."

"You never left?"

"Moved out of Wilmington for college, but have always lived in North Carolina."

"Where did you go to school?"

"A small college just north of here."

"What about your family?" she asks, rubbing her finger around the rim of her coffee mug.

"It's just my sister and me. Lindsay; you met her last night."

"Lindsay's your sister? I recognize her from the news, but I didn't place that she was your sister. She's gorgeous. So it's just you two?"

"Yep." I shift in my chair. I don't like being asked questions about our family. She senses my discomfort and hesitates before she asks me another question.

"Do you like sports?"

"Love most of them. I played football and baseball in high school. We were the state champs for both football and baseball my senior year," I say, and actually realize I sound a little too excited, reliving my glory days. "But now, I just enjoy watching sports—football, baseball, and basketball."

"State champs, huh?" She laughs.

"Hey, it was a big deal when I was in high school."

"Coming from a small town, I get it," she says. "It's actually a great accomplishment, *Champ*." She giggles at me. I love when she laughs.

"Hey, you asked," I shrug at her. "What about you?" I ask. "Family?"

"My mom and dad still live in Minnesota. Both are retired. My mom was a schoolteacher, and my dad was an accountant. I have an older brother who is in the Air Force and stationed in Germany right now. That's it. We're really boring." She laughs.

"Hardly boring," I say. If she only fucking knew how normal that sounds and how I'd take boring and normal every fucking day of the week over the shit Lindsay and I dealt with.

"What about you; do you like sports?" It's my turn to make fun of her.

"Nope. Everyone wanted me to play volleyball or basketball... you know, embrace my 'tallness,' but I had no interest. I work out; stay active, but no sports for me."

"What do you do for fun?"

"Hmm... lately, not much of anything. I've been so busy getting settled at work, and just getting my bearings on the East Coast that I haven't really done much." Her voice trails off. "Oh, I love to read!" Her face lights up.

"What do you read? Classics?"

She laughs. "Nope. Smutty romance."

"I didn't take you for that type."

"What's the saying? Don't judge a book by its cover." She picks up the flower again from the small vase and presses it to her nose. "So, your turn. What do you like to do for fun?"

I'm guessing "recreational sex" isn't what she'd like to hear. "I work out. Play basketball with my partner Matt."

"He was at the bar last night right?" she confirms.

"Yeah, that's him."

"He seems really nice." She puts the flower back in the vase.

"He is. We've been friends for six years. We started work the same day." For two people who are getting to know each other, neither of us seems nervous. In fact, this is comfortable. "Okay, lightning round. Three questions. I'll go first."

"Favorite color?"

"Green."

"Favorite movie?"

"Anything with Vince Vaughn." She giggles.

"First car?"

"A 1993 Honda Accord. I drove that thing into the ground. I think it had 150,000 miles on it!"

"Okay, your turn." I anticipate the same questions.

"Most embarrassing moment?"

"Really?"

"Answer it," she says coyly.

"The first time I had sex. Next."

"Dogs or cats?"

"Neither."

"What scares you the most?"

"Hmm… I think you've stumped me."

"Oh, come on, everyone has something they're afraid of."

"Can I get back to you on this one?"

"Sure." Her voice is quiet, yet there is a level of confidence when she speaks that I am attracted to. She knows exactly who she is, what she wants, what she doesn't want… and she's sure of herself. It's fucking sexy as hell.

"Thank you for breakfast," she says quietly.

"You're welcome. When can I see you again?" I know it's ballsy and direct. We've spent two hours getting to know each other over breakfast, but I want—make that *need*—more of her.

She sighs and meets my gaze. "I don't know." She pauses. "I am so busy, and I just—just don't really have time to date right now."

"Make time," I say firmly. "Reagan, I like you. I want to get to know you better, but I can't do that unless you spend some time with me—and I know you feel *this* too." I motion to the space between us. She swallows hard, and looks back out to the water. When she thinks, she watches the water, I've already picked this up about her.

"You're not going to take 'no' for an answer again, are you?" She smiles.

"No. So when can I see you again?"

This time, she sighs more loudly and puckers her lips in thought. "What is your work schedule?" she asks.

"I work four tens, Tuesday through Friday. Weekends and Mondays off." She stares at me and picks at the tan nail polish on her fingernails.

"I work every Tuesday, Thursday, and Friday and one weekend a month, I'm on call, the joys of private practice, so…"

"So tomorrow. We're both off on Mondays, so tomorrow it is."

"Aren't you going to wait three days to call me, you know… so you don't look desperate. Isn't that the rule?" She laughs.

Leaning in, I close the distance between us. Our noses brush and I can feel her short, warm breaths on my face. "I'm not desperate, Reagan—I'm determined. There's a big difference. And if you haven't figured it out yet—I don't play by the rules." Her breath hitches and I sit back to take in the sight of her face while she ponders what I've just said.

"Okay. Tomorrow, but this time, I choose what we're doing."

"Deal."

"Be prepared to get dirty, so wear something old and bring a change of clothes."

"What are we doing?"

"It's a surprise. I do this a couple times a month on my day off, and tomorrow, you're going to help me."

"Please tell me it isn't yoga or some crazy shit like that?"

"No, we'll do that next time." She laughs, and I roll my eyes at her. "Give me your address, I'll pick you up."

"No, I'll pick you up."

"Don't argue with me; just give me your address." She shakes her head slowly at me.

"I'll text you my address." I've got her. She gets my address when I get her phone number.

"Fine. 910-555-5175. Text me your address and be ready by nine o'clock." She winks at me and offers me a tight smile as she pushes herself away from the table and stands up. Grabbing her small purse that was hanging on the back of her chair, she catches me off guard this time when she leans in to me. "You've met your match, Champ, because I don't play by the rules either." Without another word, she pulls back and starts walking away. "Nine o'clock, be ready," she says over her shoulder.

"Fuck," I mumble and jump up from the table to follow her out of the café. Pushing through the glass door, I jog up behind her slowly as she opens the door to a silver Lexus SUV. "Reagan," I say as she slides into the driver seat. I insert myself in between the open car door and her seat.

"Yeah?" she questions.

"Game on." I step back and close her car door, and without a second glance in her direction, I walk to my car parked just three spots over. I don't know what the fuck just happened, but I think I may have my hands full with this woman—and for the first time ever, I think I'm ready.

CHAPTER 5

LANDON

Got it. 9am. Be ready Champ.

That was the text message I got in return after I sent Reagan my address last night. Nothing more. I waited all day, and into the evening, to send her my address—see if she'd sweat it a little bit, but nope. Confident Reagan replies with "Got it."

So now, I wait for her to pick me up. This is so fucked up. I agreed to let her pick me up, but I have no idea where we're going or what we're doing. What the fuck was I thinking? I wasn't, except for getting her beneath me. All night, I thought about running my hands up her long legs, over her stomach, and up to the curve of her breasts. I imagined what she'd taste like, every last inch of her. Fighting the thoughts, I imagined what she'd look like tied to my bed.

"What are you doing?" Lindsay asks, snapping me out of my daydream. She races down the hallway with her shoes and purse in her hand.

"Nothing," I respond, watching her jump up and down on one foot, trying to get her shoe on the other.

"How do you keep a job?" I ask. "You're always late."

"They love me, and I'm good at what I do, so they deal with me being fifteen minutes behind everyone else. They call it 'permanent tardyism.'"

"Is that what they call your lack of responsibility? Is tardyism even a word?"

"Shut up." She flings a coaster off the end table at me in hopes of shutting me up. Standing up, she straightens her dress and runs her fingers through her hair. "Want to talk about yesterday?" she asks with a smirk on her face.

"Nothing to talk about. It was breakfast."

"Are you going to see her again?"

"Don't know." Just then, the doorbell rings. "Fuck," I mutter. Lindsay looks at me, then at the door. Her heels echo off the hardwood floor as she pulls the front door open.

"Reagan," she says with a smile and steps aside. "Come in. Nice to see you again; we were just talking about you." Reagan steps across the threshold, wearing a pair of skintight black workout pants and a pink fitted tank top with a pair of matching tennis shoes. Lindsay crosses her arms over her chest and narrows her at eyes me.

"Ready, Champ?" Reagan asks. "I want to get this done before it gets too warm."

"Champ?" Lindsay snorts. "What are you guys doing today?"

"Lindsay, go get all investigative reporter on someone at work. You're late," I bark as I jump up from the couch and damn near push her out the front door. Both girls are laughing as Lindsay hollers her goodbyes over her shoulder to Reagan.

"Sorry about that. My sister is a pain in the ass." I grab my keys, phone, and a small bag with a change of clothes. "Anything else I need?" I question Reagan, hoping she'll give me just a few more details of where we're going or what we're doing.

"Nope." She smiles. "Let's do this."

Reagan drives us about ten minutes out of town, to a large piece of property off of a dead end dirt road. There sits an older house that has definitely seen better days. Off to the back looks to be another structure, newer—almost larger than the house.

"Where are we?"

"You'll see." We both get out of her SUV as she walks to the front door and knocks while I stay back near the SUV. I've never been out on this side of town, and I take a moment to look around at the property. While the house is older, the property is maintained well. The large grass yard has been recently cut, and the property is outlined with giant red maple trees. It really is a beautiful piece of land. I see Reagan helping the older woman who answers the door down the front steps and they walk slowly toward me.

"Landon, this is Mrs. Fitzpatrick."

"Nice to meet you." I reach out and shake her hand. She looks to be in her early sixties. Not frail, but not full of spunk either.

"Nice to meet you too, Landon. Reagan phoned me last night, telling me she was bringing a friend today." Mrs. Fitzpatrick looks me up and down and I catch Reagan smiling.

"Are they ready?" Reagan asks.

"Sure are."

"How many are there today?" Reagan inquires as she walks Mrs. Fitzpatrick back toward the front door. I follow behind.

"Four. Benny and Louie aren't with me anymore."

"Perfect. We'll be back in a couple of hours."

"Let's go." Reagan nods toward the large structure out behind the house.

"So are you going to tell me what we're doing?"

"You'll see." She picks up her pace and tugs me along by my arm. I can't help but notice how the tight black pants hug the curve of her hips and thighs and her tank top pushes her breasts together just enough to leave the perfect amount of cleavage showing. Once we get to the building, Reagan slides the large door open and steps inside. There sits twelve chain link kennels, six on each side of the building with a large center aisle down the middle.

"What is this?" I ask, confused.

"Gemma runs a dog rescue. I come and help her out on Mondays and walk the dogs for her." She shrugs and steps into the building.

"So, we're walking dogs?" I ask, surprised that this is what we're really doing.

"Yep. I do it every Monday, and figured you could help me today," she says with a giant sarcastic smile.

"Fucking great," I mumble.

"C'mon; it'll be fun." She bumps into me with her shoulder. Walking past me, she walks to the end kennel and releases the latch. A black, brown, and white medium-sized dog comes lunging from the kennel and runs right into Reagan's legs. "Ollie," she laughs, rubbing the hound behind its long ears. Squatting down, Reagan attaches the leash to Ollie's collar while he frantically licks her face. *Lucky dog.*

"This is Ollie; he's a little escape artist," she says, handing me his leash and walking to another kennel. "And this is Henry." An older dog, a much slower moving dog, wags his black tail as Reagan attaches a leash to his collar.

"They get a little excited when they see me; they know they're getting out of here for a while." She smiles at me.

"So they stay penned up in here the entire time?"

"No, Gemma has a large fenced yard out back that they run in, but I try to take a few of them away from here—to the beach to run." Reagan hands me Henry's leash as she walks to the third kennel and two smaller dogs meet her at the gate.

"And this is Mo and Curly." She reaches her finger through the chain link and scratches their curly haired heads one at a time.

"So we're taking all four to the beach?" I ask her as Henry and Ollie tug me toward the door.

"Yep. This is easy. I usually take four to six by myself."

"You're insane, or a goddamn saint," I mumble as I finally let the two dogs pull me toward Reagan's car. They know exactly where they're going.

We load all four dogs into the back of her SUV and I take the passenger seat again while she navigates the bumpy dirt road.

"So, how did you find this place?" I ask curiously.

She lets out a little laugh. "Let's just say that I spent a lot of time here growing up."

"You know Mrs. Fitzgerald?"

"Yep. Gemma and my Uncle Mac used to be married. They divorced the second summer that I was here. Gemma has always been wonderful to me, so I help her out when I can."

"Seems like you help everyone out."

"I try to. I really do. Mac and Gemma were so kind to me… and… just… I have a lot to thank them for. I'll always help them." I notice her grip the steering wheel a little tighter and blink her eyes as if she's fighting back tears. She takes a deep breath and glances at me. "Gemma has the kindest heart. She was always taking in strays, so a few years ago, she finally decided to open a small rescue group. Mac built her that kennel. Even though they're divorced, he still pretty much does everything for her."

"It's a little unusual," I mention. "But hey, if it works for them, so be it."

"I don't disagree with you and yes, it works for them," she says as she pulls into a small parking lot that is set off from the beach. Putting the car in park and killing the ignition, she looks at me with her bright blue eyes.

"Ready?"

"Ready as I'll ever be," I grumble. Walking dogs was not what I envisioned doing with Reagan today, but if it means spending time with her, I'll fucking walk some mutts. We meet at the back of the SUV and, as she opens the back door, the four dogs come bounding at us.

"Grab the leashes," she yells as we both scramble to collect the tangle of leashes. Once we're all sorted out, we walk through the thick sand down the beach.

"I walk them for a couple of miles; hope you're up for a walk." She smiles again. Twisting the leash around her wrist, she shortens the length on Ollie.

"This one," she tugs at Ollie's leash, "is my trouble maker." She rubs his long ears and down his neck. "He doesn't listen and does everything he's not supposed to do. I swear he's untrainable—until he's worn down, then he listens." I laugh at her description of Ollie; if she wasn't describing this beagle, her description could fit me. "Here, I'll let you take Ollie today." She cocks her head to the side and gives me a sarcastic smile.

"Jeez, thanks." I take the leash from her hand and that of one of the smaller fluffy dogs. Ollie knows the routine. He pulls me down toward the water line, and Reagan and the other dogs follow us. It's warm and humid, but the breeze off the ocean keeps it from being unbearable.

"So you mentioned you spent summers here growing up, but when did you officially move here?" I ask, eager to learn more about her.

"Actually, just about six weeks ago. I'm still really just getting settled." The wind is whipping her long, dark hair all around and it's giving me a perfect view of her neck. "I couldn't pass up this job—it was basically handed to me on a silver platter, and I love North Carolina and the ocean." She pauses. "It's always been my home away from home, I guess," she says, smiling. "So how old were you when you became a police officer?"

"Is this your way of asking me how old I am?" I laugh.

A light blush sweeps across her face and chest. "Maybe," she says, tucking some hair behind her ear.

"I was almost twenty-four when I started and I just turned thirty, if that's what you really wanted to know," I smirk. "Speaking of age, you seem really young to be in a private practice," I observe.

"Is this your way of asking me how old I am?" She laughs and bumps her shoulder into mine. She pauses, and I can see her thinking.

"I'm thirty-one," she says quietly, pausing again. "I graduated from high school when I was seventeen." *What is it with me and girls that are so ambitious with their schooling?* "I spent the next three years and those summers working on my undergraduate degree in biology, and I was accepted into medical school when I was twenty-one. I've done my time when it comes to school and my residency." She laughs.

"You don't look like you're thirty-one," I remark. She doesn't. I pegged her for mid-twenties.

"Well, thank you for the compliment," she jokes.

"I don't know how I feel about dating an older woman," I say, just as she snaps her head to look at me.

"Who said we were dating?" She raises her eyebrows at me.

"No one. I'm just saying I've never dated an older woman before." She doesn't say anything, but just stares at me with narrowed eyes. I can see her thinking.

"Landon, I told you I don't really have the time to date anyone right now," she says quietly. "But... I like you..."

"I like you too, Reagan," I interrupt her, "but I'm not going to lie to you. I'm not really a relationship kind of guy."

"What does that mean?"

Shrugging, I take a deep breath. "I don't know. I guess I just like to have a good time, without all the seriousness of a relationship."

"So you like to fuck around," she states matter-of-factly. "Relationships are too difficult for you to manage, so you fuck who you want when you want, and since there's no commitment, it doesn't complicate things, am I right?" It sounds so harsh when she says it, but yeah, that's exactly what it is.

"Yeah, I guess that's what it is." Why am I so embarrassed to admit that to her?

"I've done the friends with benefits things in college," she says. "It never works out. Someone always develops feelings. Always," she says, kicking at the sand. We've slowed down considerably and the dogs are tugging at the leashes.

"Yeah, that's what I've heard. That's why I've never slept with the same woman twice."

She stops abruptly. "Are you kidding me?" I shake my head

to answer her. "Shit," she whispers. "So, you've never been in a long-term relationship?"

"Nope. I've never been in a relationship, period."

"Have you ever loved a woman? Sorry, I know that's a personal question."

"That's okay. I had feelings for someone, and I cared about her—a lot, but I wasn't who she loved—who she needed." I think back to Jess, and how it was the first time I ever felt compassion or cared for a woman and her feelings. It was the first time I'd felt the instinctual need to protect someone other than Lindsay and the first time I felt another person's pain.

"What happened?" Reagan asks.

"I pushed her back into the arms of the man she needed."

"That sounds like love," she whispers. "Or complete stupidity."

"Thanks."

"Sorry," she says.

"No, it was for the best. What about you?" I ask. "Ever been in love?"

"Just once. It didn't work out. End of story." I can tell this is a sore subject for her.

"How long ago was this?"

I see her swallow hard. "It was a really long time ago. First love. You know, the one you think you're going to be with forever, the one who will never hurt you. Yeah, that's a bunch of shit. It just didn't work out."

"Why?"

"Long story."

"I've got all day."

"Not today, Landon. Not something I'm ready to talk about."

"Got it, okay. Such serious conversation we're having and we met, what, like thirty-six hours ago?" I joke with her.

"Here." She reaches for the leashes in my hand and unhooks Ollie and Mo. When she unhooks Henry and Curly they all take off running down the beach. A small pack of dogs, barking, yipping, and running together. She walks up to where the sand is dry and sits down as she watches the dogs race down the beach.

"They're tired enough that they'll run for a bit, but won't run away. They always turn around and come back," she says, nodding at them. I take a seat in the sand next to her. Our shoulders are almost touching.

"So you're like a modern-day saint," I say. "Saving people, dogs... what else do you have up your sleeve?"

She laughs. "Ha! Hardly. I don't save anybody or anything, I just like to help."

"I like that about you, Reagan. I like that you like helping people—even dogs." She picks up a small handful of sand and lets it run through her fingers. "And I'd like to see you again, but I'm not sure I could give you what you want or need."

"How do you know what I want or need?"

"I guess I don't. But what I do know is that I like talking to you."

"You're breaking your own rules, Champ. You've seen me twice—yesterday and today. You said it yourself you don't see someone more than once."

"Ah, you're wrong. I don't sleep with them more than once, not *see* them more than once."

"Oh, that's right; as long as we don't sleep together, we can be friends—hang out, and see each other again and again," she says sarcastically. Turning toward me, she leans in too close, her nose pressed against the side of my face. I can feel her lips hovering just next to my ear. "But what happens when one of us wants more?" she whispers. "Because one of us will, it's inevitable. What happens then? You fuck me and leave me—never see me again?"

I turn to meet her crisp blue eyes. She's leaning in to me—staring at me.

"Do you want to fuck me, Reagan?"

"Not if I can't see you again—no."

Goddamn, this woman is going to drive me insane. I let out a frustrated laugh. She rests her hand on top of mine, giving it a gentle squeeze. "I want to see you again, Landon, so there will be no fucking, understand?" I drop my head back and close my eyes.

"Got it, Doc."

"Good, now let's get these dogs back to Gemma."

She gives out a whistle and all four dogs come bounding down the beach. She stands up with all four leashes while I sit and watch her. What the hell is it about her? Why do I suddenly want something I've never had before? Why do I want her?

"Ready, Champ?"

"Ready."

CHAPTER 6

Reagan

I reach over and shut off the water just as the bubbles reach the top of the bathtub. Sliding into the hot water, I glide down the back of the porcelain tub and rest my head on the edge with a rolled up towel propped under my neck to keep me comfortable. I could lie in this water forever. Baths are my escape, my place to decompress and let go, except tonight, I can't stop thinking about Landon. Something about him makes me question everything I think I know—everything I think I want.

He's dangerous... he admitted it. But damn if I'm not attracted to that danger—knowing that if I succumb to it, it would be nothing but heartbreak for me. "Shit," I say out loud. I can't do this. Not now. I need to keep my head clear and focused on my job. I've studied and worked too hard to get this far to let myself get distracted by a man, by Landon.

"Focus," I tell myself. "Remember how far you've come." I push thoughts of Landon to the back of my head and try to relax. I let the warm water carry away the stress and anxiety as I relax, but my thoughts are never far from the dangerous man who has me hooked. I see every line and every color of the tattoos that cover both of his arms—wondering what it would feel like to lie in those arms, wrapped around him.

"Let him go, Reagan," I tell myself as I climb out of the bathtub. The bath was hardly relaxing, as all I could think about was *him*. Drying off, I pull on my negligée and let my hair down, running a brush through my long hair. Looking at myself in the mirror, I see successful and accomplished—a doctor, but not far hidden behind the façade is the scared, weak girl I once was, afraid of love, of letting someone into that place within—only to have them disappoint me and leave me broken again.

I plug my cell phone in to charge and set it on my nightstand, glancing at it one last time to see what time it is, eleven o'clock exactly; that's late for me—yet I'm not tired. I thumb through the book I've been reading for the last few nights, finding I can't stay interested in the story as my mind wanders back to *him*. I see his lips, his muscular tattooed arms, his chiseled face… and I can't seem to think of anything else.

Reaching over, I shut off the bedside lamp and open the drawer, pulling out my vibrator. I slide it under the covers and between my legs and with the press of the button, it hums to life as I guide it to the spot that's been throbbing since this afternoon.

Pressing and gliding, it doesn't take long for me to orgasm, my legs twitching and my breathing rapid as I recall the sight of his face. It's been far too long that I've let that little piece of plastic and AA batteries bring me pleasure, and not a man. Tossing the vibrator aside, I curl up into a ball. I close my eyes and fall asleep to the thought of those piercing blue eyes and inked skin lying next to me—touching me.

Tuesdays are always busy for me—I see more patients on Tuesdays than I do any other day of the week. When I close the door to the exam room as I exit, there is a small group gathered around the horseshoe-shaped desk in the back office. This is where the medical assistants chart, and where pharmaceutical reps tend to make themselves at home.

"What's going on?" I ask, wondering what I'm missing out on. There is a group of girls huddled around, looking at a cell phone.

"Look, I snapped a picture this time," Melissa says, handing me her iPhone. Melissa is my medical assistant and is absolutely hilarious.

"Who is this?" I scan the picture briefly.

"That is Tony. Tony Puchello—or affectionately known as the Italian Stallion." I can't help but laugh at their reference. "What do you think?" Melissa asks as all the girls *goo* and *gah* over him.

"I think he looks like a nice, good-looking young man… who also happens to be one of our pharmaceutical reps… which means he's off limits."

"You're just saying that because you want him, huh, Reagan."

"Uh, no. I'm not interested in Mr. Italian Stallion, thank you very much." The girls all laugh at me using their reference to him.

"Are you dating anyone?" Ashley asks. Ashley is Dr. Gerard's medical assistant and your true Southern belle. Her

Southern accent is extremely thick, so much so that I really have to focus on what she's saying to be able to understand her. I know I'm new here, and I know the staff is trying to get to know me, but my personal life is off limits.

"Not right now." I leave it at that. Short and sweet. Saved by the buzz of the intercom from Sally at the front desk. "Dr. Sinclair, you have a delivery up front that needs your signature." I look at the group of girls still eyeing the cellphone and shake my head.

"Melissa, would you mind going to sign for my package. I'm going to try and eat something really quick before my next patient."

"Sure thing." She hops up and strides through the door to the front waiting area. The rest of the medical assistants scatter and make themselves busy around the back office.

Before I can even make it to my office to grab my sandwich, she's shouting down the hall, "Sinclair, they need *your* signature. They won't accept mine as proof of delivery." She giggles and wags her eyebrows at me.

Frustrated that my ten-minute lunch is being taken up by the UPS man, I shove the door open and am met by the beautiful blue eyes I dreamt of last night.

"Hey, Doc," he says as he pushes himself away from the reception counter. The lean muscles in his arms flex as he pushes himself back from the front counter. Megan, who manages the phones up front, blushes as Landon smiles at her before sauntering over to me. I hold my breath for a second when he begins walking toward me. He is wearing a pair of faded blue jeans and a black polo shirt, and his bright blue eyes stand out against his tan skin and light brown hair.

"What are you doing here?" I question him suspiciously.

"On my way to work, but wanted to drop this off." He points to a giant vase of flowers on the counter. "They're for you."

"Why?"

"Because." He smiles at me. My eyes fall to his lips and I fight thoughts of his mouth all over me. My heart races as I stand watching him. Glancing away, I look around the waiting room and it's full of patients. One lady has set her magazine down and is listening to us and Megan pretends to busy herself while watching us out of the corner of her eye.

"Thank you," I whisper as he steps in closer to me. Standing almost too close, he pulls at the stethoscope I have hung around my neck.

"You look sexy in scrubs," he whispers back with a quick wink. "Have a good day, Doc," he says, pressing a light kiss to my cheek. Instinctively, I reach out and place my hand on his chest as I inhale the light scent of him.

"Be safe, Champ."

"Always am," he says as he pulls away and walks toward the door. "Bye, ladies." He waves to Sally and Megan at the front desk.

"Bye," they both say in unison. I walk to the counter and grab my vase of flowers, making a hasty retreat to the back. Entering my small office, I set the flowers on my desk and stand there admiring them while I think of him. I take my time and smell each flower, smiling because he remembered—peonies.

I slide the small card out of the plastic holder and open the envelope. The card is simple, but it's the words that melt my heart.

"*Just because I think you're beautiful.*" I press the small card to my lips as I stare at the giant bouquet in front of me.

"And who in the hell was that," Sally screeches as she pushes her way into my office. "That man was simply beautiful," she says, fanning herself.

"I know," is all I can manage to say.

"So who was it?" she asks again.

"Out!" I point at the door, laughing. I'm not sharing anything with these gossipy ladies. "And close the door behind you."

"I want details," she says as she closes the door.

Holding the card against my chest, I can't contain the smile on my face. Pulling my phone out of the pocket of my lab coat, I run my hand over the smooth surface, unlocking the screen. I type out a quick text to Landon.

I need to see you tonight. I know you're working, just give me 5 minutes.

I drop the phone back into my pocket and stare at the large bouquet of bright pink and white peonies, just as there is a little knock on my door.

"Your one o'clock is here."

"Thanks. I'll be right there," I announce over my shoulder to Melissa. I drop the little card into my pocket next to my phone just as I feel it vibrate. When I glance at the illuminated screen, anxiety courses through me until I tap the messages icon and see his response.

Sure thing Doc. Text me later.

The rest of my day is full of patients, exams, and babies. Fortunately, I'm too busy at work to be distracted by thoughts of Landon; however, as usual, he is not far from my mind. After the last patient leaves, and we've charted, cleaned, and locked up the office, it is after six-thirty.

I sit in my car and contemplate seeing him. I know he's right in the middle of his shift and I don't want to bother him, but there is something I need to do—*want* to do. Pulling my phone from the pocket of my purse, I stare at the screen for a few seconds. I shiver slightly when I notice how fast my heart is beating.

It's been years, make that over fifteen years since I've felt these emotions, felt this way about a man—it's a foreign, yet welcome feeling.

Just leaving work. Let me know when you're available and where I can meet you.

I start my car and head in the direction of home. I glance occasionally at my phone, which I've tucked into the cup holder, just within my reach. I check it at every red light, at every stop sign—and no response. Pulling into my condominium complex, I reach up and push the garage door opener and wait while the door slowly lifts. Behind me, I see the police car and I know it's him. My heart races and my hands begin a steady shake.

"Breathe," I whisper to myself as I pull into my garage. Cutting the ignition, I slide down from the SUV and walk to the garage entrance. I hear him before I see him.

"Hey, Doc."

"Hey, Champ."

"You wanted to see me?"

"How did you know where I live?"

"We actually saw you a couple of miles back. I recognized your car, so we followed you. Is everything okay?" he asks, stepping in closer to me.

I nod my head and realize just how nervous I am. My stomach is in knots, and I can hardly breathe. But I decide in that moment, when you want something badly enough you have to take risks. I'm not playing it safe anymore. One foot in front of the other, I take two steps and find myself chest to chest with him. He's only a few inches taller than I am, and our lips almost meet. Almost.

Time stands still while I study every feature of him—his chin, his lips, his jaw, the colorful tattoos that line his arms, and those beautiful blue eyes. I notice the defined muscles in his neck when he swallows, and how he runs his tongue over his bottom lip as he watches me study every last inch of him.

Raising my hand, I place it on his bicep to balance myself as I lift my head and meet his eyes. Those beautiful eyes hold so much mystery, so much danger. Before I convince myself otherwise, I press my lips to his, tasting him for the first time— and maybe the last time when he suddenly pulls himself away from me.

CHAPTER 7

LANDON

Why the fuck did I pull away from her kiss? Why? She takes a quick step backwards and I instantly take notice of her shaking hands. Her eyes are shifted downward to her feet and her long brown hair covers most of her face.

"Reagan," I say, urging her to look at me.

"I'm sorry," she whispers and quickly turns around. Her feet carry her quickly away from me and I see where she is headed, to the door at the front of the garage that must lead into her house. I pause momentarily, but know I need to fix this. She is only steps away from her escape. *Run. I'll only hurt you more.* I know I've crushed her. *Run.*

"Stop," It's an order, not a request. My voice is firm—angry. She stops just in front of the door. The keys are jingling in her shaking hand, but she doesn't turn around as I approach her. She knows I'm right behind her; I see her shoulders tense as I stand mere inches from her.

I brush her dark hair off of her right shoulder and over to the other side, freeing up the side of her neck. Resting my chin on her shoulder, I can smell her—a combination of citrus and vanilla.

"Don't open that door, Reagan," I growl in her ear. I can hear her swallow and, with a deep inhale, she inserts the keys into the lock and twists them, letting her hand fall to turn the doorknob. She's defying me. She pushes the door open slowly just as I reach around her and pull it closed with a quick pull of my hand. My hand remains pressed on the door handle, pinning her between me and the large door. Her breaths are short and heavy, her body trembles in fear. She's afraid of me... she should be.

"I said don't open the door, Reagan."

"I'll open my goddamn door if I want to," she snarls at me, her voice shaking and full of anger.

"No, you won't. Not until you listen to me, do you understand?" She doesn't respond, but she doesn't challenge me either. With one hand on her shoulder, I remove my other hand from the door and run it along the side of her cheek and down the front of her neck. My chin rests gently on her shoulder, inhaling the scent of her. The sound of her breath hitching as I run my hands over her turns me on.

"Turn around," I whisper in her ear. She remains still. "Turn around, Reagan." My voice is less aggressive, but still demanding. We stand like this for a few moments, my hand gently wrapped around her neck. A sign that I am in control here... me—not her. I hear her breathing finally calm, and her head falls back gently onto my shoulder.

"I'm going to break my rules for you, Reagan," I whisper in her ear. "Rule number one. I never fuck the same woman twice. Rule number two. I don't kiss women," I say, pressing a gentle kiss to the side of her cheek. I turn her around gently by the shoulders, positioning her in front of me. With the tilt of her chin, I kiss her. Softly and gently, I kiss her, succumbing to the feel of her soft lips on mine.

Holding her head in my hands, I whisper against her lips, "I'm sorry for pulling away from you, it's just that..."

"You don't kiss women. Got it. I'm sorry... I didn't know," she whispers back. "But who said we were fucking?" Before I talk myself out of this, I'm kissing her again. This time, my kiss for her is hungrier, needier. Her head falls back as my tongue rolls down her neck. I taste the soft skin from behind her ear down to her collarbone. I can hear a low hum from the back of her throat as I kiss her neck—and I know she's mine.

In one quick movement, I lift her onto the hood of her SUV. A loud gasp escapes her as I bite at her neck.

"Landon."

"Shh," I whisper against her neck. "I don't kiss women, Reagan, but let me kiss you." Her lips move with mine and I'm lost in her. Her fingers tug at my short hair, trying to find something to hold onto. As I am standing between her legs, she's propped at the very edge of the hood of her car. I can feel the heat from between her legs through her thin scrubs and I'm instantly hard. I want nothing more than to take her on this car—right now. Pressing myself into her gently, I let her feel what she's done to me. She gasps again when she feels me press against her, rolling my hips into her. Guiding her slowly to her back, she's now lying down—her long legs dangling from the hood of the car. I can see the rise and fall of her chest through her light green scrubs. Her legs tighten against my sides. She knows she's in a vulnerable position, lying like this with her legs spread and me standing between them.

Leaning over her, I press a kiss to her neck again. I can feel the heat from my breath ricochet off her neck and back onto my face as my breathing becomes heavier. It's taking every ounce of self-control not to continue grinding myself into her. Both of my hands find the sides of her firm waist, holding her in place. I can feel her stomach muscles tighten as my thumbs rest on her abdomen.

My hands move slowly to the edge of her pants. I have her where I want her. I want her to know if I wanted her, she'd give herself to me, although I have no intention of taking her here on the hood of a car. With my left hand resting on her chest between her breasts, I hold her gently in place. I tug at the tie on the waist of her scrub pants and, with one quick tug, they are untied and the waist is loose. Running my fingers just inside the waist of her pants, I touch just the top band of her panties. She gasps loudly and tries to sit up, but I hold her down with my hand on her chest. I press my erection into her warm center. "Feel that, Reagan?" I hiss through my teeth. She nods quickly as she lets out a moan. "That's what you do to me."

I continue to hold her down—leaning in to kiss her again while my other hand taunts the soft skin just inside of those scrub pants.

"As much as I want to fuck you on the hood of this car, I'm not going to, Reagan. But this isn't done, understand? I will fuck you. " I press a long kiss to her lips. "I have to go," I whisper and pull her down from the hood.

She immediately begins tying her pants, but never removes her eyes from mine. Her breathing begins to settle and we maintain eye contact with each other—a power struggle that I will win. Her flushed cheeks and full lips taunt me, but I want to show her who's in control.

"We good?" I ask quietly.

"We're good," she whispers.

"We're not done here."

"Agreed," she says confidently, trying to reestablish some form of control over me. It's not working.

This woman will be the death of me; she's feisty, yet vulnerable. Confident, yet insecure. Dominant, yet submissive, and she wants me, I know she does.

"Do *you* want to fuck me, Reagan?" My words catch her off-guard and she stills momentarily. The corner of her mouth turns up just slightly.

"No, because I want to see you again." With no other words, or even a goodbye, she turns and walks into her condo, shutting the door behind her. And as much as I want her too, she's so frustrating.

Jogging back to the patrol car, I can see Matt on the phone. I pull on the door and slide into the seat, just in time to hear him tell whoever he's talking to that he has to go.

"Who was that?" I ask, since Matt never talks on the phone.

"Ah, no one. What'd she want?" he inquires as he tucks his phone into the side pocket of the door.

"Just to thank me for the flowers."

"That was a long thank you," he smirks. "And you bought her flowers?"

"Yeah, what's wrong with that?"

"Have you ever done that before, bought flowers for someone?" he asks with a look of genuine shock on his face.

"No. I haven't," I admit.

"Well, holy fuck," he bellows. "Someone is pussy whipped!" He laughs, throwing his head back against the headrest of the seat.

"Shut the fuck up; no one is pussy whipped."

"I'll be damned, I never thought I'd see the day," he continues, laughing at me, "and I take it you took my advice and haven't tapped that piece of ass yet?" Something in how he says that bothers me.

"She's not just a piece of ass," I mumble, shutting him up. He puts the car in drive and starts driving, but I hear him say it under his breath, "pussy whipped." For once, that fucker might be right.

The rest of the night is uneventful, which gives me a lot of time to think about Reagan. Too much time. Of course, my mind goes to what she'd look like lying on top of her car naked while I fuck her senseless, to thoughts of how every inch of her would taste in my mouth.

We turn in our paperwork for the night, and I change in the locker room—tossing on my jeans and a white t-shirt.

"Christianson, I need to see you out here when you're done," I hear my sergeant say.

"What the fuck does he want?" Matty eyes me suspiciously.

"No fucking clue."

"Want me to hang around and wait for you?" Matt is always looking out for everyone—especially me.

"Nah, go ahead. I'm sure it's nothing and should only be a minute. See ya tomorrow, man."

"Sounds good. Night, brother," he says with a fist bump.

Tying my tennis shoes, I grab my wallet, phone, and keys and head down the hallway to Sarge's office.

"Sarge," I acknowledge him.

"Christianson, have a seat." He points to the chair sitting in front of his large wooden desk. I take a seat, waiting for him to tell me why I'm here. "Congratulations, son. Starting Monday, you've been assigned to Narcotics," he says with a giant smile.

"Seriously?"

"Yes, congratulations—looks like someone is following in their old man's footsteps." His reference to my father just sends bile rushing to my throat. That is one man I never want to be compared to, except around here, he was an icon. I don't respond as I let my stomach settle. "You okay?" he asks as he steps around the front of his desk.

"No, yeah, I mean, I'm just surprised," I say, trying to deflect conversation away from his reference to me being like my father.

"Don't be. You deserve this. I'm very proud of you, son. And we're going to miss you on patrol." He reaches out to shake my hand.

"Shit, I need to tell Matt."

"Let him know sooner rather than later; you're off until Monday. We've got him training the new kid beginning tomorrow." He laughs.

"He's going to be pissed." I laugh back.

"Yeah, I'm going to let you break the news to him."

"Fucking great," I mumble.

<hr />

I waste no time getting out of bed this morning—I feel good, even though I barely slept. Excitement with news of my job and yesterday's events with Reagan kept my already busy mind working overtime and not allowing me to rest. I meet Lindsay in the kitchen, where she already has the coffee brewing.

"Where did you stay last night?" I ask her. She wasn't home

when I got home from work and I heard her come in early this morning.

"None of your business," she says as she cuts up fruit on the kitchen island. "And since when do you care where I stay?"

"You've been gone a lot lately. Seems like whoever you're seeing, things are getting serious." I see the knife still as she is about to slice the last piece of peach.

"Nope, nothing serious. Just having fun." She offers me a reassuring smile.

"Be safe, Linds."

"Really, you're going to offer *me* the 'be safe' speech? Pfft." She has a point, but it's my job to protect her—and I'll be damned if I let anything or anyone hurt her.

"Fine, all right. Lecture's over."

"Good," she says, pouring us two giant mugs of coffee. "So how are things with Reagan?" she asks, setting a steaming mug of coffee in front of me while she goes back to cutting fruit. When I don't immediately answer, she stops cutting and turns her head, narrowing her eyes at me. "Please don't fuck this one up. I actually like her," she says. I can't contain my laughter as it gets the better of me.

"You met her in a bar, Lindsay, and talked to her for all of five minutes. How do you have any clue if you like her?"

"You met her in a bar too, Landon, and I just have a gut instinct about people and I can tell she won't take your shit, so that means I like her. That means I *really* like her." She sets the knife down and crosses her arms across her chest. "So dish it, brother."

"It's good, I guess. I mean, we're just hanging out."

"How was your date the other day?"

Sipping the coffee, I set the mug down. "Oh, you mean walking the stray dogs?"

"What?" she says, laughing.

"Yeah, Reagan is a modern-day Mother Teresa. She saves people... dogs... who knows, maybe she can save me." I wink at Lindsay and pick out some berries from the fruit bowl she has on the island.

"What do you mean she saves people and dogs?"

"She's a fucking doctor, Lindsay, not some barmaid like I thought she was, and she walks the stray dogs from her ex-aunt's animal rescue on her days off."

"Jesus," Lindsay says, pouring creamer into her coffee. "She's really a doctor?"

"Yep. Catches babies all day," I joke.

"Then what was she doing working at Mac's?"

"I asked the same thing. Her Uncle Mac owns the place and on occasion, she helps him out. Sounds like it's not often. Just happened to be my lucky night last weekend."

"That's called fate, Landon. Don't fuck with fate. Trust me."

"I don't believe in signs and fate and all that bullshit, you know that."

'Well, whatever the hell you believe in, that was it—last weekend. Divine intervention or whatever. That. Was. It. Don't fuck this up," she says, pointing at me. I actually roll my eyes at my sister.

"Yeah, okay, Linds, I'll try not to fuck this up like I do everything else."

"Hey, I didn't say that." She lowers her voice.

"I know. But hey, I actually have some good news to share."

"What?" she asks skeptically.

"I made detective. I got the job." With a squeal, she lunges at me and wraps her arms around my neck, squeezing me.

"I knew you would get it. I'm so proud of you." She continues hugging me. "Now don't fuck this up either." She fake punches me. "I'm really happy for you," she says.

"I'm happy too," I whisper. And I am. For the first time ever, I feel like the fucked up pieces of my life are falling into place.

CHAPTER 8

Reagan

I can barely make out the sound of the vibration from my cell phone buzzing against the wooden nightstand, but it's just loud enough to pull me from my morning slumber. Cracking one eye open, I give myself time to adjust to the morning sun seeping through the slats on the wood shutters that cover the oversized windows in my room.

"What?" I grumble when I hear the vibration again. "It's my day off. Let me sleep," I say as I roll over and pull it off the nightstand. Sliding my finger across the screen, I see I have missed a call from my mom and another one from Landon. Landon; my heart jumps momentarily at the sight of his name on my screen. Debating whom I should call first, I decide that coffee is more important.

I shuffle down the long, tiled hallway to the kitchen. The kitchen is bare, with only a few small appliances on the counter top, and the large bouquet of peonies from Landon adorning the granite kitchen island. Pulling the coffee grounds from the freezer, I prep the coffee pot and start it. Leaning on the island, I close my eyes and press my nose to one of the large flowers that has opened as I inhale the fresh scent of the flowers that remind me of home. The flowers put a smile on my face when I think of Landon and the bright pink color stands out against the modern cream cabinets and light granite counter tops of my newly remodeled kitchen.

The kitchen is filled with the smells of the peonies and the freshly brewed coffee, and the only thing that could make this morning any better was if Landon was sitting here in the kitchen with me. Thinking of Landon, I grab my cell phone and slide my finger over the recent calls screen, tapping his name. My heart flutters inside my chest as the phone rings... once... twice...

"Hey, Doc." His raspy voice puts a smile across my face.

"Morning, Champ. I saw you called—what's up?"

"Wanted to steal you for the day. I know it's your day off."

Various thoughts cross my mind as he asks me to spend the day with him, but right now, my need to see him, to smell him, to touch him is greater than the voice in my head telling me to slow down and take this slowly. There is something dangerous about him—but it's something I want, something I need.

"Sure, but aren't you working?"

"Not today. I'll explain when I come over."

"It'll have to be a while; I just woke up and just started a pot of coffee."

"Perfect. I'll be over in fifteen minutes. Save me some coffee." Before I have time to say anything, he's hung up on me.

"Shit," I mumble to myself as I run down the hallway to the master suite, stripping out of my negligee and panties as fast as I can. I turn on the shower to warm up the water. I brush my teeth quickly and swish some mouthwash around, before spitting it into the sink. Stepping into the warm shower, I immediately lather up my body with the sponge and body wash. It's mornings like this that I thank myself for spending a small fortune on laser hair removal, never having to shave my legs, bikini or armpits ever again. The time saving alone was worth the thousands I dropped as a medical school graduation gift to myself.

Lathering up my long, dark hair, I massage my scalp for a few seconds, hoping to relieve what I hope is not the start to a migraine. Ever since that day, fifteen years ago, I've battled migraines. I swear it's because I've never cried so hard over anything ever, and I've convinced myself that I damaged myself from crying and lack of breathing and not sleeping for what felt like months. As a physician, I know that's not the case, but I never had headaches before that day.

Rinsing my hair, I condition it quickly and rinse—grabbing an oversized towel and wrapping it around myself. I pull my hair into a smaller towel, twisting it on top of my head. Careful to move quickly, I apply lotion, deodorant, and pull my wet hair down from the towel. Checking the time, I realize that Landon should be here any minute, so I rush to the large walk-in closet and sift through some casual dresses. It won't be too much longer and the weather won't allow for dresses, so I'm taking full advantage of it while I can. I pull down a navy blue cotton dress and pair it with nude flat sandals, gold hoop earrings, and a gold charm necklace with matching bracelets. I love this outfit; it's cute, casual, and comfortable.

With no sign of Landon yet, I apply make-up and begin blow-drying my long locks, running a round brush through my hair in hopes of creating some waves. My eyes wander nearly every minute to the cell phone that is sitting on my bathroom counter—tormenting me. I keep watching the clock, wondering where he is. Just as I'm putting the blow dryer away, I hear the chime from my doorbell. My heart races and I stride down the hallway to the door.

With a deep breath, I turn the knob and open the door. He is standing in a light blue shirt and faded blue jeans with a pair of aviator glasses and I literally stop breathing.

"Hey, Doc." He leans in, pressing a quick kiss to my forehead.

"Come in," I say, stepping aside as he crosses the threshold into my home. I notice immediately how observant he is. He scans the kitchen, the living area, and the hallway. Maybe it's the cop in him, or maybe it's just him—but I love watching him. Dressed in a pair of jeans and a light blue polo shirt that hugs the muscles in his arms perfectly, I can't take my eyes off of him.

"Nice place, Doc."

"Thanks," I say quietly, dropping my eyes from him. This condo is gorgeous—stunning. I know it is, but it is also almost embarrassingly so. It's so not me, but I fell in love with this place when I was looking at homes. In reality, I'm much more modest than this condo appears, but the luxury kitchen with high-end appliances sold me. "So why are you off work today?"

"We're celebrating."

"Celebrating what, exactly?"

"My new job." He smiles and I lunge at him, throwing my arms around him in a giant hug. His arms fall into place, holding me tightly in return. My nose is pressed against the side of his neck as I breathe him in.

"Congratulations," I breathe against his neck and he squeezes me a little tighter. "I'm proud of you," I say, pulling out of his embrace.

"Thank you," he says, pressing a kiss to my forehead. He's holding my forearms, not letting me out of his immediate space.

"I was thinking we could go to the shooting range and then grab lunch, unless you already had plans today."

"Shooting range?"

"Yeah, shoot some guns," he says excitedly.

"Sure, but I wanted to talk to you about yesterday." I hang my head, slightly embarrassed about yesterday's events in the garage.

"What about it?" He tips my chin up so that we're looking directly at each other. I don't even know what to say; I'm just embarrassed, so I shrug and take a deep breath while trying to form the words to a coherent sentence.

"You were kind of aggressive."

"And?"

"And, I don't know." I study his blue eyes. There is so much hidden in those eyes, compassion, danger, fierceness, pain, and maybe even love.

"Are you afraid of me?"

"No."

"You should be."

"Why?"

"I'm going to hurt you, Reagan. It's who I am; it's what I do. I will never physically hurt you—but emotionally, I will wreck you, and I don't want to fucking hurt you. I like you—a lot. But it's inevitable, I'm going to hurt you and I'm going to hate myself when it happens." He drops his head and his shoulders slouch slightly. He shoves his hands into his front pockets and stares at his feet.

"So don't hurt me." Where did those words even come from? "I *know* you won't hurt me."

"You don't know that," he says, lifting his head, but he turns and looks away from me. "Give me your hand." He pulls his right hand out of his pocket and I reach for it. Placing his hand over my heart, I hold it there. I want him to feel how rapidly it's beating—for him.

"Feel that?"

He nods his head.

"This is what happens when I'm near you. You scare me in a good way. This…" I press his hand tighter to my chest, "doesn't happen for just anyone. I know you won't hurt me." I say those words with confidence, a little louder than I normally would have.

He turns back and catches me with his eyes. There are so many unspoken words just sitting in those eyes.

"So I scared you last night. I was too aggressive?" My eyes fall from his to those lips, then to his jawline, which is lightly covered in day-old stubble.

"Yes, a good scared," I whisper. "You were aggressive *and* sweet." I swallow hard and inhale deeply. "And I liked it—all of it."

We stand staring at each other. My arms have since fallen to my sides and I stand as his large, firm hands hold me by my upper arms. He moves quickly, pulling me to him—our lips connecting. His full lips press against mine and I lose myself in his kiss.

Guiding me back until I rest against the kitchen island, our tongues dance as our kisses deepen. My heart races as I lean back and he lowers his mouth to my neck and I let him consume me. Grabbing my hips, he lifts me and sets me gently on the edge of the island, my long legs dangling off the side. My arms are wrapped around his neck as he peppers the sensitive area just behind my ear with kisses. He positions himself between my legs much like he did yesterday, only today I'm wearing a dress and the hem rises higher, the further my legs spread apart. His firm hands rest on my bare thighs and he squeezes them lightly as his kiss intensifies.

My breathing becomes more rapid and his lips move from behind my ear along my jawline, taking his time as he moves slowly back to my mouth. He tugs gently at my bottom lip with his teeth and his hand slides further up my thighs, finding the junction of my hips. My breath catches when his thumbs finally come to rest at the edge of my panties. His mouth leaves my lips as he kisses a slow trail down my cheek to my neck as he settles in and sucks gently on my neck just above my collarbone. Goose bumps break out across my skin as he nips tenderly at my neck.

"You like that, huh, Doc?" he whispers as his hands move higher under my dress, resting just under my bra. His thumbs brush over the lace that is doing nothing to hide my tight nipples and I gasp.

"God," I mumble as he continues his assault on my neck, kissing, sucking, and nipping. My fingers dig into the firm flesh of his shoulders and he bites at my neck a little harder. I flinch slightly at the little bite, and I hear a low growl in the back of his throat. I know that if I don't stop this, we'll never make it to the gun range, not that I really want to go shoot guns—but if it means spending time with him, I'll do it.

"Landon," I mumble as a shiver rolls through me.

"Yeah, Doc." He continues kissing, sucking, licking, and my head falls back even more.

"We need to stop, or we're not going to make it to the range, or lunch."

"This is lunch," he mutters against my neck.

"Do you want to fuck me?" I ask him directly, just as he asked me. He stills, his lips still pressed against my neck, his nose tucked behind my ear. I can feel his hot, heavy breaths just behind my ear. Pulling himself off my neck, he steps back and looks at me—searching my eyes. His breathing is still heavy, labored, and his light eyes have darkened.

"Yeah, Reagan, I want to fuck you," he says quietly. He releases me from his arms and steps away from the kitchen island. I tug at the hem of my dress, pulling it down to cover more of my thighs before I slide off the island and walk over to him.

"I want to fuck you too, but my need to see you again, to have you be a part of my life is greater than my need to fuck you. Does that make sense?"

"Jesus Christ, Reagan," he mumbles and rakes his hands over his face. "Look what you do to me." I smile when I see how flustered he is. Taking a moment to compose himself, he reaches out and fixes a piece of my hair. Running the backs of his fingers over my cheek, he stands and shakes his head at me before a smile breaks free from his lips.

"Let's go to the gun range before I change my mind and tell you how much I hate guns, Champ." I lean forward and kiss his cheek before grabbing my clutch and cell phone off the counter. He's still shaking his head as he follows behind me, opening the door for me.

"Do you really want to…"

"Landon." I stop him.

"Fine, let's go shoot some guns," he says, closing the door behind us.

CHAPTER 9

LANDON

The entire drive to the shooting range, we hardly say anything to each other. She sits with a smirk on her face and giggles while I try to think of kittens and unicorns and girly shit to make my hard-on go away. It doesn't work. My hand rests on her thigh in a possessive manner, as if she was mine—because she is, kind of. My thumb rubs small circles along the soft skin just at the hem of her dress. I want to see everything under that dress.

"So what's with the car?" she asks, finally breaking the silence as she turns away from the window to look at me.

"What do you mean?"

"What's with this car? I mean, I like it, it just doesn't seem like something I thought you'd drive."

"What did you envision me driving? A mini-van?"

"No, but a completely blacked out Camaro wasn't what I envisioned—it's very 'bad boy' of you." She flashes her sweet smile at me. The one that lights up her whole face and makes her blue eyes sparkle.

"Did you really just say that? I'm selling this car now," I joke with her.

"I'm just giving you a hard time. I actually really like it. It's fun and sporty—where my SUV is practical."

"Maybe that's what I like about you. You're smart and sexy and practical." She doesn't respond, but I see her thinking. She's quiet the remaining few miles until we get to the range. Cutting the engine, I look at her and she looks terrified.

"Ready?"

"No, not really." She runs her palms over her blue dress nervously.

"Look, there's nothing to be nervous about. You're here to learn. I'll be with you the entire time." I reach out and hold her hand, giving it a little squeeze. "I promise it won't be as scary as you think it's going to be."

"Everything with you is scary," she says under her breath, but I hear it. She reaches for the door handle and opens the door. As she steps out into the humid air, I see her chest rise and fall as she takes a deep breath. I meet her on her side of the car just as she's closing the door. Walking back to the trunk, I pop it open, taking out my 40mm Glock and a smaller nine-caliber Glock for her. Meeting me at the back of the car, she stands to the side of me, fidgeting with her purse.

"Ready?" I ask as I take a few steps, heading toward the entrance of the range. When I see she's not following, I walk back to her and lace her fingers through mine. No words are said as I slip her soft hand into mine and gently tug her behind me to the entrance.

I open the door for her, and she steps into the shop. Her grip on my hand tightens. Before we approach the counter, I pull her aside.

"Look at me," I demand quietly. Her large blue eyes find mine. "Something else you have to know about me, okay?" She nods. "I don't make promises. But I'm going to promise you something, Reagan, right now. I'm not going to let anything happen to you, okay?" She stares at me and, if I'm not mistaken, her eyes are slightly pink and misty. "You're safe with me right now—here." She nods again in understanding.

At the counter, we hand over our driver's licenses and sign the required waivers. Her hand shakes the entire time she signs and her fingers are white from pinching the pen so tightly. Maybe this wasn't such a good idea.

"You're all set, window four," the man instructs us. "You're lucky; it's dead today. No one is here but you. Have fun and take your time."

Taking her hand in mine again, I walk her slowly to the sliding glass doors that open and lead us toward the range. I guide her inside and wait for the next set of doors to the shooting range to open. When they open, I nudge her gently and we walk down to window four—all the way at the end of the range. I set the guns and ammunition on the small ledge, as Reagan steps back from the window. Her blue eyes dart from window to window, to the ceiling to the floor as she takes in the open space of the range and its surroundings.

"Doc, it's going to be okay. Calm down," I nearly beg her. Reaching out, I hold her firmly by the shoulders. "I won't let anything happen to you." God, I wish those words were true. I won't let anyone else, or anything hurt her, but I can't promise that I won't hurt her.

"I just really don't like guns. I should never have agreed to this."

"But you did, and I already told you, I'm not going to let

anything happen to you, okay?" I press a tender kiss to her temple.

"Okay," she whispers.

I tuck a piece of her long, wavy hair behind her ear, and drop my hands from her shoulders down her arms. Leaning in, I kiss the tip of her nose and whisper, "Don't be afraid." With a tight smile and a hard swallow, she nods her head.

"I'm going to go first. Watch me. Watch how I stand, where I put my hands on the gun, how I lean. Just watch." I push bullets into the magazine and she fiddles with the protective glasses in her hand. Setting the gun down, I take the glasses and slide them onto her face. Her blue eyes watch me nervously through the clear glass lenses as I take the ear protection and slide it onto her head and over her ears.

"Watch me," I mouth to her and she nods again in understanding. I clip the target and push the button on the wall to send it down the range. Taking my position, I grab the gun and take my stance. Glancing over my shoulder to her, I can see she's watching me intently.

With steady pressure, I pull the trigger and *pop, pop, pop*, I empty all sixteen rounds into the target down range. Setting the gun down, I push the button to bring my target back. I nailed the target. All sixteen rounds hit exactly where I wanted them to. I pin a new target on the clips and send it down range for Reagan to shoot at. I fill her magazine while she stands anxiously picking at her fingernails.

"Ready?" I say loudly, hoping she can hear me.

"Ready as I'll ever be," she yells back as she steps up to the open window. Positioning myself behind her, I press myself against her back. Her shoulders are tense, and her long hair hangs down the middle of her back. I adjust her grip and straighten her arms. I breathe in the smell of her shampoo mixed with the light floral perfume she's wearing. Her smell is feminine—sweet. With my chest pressed firmly against her back, I wrap both arms around the front of her, placing my hands on top of hers. She's shaking, so I hold her for a moment and try to calm her. Her slender fingers are locked around the handle of the gun and her forefinger rests on the trigger. I pull back the ear protection from her left ear and she turns her head just slightly.

"Look straight ahead at the target." She nods in acknowledgement. I nudge her leg forward just a little bit with my knee. "I'm going to put the ear protection back on. Just follow my direction. When I tap your shoulder, shoot. Hold the trigger and pull it back slow and steady, okay?"

She nods and I place the ear protection back on her ear. I straighten her arms and reposition her hands. My left arm is snaked around her waist, holding her against me. I check her form one last time and tap her shoulder. She hesitates, then empties the entire magazine into the target. I can tell from where I stand behind her that every bullet hit the target somewhere between the head and chest area. She sets the gun down on the ledge and pulls off her ear protection, turning toward me.

"You fucking know how to shoot?" I say, pulling off my own ear protection.

"Yep. I didn't say I didn't know how; I said I didn't like it. I never have. My dad used to take me shooting, and to this day, my blood pressure rises to unhealthy levels when I'm near a gun."

"You could have told me you'd shot before," I say, stepping around her to pull in her target. As it nears, I see a smirk settle on her face.

"Not too bad, huh, Champ?"

Every hole was center mass, and one to the neck. I roll my

eyes and refill both magazines. "Put your ear protection back on," I say. I make mental note of the video cameras and where they're positioned, as well as check out if the guy at the front desk is watching us. He's not. I send another target down range, ready for her to empty sixteen bullets into it.

Stepping back, I let Reagan insert her magazine into the gun. She positions herself before I sidle behind her. "I want you to aim for the head. I want all of your bullets in that head, got it?" She nods and I pull her ear protection from around her neck and place them on her head. I position myself exactly as I did before, behind her, but this time I don't hold her arms. I keep both of my palms pressed to her stomach; my left hand up higher under her rib cage and my right hand pressed flat across her abdomen.

She finds her stance and, before she shoots, I drop my right hand a little lower. She turns her head toward me, and I nudge it back with mine. She readjusts her shoulders, and I drop my hand lower. I can feel the little waist band of her panties through her thin cotton dress as my hand trails lower.

With her arms raised, the length of her dress is mid-thigh and my hand drops lower as I reach under the dress, placing my hand on her right thigh. She lowers her arms, but I nudge her again and she raises them, repositioning herself for a third time. My chin is resting on her shoulder and her arms have started shaking. My hand snakes higher and I make my final move, pressing my fingers against the soft silk just between her thighs. Only this time, she doesn't budge. Her arms are straight and her stance is perfect.

Her thighs are separated just enough, allowing me enough room for a finger to glide over the center of that small patch of silk. I feel her inhale deeply as I brush across her again, just as she pulls the trigger, emptying her magazine. Placing the gun on the ledge, she pulls off her ear protection and glasses, setting them down next to the gun.

"What the hell was that?" she barks at me. I place my glasses and ear protection next to hers. "You don't play fair," she says, her voice seething.

"Never look away from your target." I point at her. "Distraction will get you killed." Her face is red and full of anger, or maybe embarrassment, but I'm pretty sure it's desire that has her reacting this way. Stepping up to her, I take her hands in mine, not saying anything— holding them against my chest.

"Your finger brushing my…" She turns her head. "My…"

"Wet lips?" I say, cocking my head to the side.

"Panties. Your finger brushing my panties will get you killed." She crosses her arms over her chest.

"I'm sorry. I was trying to see how you'd react to being distracted." She narrows her eyes at me.

"Don't distract me when I'm holding a gun," she whispers.

"Forgive me?"

"Yeah," she says, laying her forehead against my chest. I wrap my arms around her and she mimics me, wrapping hers around my waist. I hold her—as I fight with new feelings that are simmering just below the surface—the need to protect her and care for her.

"I'm ready to go," she mumbles against my chest. She pulls herself out of my arms and I begin collecting the guns and ammunition as she takes the glasses and ear protection. She waits for me at the first glass door and we step through it as it opens.

"I'm sorry if I made you mad," I say apologetically.

"I'm not mad at you; you just caught me off guard."

"That's what I was trying to do," I smirk. "It worked, didn't it?"

"Shut it, Landon." She tries to contain her smile as she shoulder bumps me just as the second set of doors opens. Stepping into the retail area, we return our glasses, ear protection, and get our licenses back. There is no hesitation or falter in her step as she heads straight for the main entrance and into the safety of the outside.

"Whoa, wait up!" I holler from behind her. "So I take it we won't be doing this again, will we?" I joke as I unlock the car. Her eyebrows raise, and her lips pull into a snarky smile.

"Uh, no."

"Well, I think we're even… I walked dogs, you shot guns."

"That's even? Dogs are sweet. They lick your face and give you love. Guns are dangerous and icky."

"Icky?"

She rolls her eyes at me and slides into the front seat. "Deal. No more dogs, no more guns."

I chuckle at her. "Hungry?"

"Starving." She smiles at me. That smile. Every time she smiles at me, a little piece of the concrete walls I've built around me crumbles and falls away. Everything good about her lies within her eyes and that sweet smile.

"There is a little Mexican restaurant down the road that has the best margaritas I've ever had, and the food is amazing too."

"I could live on a supply of good margaritas," she says. "It sounds perfect."

She leaves her window down as we drive the few miles to Armando's. With her head resting against the headrest, her eyes are closed and the wind whips her long hair around, but she doesn't seem bothered by it. If I weren't driving, I'd study every one of her features better. I could watch her for hours, days— drinking in her beauty. Her profile is stunning. Her fair skin set against her dark hair isn't something you see all that often. She's beautiful.

"We're here," I say as I pull into a parking spot. The parking lot is empty, as it usually is in the early afternoon. "Have you eaten here before?" I ask, as we both step out of the car.

"No, but I've heard it's amazing. Most of the small restaurants in town are," she says as we step inside the restaurant. Just inside the double doors, we're greeted by the cool air conditioning, the modern décor, and the aroma of freshly made tortillas. The restaurant is small, but it's clean and recently remodeled. I point to a small table tucked away in the far corner. As we settle in, our server greets us and we each order a margarita as we look over the extensive menu.

"There's so much to decide from and it all sounds amazing," she says as she flips each page of the menu. "What's good?" she asks me.

"My favorite is the *carne asada* tacos. The flavors are phenomenal."

"I think I'll try that," she says as she sips her margarita.

"So your dad used to taking you shooting?" I'm curious to know how she became such a good shot.

"Yeah, he felt it was important that I knew how to handle a gun, especially because I'm so afraid of them."

"Why are you afraid of them?"

"No reason really; I just don't like guns."

"Huh. Fair enough. I don't particularly like them either, but they're an evil necessity for me."

"I understand that you have to be comfortable with them." She shrugs. "Thanks for taking me with you today."

"You're welcome. I really like spending time with you," I admit.

"Me too." She runs her finger around the edge of the glass, collecting salt on the tip of her finger. She brings it to her mouth slowly and her tongue peeks out from between her teeth to collect it. We sit in comfortable silence for a few moments as I watch her strum her fingers on the table gently and twirl a piece of her long brown hair around her finger. She takes a sip of her margarita and I find myself lost in a world of thoughts as I focus on her lips.

"So, I feel like I always do all the talking," she says, setting her margarita on the table. She meets my gaze and pauses for a moment. "I'd love to learn more about you and about your family." *Shit.* I catch her looking at me, studying me, as I sit and say nothing. I play with the salt that has fallen off the rim of my glass when I finally speak.

"Like I mentioned before, there is really nothing to tell you. My family is just Lindsay and me."

"What about your parents?"

"Don't have any."

"What do you mean, you don't have any?"

"My dad is dead, and I haven't seen my mom in over twenty-two years. No clue if she's dead or alive." I know my tone seems abrupt, but I hate talking about my family. This is shit she doesn't need to know about me.

"Why did she leave?" she asks quietly. I can tell her inquisition is sincere, but it's just not something I'm willing to talk about with her, at least not yet.

"Look. I know we're learning about each other, and part of that is finding out who we are and where we came from, and that means asking questions about our families… but my family was so fucked up, Reagan. We were so beyond the scope of normal that there really aren't accurate descriptions of how fucked up we were, okay?"

"Landon, I would never judge you based upon your family. I don't give a shit how imperfect your family is or was. What I care about is learning more about *you*."

"And I want to learn more about you too, but right now, I want to leave my family shit where it belongs—in my past."

And this is where the dark secrets I keep want to come out. There is something about Reagan that makes me comfortable, makes me want to tell her everything about me, and it scares the hell out of me. I wonder if I'll ever be able to share those secrets, or if they'll haunt me, taunt me for the rest of my life.

"You know, sometimes talking about it helps," she says, resting her hand on top of mine. I know she's not going to let this go, and maybe in time, I'll be able to share bits and pieces, but for now, she humors me, "So tell me more about Lindsay."

"She's everything to me. It's pretty much been her and me since I was eight and she was four. She's the only person in this world I'd lay down my life for."

"You're wrong," she interjects. "Your job puts you in the position to lay down your life for complete strangers."

"I guess, but maybe what I was getting at, is that she's the only person I would intentionally put down my life for."

"You're wrong again," she corrects me. "You intentionally put yourself in harm's way every single day—for what? Because whether you believe it or not, you care about others."

She's right. I decided to become a police officer because I wanted to prove that officers were meant to help people, not hurt them, like my dad. I nod at her and smile.

"You know, Doc, you're too smart for your own good sometimes, you know that, right?"

"I may have heard that before." She smiles. "So, Lindsay," she reminds me.

"I mean, I don't know what to say about her. She's more than just my sister—she's the one person who knows everything about me: the good, the bad, and the ugly, and doesn't judge me. Well, her *and* Matt." I laugh. "She loves her job and she's damn good at it."

"She is," Reagan interjects. "How long has she been a reporter?"

"Almost a year. She really wants to anchor, so she busts her ass around that TV station. I don't know anybody that puts in more hours than her."

"You sound proud of her," Reagan says, sipping her margarita just as the waiter delivers our food.

"I am. Damn proud."

"Obviously, I don't know her well, but I'd love to spend more time with her. I love her sense of humor."

"She's witty all right, and sarcastic, and a pain in the ass. I seem to surround myself with women like that."

"Oh yeah?" Her eyebrow arches as she says it.

"Yeah."

"Well, maybe you should choose better company," She takes a bite of her taco and rolls her eyes at me.

"Nah. I actually kind of like the company I've been keeping lately." I look away from her—these little admissions scare me almost as much as my past does.

"I like it too," she whispers as she sets her napkin on the table. "I'm really happy we've been spending time together."

"That's the margarita talking," I joke with her and she laughs at me, but her eyes tell me otherwise.

"So what did Matt say when you told him about your new job?"

"He's really happy for me. He is the only person other than Lindsay who has really ever supported me. It's going to be weird not riding patrol with him every day."

"Has he ever considered applying for a detective position?"

"We've talked about it. He's interested in homicide. Not a lot of that here in this department—which is good, but doesn't really open up any opportunities for him here."

"We should all celebrate together, maybe we can all go out this weekend," she says excitedly. "I'd love to get to know Lindsay better, and Matt too. We could go to Mac's—have some drinks, dance; it would be a lot of fun. What do you think?" She's almost bouncing up and down in her seat, she's so excited.

"Let me ask Matt and Lindsay, but it sounds like it could be fun. Trouble, but fun."

"Trouble?" Reagan inquires. "Why?"

"Matt hates dancing and doesn't drink much, and let's just say Lindsay likes to indulge on her nights out and dance her ass off. When she doesn't have her boyfriend of the month with her, poor Matt gets sucked into being her dance partner."

"Is that why he looked so miserable last weekend? I thought maybe he didn't feel well or something."

"No, that look was straight up pain from having to dance with my sister."

"That is so funny." She laughs. "I hope they'll want to do it again. Maybe Mac's two weekends in a row isn't such a great idea."

"I'll ask them. You never know until you ask, right?"

"If it's for you, I'm sure they'll agree." The server interrupts us as he takes our plates and empty glasses.

"Thanks for lunch. I feel like I should be paying since this is a congratulatory lunch for you."

"Never. You may make eight times as much money as I do, but you'll never pay if you're with me."

"Thanks," she says quietly as she blushes. "You ready to go?" I'm not. I could sit here and talk to her all day long, then take her home and touch her, taste her all night long.

"Yeah, let's get you home."

Something stirs inside of me when I say that, a possessiveness I've never felt before. I don't want to take her to *her* home; I want to take her to mine. But I can't, I won't.

CHAPTER 10

Reagan

Locking the door behind me, I traipse over to the oversized white leather couch in my living room, tossing my clutch onto the sofa table as I pass it and throw myself down on the couch. I've known this man for all of five days, *five days...* and everything about him consumes me. He consumes my thoughts and my emotions—a reminder of what it feels like to care about someone, an emotion I've buried so deep inside of me that I had long since forgotten what it felt like. I like it. I like him. I want him, and I may even need him.

My cell phone rings, pulling me away from my thoughts. Reaching for my clutch, I unsnap it, pulling the small, thin phone out as my mom's name illuminates the screen. "Shit," I mumble to myself. I slide my finger over the answer icon and clear my throat.

"Hey, Mom! Sorry, I was just about to call you back."

"I called you over seven hours ago, Reagan. You never wait that long to return my call."

"I know, I'm sorry. I was out and about this morning

running errands and it just slipped my mind."

"How is Wilmington, more specifically, how is Mac?" she asks me, her tone more serious.

"Wilmington is good. I'm finally feeling settled and Mac is doing really well. He seems to be responding to the radiation, which is great. I spoke to his oncologist the other day, and his prognosis is really, really good so long as he keeps responding this well to the treatments."

There is a sigh of relief on the other end of the phone, "Thank God, Reagan, that is fantastic news! How is Gemma?"

"She's doing well too. She's still taking in strays—still eccentric Gemma," I say with a smile on my face. I've always loved that Gemma was a little different. Not afraid to buck the trend, or tell it like it is.

"Please send my love to her. I haven't talked to her in ages. Has Mac sold the bar yet?"

Now I sigh, and she hears it. "No, not yet. He's not ready… and don't give him a hard time about it. This is all he has left, Mom. Sam is ready and willing to buy it when the time is right, and the time is not right, okay?"

"As much as I hate you living so far away, I'm so glad you're there with them," she says, her voice cracking. "I know how much you love Mac and Gemma, but please see if you can get him to sell that shithole. He needs to focus on his health."

"Mom, he needs to focus on what makes him happy. That shithole gives him a purpose right now, so please back off of him about selling the bar. He'll know when it's time."

"Okay," she says quietly. "So another reason I wanted to call was your Dad and I were wondering if you were going to come home this year, you know for…"

"I don't know, Mom," I cut her off. "I'm finally settled at work, and I just don't know if I can get away."

"Just for the weekend," she says.

"I'll think about it, okay? Hey, I have to get going. I have to pick up dry cleaning before it closes and run to the grocery store, okay? I love you, Mom. I'll call you soon."

"Love you too, Reagan."

I disconnect the call much like I disconnect the pain, the memories—the feelings. Every September fourth, I spend the day in front of that headstone, reliving that pain. I've never missed September fourth before, and I don't intend to this year, either.

Pulling myself up from the couch, I walk down the hall to the master suite. I stand in the oversized walk-in closet and strip off my blue dress and change into a pair of dark grey yoga pants and a black tank top. My body stills in the closet for a moment as I will myself not to look on the top shelf—but it happens every time. My eyes find it. There sits the box that holds my broken heart. My stomach churns with sadness.

Pulling it down from the shelf, I walk out to the bed and sit down, my fingers wrapped tightly in place, holding onto the box as if my life depended on it—and in a sense, it does. Setting the box on my lap, I rest my hands over the top of it, loosening my grip. My pulse races, and I feel the sting of tears behind my eyes as I run my fingers over the square edge of the box. My throat is dry, making it hard to swallow as I try to force down the lump in my throat. *Don't open the box. Don't open the box.* My fingers find the edge of the box and gently lift the lid, carefully setting it to the side.

I pull out the five pictures I have and set the box down on the comforter. My hands shake violently as my eyes slowly absorb every detail in those pictures again, as if it's the first time I've seen them. I study every minute detail as the tears finally take over and spill from the corners of my eyes and I can no longer see. My body slides off the edge of the bed and I find myself on my hands and knees, sobbing. I haven't cried like this in a long time and for that, I feel guilty. Knowing I've made great progress in moving forward, I realize that I've learned to cope, but you never really heal.

With my face buried in my hands, I let the tears flow. I let my frustrations out and hit the floor with my hands. Momentarily, the physical pain of hitting the floor takes away the emotional pain that after fifteen years still rips through me. Sitting on the floor, with my face still buried in my hands, I allow myself to hurt today, to cry—to feel.

Pulling myself together, I wipe the tears and work to compose my breathing. Rising from the ground, I walk to the bathroom and stand before the sink. Pulling my hair back into a long ponytail, I rinse my face with cool water—allowing the water to wash away the few tears that still run from my eyes.

"Get it together, Reagan," I whisper to myself, drying my face with the hand towel. Deciding to force myself to run those few errands I just lied to my mom about, I bury the pain again as best I can, or save it for another day.

"Be gentle with yourself," I hear my mom whispering to me. She always told me not to be so hard on myself. I smile when I think of her comforting words when I need them most.

Passing through the bedroom on my way to the kitchen, I see the little box still sitting open on my bed, and the photos are spread across the comforter. Grabbing my wallet and keys off the counter I mentally make a list of the errands I need to run. Two hours and three stores later, I finally toss the last of my grocery items into the cart. Grocery shopping is the one task I despise more than anything.

As I toss my reusable shopping bags onto the belt, I empty the cart of my week's worth of groceries. The hair on my neck rises, and my skin tingles with familiarity. I don't need to hear his voice to know that he's standing right behind me; you can say it's a sixth sense. That feeling that you just know someone is there, whether you can see, hear, smell, or feel them. He's here. I turn around slowly to confirm what I already know.

Gorgeous blue eyes meet mine, and a smile that melts me instantly awaits me. "I was wondering if you were ever going to turn around," he says, leaning into me.

"Are you following me, Mr. Christianson?"

"I was just going to ask you the same thing, Ms. Sinclair." His voice is a bit raspy and it sends a shiver through me. "But I'm glad I ran into you. I'm making dinner for Lindsay and me. Maybe you should join us. You said you wanted to get to know her better, so here's your chance." Everything inside of me is screaming *yes*, but the sensible part of me knows I've seen him every day since we met. This is fast, even for being just *friends*.

"I don't know. I have to work tomorrow and get these groceries home and put away…"

"Just think about it." He taps the tip of my nose gently with his forefinger and steps back to begin unloading his cart onto the belt behind my items. I stand, deep in thought—fighting the internal battle of wills.

"Okay, I'll think about it," I say quietly, stepping up to pay for my items. I watch him out of the corner of my eye and take in the sight of him in a pair of red basketball shorts and a tight black t-shirt that hugs every curve of his arms and chest. I can't help but feel a little guilty looking at him like this. The young man bagging my groceries sets the last bag in my cart just as the cashier hands me my receipt.

"Bye," I mouth and give him a small wave. Pushing my cart away, I hear him clearly say, "See you tonight, Doc. Six-thirty."

"Six-thirty," I confirm with a smile. "Maybe I'll see you. If not—I'll call you sometime." The look on his face is priceless, but shit, that leaves me less than ninety minutes to get home, unpack, and get ready.

Saying a quick prayer that I don't get pulled over, I speed through the small residential streets on my way to Landon's. I'm almost fifteen minutes late—which is not like me, but after shopping, and crying, I just needed to shower and change and it took me longer than expected. I'm mentally kicking myself for not putting the box away. The pictures are still scattered across my bed, but it was not something I wanted to deal with before heading over to Landon's. I know I'm still fragile from this afternoon, and another breakdown was not what I needed.

Pulling up to the modest-looking ranch-style house, I put my car in park and kill the engine. I sit for a moment and take in the neighborhood with perfectly manicured lawns and recently updated homes. I watch a father and son play catch with a baseball in their front yard a few houses down, while a young mom pushes a stroller and walks a dog down the street. This reminds me so much of the Midwest and where I grew up, and I instantly feel comfortable here.

Grabbing my purse, I lock the door behind me and walk as quickly as I can to the front door, cursing myself once again for being late. Just as I'm about to push the doorbell, the front door opens and Lindsay greets me, holding two glasses of sangria.

"'Bout time you got here, come in." She laughs, stepping aside so I can enter. "Hope you brought your swimsuit," she says, shoving one of the glasses of sangria into my hands.

"Uh, no." I laugh. "Didn't know I was supposed to bring one and not sure I would have anyway," I say under my breath. Probably not the best idea to put Landon and me in close proximity to each other with very little clothing on, I think to myself.

"You can wear one of mine," she says nonchalantly as she walks past me. "Size ten, right?" she asks over her shoulder.

"More like a twelve," I say, rolling my eyes, but she just scored major points in my book for skewing me down in size.

"Hey, Doc," I hear from the other side of the room. Landon walks through the entrance from the kitchen, carrying a pair of grilling tongs and wearing nothing but a pair of swim trunks and a loose tank top.

"Hey, Champ."

"Glad you could make it," he says as he pulls me into a sideways hug.

"Didn't really have a choice, did I?" I say sarcastically.

"You always have a choice, Doc. But I knew you'd come." His voice is low and sexy and full of arrogance. Why does his voice get to me?

"Pretty confident, aren't you?"

"I always get my way, Reagan. The sooner you remind yourself of that, the better off we'll be." He laughs and walks back toward the kitchen. "Go get one of Lindsay's swimsuits. I heard you two talking. Meet me in the backyard." Goddamn him, I think to myself. Tossing my purse on his leather couch, I walk down the hall to Lindsay's room. The door is cracked open and she's pulling swimsuits out of her dresser, laying them across the end of her bed.

"Hey," I say, pushing the door the rest of the way open.

"Hey, take your pick. I have a bunch of suits in different styles, cuts, and sizes," she says as she places at least six or seven suits on the bed. "I'm going to change in the hall bathroom. Take some suits and go to Landon's bathroom to try them on. He has a full length mirror in there so you can see which one you like on you." She smiles at me as she walks away. "His room is across the hall," she says, shutting the door to the hall bathroom.

Setting my drink on Lindsay's dresser, I pick through the suits on her bed, and there are only two that look remotely conservative enough for me, and I have anxiety about wearing either of them. I scoop them up and find my way across the hall to Landon's room, pushing the door open. The lights are off, but soft daylight filters in through a skylight, illuminating the room enough to see without a light.

I notice the masculine furniture and décor as I find the open door to the bathroom in the master suite. Closing the door behind me, I set both swimsuits on the counter as I pull off my khaki shorts and navy tank top along with my bra and panties. Folding them all into a pile, I set them off to the side on the long granite counter.

Going with my gut and the swimsuit that looks like it has the most coverage, I step into a pair of black bikini bottoms. They're snug, but they fit, and at least they don't have the little ties on the sides that could come loose. They actually feel comfortable—which eases some of my anxiety. The solid black top is halter style, which I hope will help hold my boobs in place, as they're not exactly small. Tying the straps behind my neck, I study myself in the mirror for a second and actually don't feel completely uncomfortable.

The swimsuit shows off all of my curves, and it's a small miracle I fit into a size ten, but I'll take that miracle and own it. Feeling confident and comfortable, I take the suit I didn't try on and open the bathroom door leading to Landon's bedroom.

My feet sink into the plush carpet as I walk toward the door that leads to the hallway. Noticing that it's closed—I stop, not remembering closing it when I came in. Reaching for the handle a firm arm catches me around the waist from behind, pulling me backwards.

"You look amazing, Doc," he breathes into my ear from behind, pressing his hard stomach against my back.

Wiggling out of his grasp, I reach for the door handle again, only to have him pull me back to him again. "We can't keep doing this, Landon," I whisper, not wanting Lindsay to overhear us. I know she's just across the hall.

"Doing what?"

I escape his grasp again and turn around to face him. "This," I motion between us. "The touching, the kissing, the... the... the touching."

"You already said that."

"I know, dammit. You can't keep touching me."

"What if I want to?"

"Well, you can't, okay? We're friends, remember? Just leave it at that."

I know my voice sounds angry, because I am angry. I'm angry because deep down, I want to be more than friends, I want him—and I want him to want me, more than once.

"Okay, Doc." He opens the door and leaves me standing in his room. Just like that, he's gone—and I suddenly realize how disposable I am to him. My hands begin shaking, and I can feel the hurt simmering inside. Walking to Lindsay's room, I set the swimsuit I haven't used on the bed and grab my drink from her dresser.

"Three deep breaths," I tell myself quietly. It's my calming mantra, something I've always done to help me calm down. Tipping back the large glass, I damn near finish the entire glass of sangria. Walking to the kitchen, I see the red wine and fruit soaking in the glass pitcher and I pour myself another glass. I can see Lindsay and Landon talking through the kitchen window, both of them smiling. Landon wraps his arm around her neck and pulls her into a hug. I love how protective he is of his sister, and it warms my heart to know he's not a complete asshole.

Opening the French door that leads to the back patio, I step onto the paved patio. Lindsay turns to see me and walks over. "Let's float." She drags me by the arm toward the pool. "I bought new rafts this weekend."

"The sun isn't even out," I say as she continues dragging me toward the pool.

"We don't need sun to float and talk." She makes a valid point. "Plus, we only have a couple of weeks of warm weather left to do this. Before we know it, we'll be out here hovered around that damn gas fire pit he built last year." She points to the large circular fire pit built out of stone—it's gorgeous.

I glance at Landon, who is leaning against the large outside island. His eyes bore holes through me as he stands with his arms crossed over his chest, holding a bottle of beer. I stare back at him and neither of us makes any effort to look away.

"Here," Lindsay says as she hands me a raft and steps into the pool on the oversized step. I follow her into the water and get settled onto my back on the raft.

"I'm really glad you came over." She pulls my raft toward hers and holds onto it so I don't float away.

"Thanks for having me." I glance at Landon again and he's still leaning against the wall and opening another beer. He smirks at me and I finally look away.

"So Landon tells me you're a doctor?"

"I am. Just moved here and am working in private practice. I'm an OB/GYN."

"So you deliver babies?"

I laugh at this, because everyone thinks all I do is catch babies all day long. In fact, I go days without delivering a baby.

"Not every day, but yes, some days, I deliver babies."

"You don't look old enough to be a doctor, and I mean that in the nicest way possible." She laughs.

"Thank you, I guess. I was blessed with good genes, and I'm probably a lot older than you think I am." I wink at her.

"Hey, Landon," Lindsay yells out. "Can you bring us our drinks?" He picks up the two glasses of sangria that we had set on the tiled island and walks to the edge of the pool, handing us each our drink. I drink in the sight of him—the way the setting sun casts an amber haze on his already bronzed skin and how his blue eyes seem even brighter in the dusk. Lindsay and Landon share the exact same eyes—there is no mistaking them for brother and sister.

"Thanks," I mumble as Landon hands me my glass of sangria. His hand brushes mine as I wait for a response, but he turns and walks away, assuming his position back by the island, pretending not to listen to us, although I know he can hear every word.

"Everything okay with you two?" Lindsay asks me quietly.

"I have no idea. I don't even know what *we* are," I admit.

"Look, he's complex, Reagan, and complicated, and difficult. He's my brother—I know this. Give him a chance," she whispers.

"He's explained everything to me, Lindsay. He's not looking for a relationship, and I'm not looking for a quick fuck." I pause, and carefully choose my words. "I like him, a lot. I really do—but I'm thirty-one years old. I'm past friends with benefits and one-night stands."

"Is that what he said he was looking for?" She raises her eyebrows with a look of concern. Landon still leans against the tiled island, but our hushed conversation has him narrowing his eyes at us.

"Well, not really. He basically just said that he doesn't do relationships and he doesn't sleep with the same woman twice. That's not me, Lindsay. I can't do that, I can't be that."

"And you shouldn't have to be," she says, rolling over on her raft. "Look, my brother doesn't buy women flowers, or take them out for dinner, or invite them over to hang out with me. He likes you, Reagan, but he doesn't know how to show you." She raises her head and we both look at Landon. He stands there, with a beer in his hand, watching us, but again, never makes a move to join us.

"Reagan, there is so much I want to tell you, but it's not my story to tell." Lindsay sighs and looks at Landon before looking back to me. "Just give him a chance, Reagan. There is a lot about him that you don't know—but again, it's for him to tell you, not me."

"How do you give someone a chance when they won't take it?" I watch him as he watches me in return. It's a peaceful, yet strained silence. He shows no emotion as I try to see through his exterior, see the innermost parts of him that he's unwilling to show me on his own.

We float in silence for a few minutes while I take in the little bits and pieces I've just learned, Landon is a complex puzzle—and I hold in my hand only a small handful of the pieces that I need to put him back together. My fear is that I'll never have all the pieces I need.

Finishing my second sangria, I float over to the steps in the pool. Sliding off the raft, I take the steps out of the pool to be greeted by Landon, who takes the glass from my hand.

"Enjoying your time with Lindsay?" he asks as he unfolds a towel and wraps it around me. Even though it's late summer and still warm outside, the light breeze makes the evening air chilly when you get out of the water. Landon rubs his hands over the towel, up and down my arms to warm me up.

"I am. I really like her," I tell him, backing away. I grab my glass and hold it up, motioning to the kitchen door. "I'm going to go get another one."

He nods at me as I step around him and open the door. Stepping into the cool air-conditioned house, goose bumps prick at my skin. I pull the towel around me tighter, tucking it under my armpits. I note his clean, modern kitchen. Everything is perfectly in its place. Not a towel on the counter, not a dish in the sink.

I pour another glass of sangria and set the large glass pitcher back on the kitchen island. Through the kitchen window, I see him squatting down next to the pool, talking to Lindsay. His body language is telling me he's not happy.

Opening the door quietly, I step out onto the patio, and walk over the large flagstone pathway that leads to the gas fire pit. In a circle around the fire pit sits a group of six oversized cushioned chairs. I sit in one and prop my feet on the edge of the unlit fire pit.

"What'cha doing, Doc?" he asks as he pulls a chair up, closer to mine. He sets the chair so close that the arms of the chairs are touching. I like when he's near me; it's a safe, comforting feeling.

"Just came to check out the fire pit. Is everything okay over there?" I motion to Lindsay, who is still floating in the pool.

"Everything's great," he says with a hint of sarcasm in his voice.

I damn near polish off my third glass of sangria and I can feel the red wine's effect on me as my body warms and my head becomes just a little fuzzy. We sit and stare at our feet, which are both propped on the edge, but neither of us talk to each other. Oddly, it's comforting—but I have so many questions for him.

"Remember when we were walking the dogs?" I break the silence as he turns to look at me.

"I do," he responds, tilting his head slightly.

"You mentioned you had feelings for someone before—that you thought you loved her." He swallows hard.

"Mmm hmm."

"Be honest with me. Did you love her?"

"Jesus, Reagan, no. Where is this coming from?"

"Honest, you don't still have feelings for her?"

"No."

"What was her name?"

He takes a deep breath and I feel his arm go rigid next to me.

"Jessica," he says quietly. "The honest answer is, no. I don't love her."

I sip the remaining few swallows of sangria and turn to face him.

"Why are you so afraid of me?"

He laughs, and closes his eyes. "I'm not afraid of you, Reagan."

"Yes, you are. You're afraid to let me in. Why?"

"No, I'm not afraid of you." He sits up straight in his chair, pulling his legs down. His voice is raised and I see Lindsay slip out of the pool from the corner of my eye.

"Then why…" My voice breaks. Goddammit, I curse at myself for letting my emotions get the better of me. "Then why won't you try to be what I need?" I whisper because it seems easier than yelling.

"What is it that you need, Reagan? You want a boyfriend that isn't going to hurt you—that is going to worship you like you deserve and not fuck up, right? Someone that isn't going to hurt you… because, Reagan I don't want to hurt you, I already told you that. And I will hurt you."

"You know what? Fuck you, Landon!" I stand up quickly from the chair. Pulling the towel off that is wrapped around me, I toss it in the chair. Stepping around the chair, I walk briskly toward the house.

"Where in the hell do you think you're going?" he bites out.

"Home," I yell, slamming the door behind me. I damn near run down the hallway to his room, shutting the door behind me. I lean against his door as my stomach turns and tears sting my eyes. I'm hurt and frustrated that he won't let me in, but more importantly, I'm angry with myself for letting me fall so quickly for someone I know so very little about.

Walking into the bathroom, I lock the door behind me and change quickly. Grabbing the wet swimsuit, I find my way to the living room where I set my purse.

Lindsay rounds the corner from the kitchen. "You okay?" I nod, for fear if I try to talk, I'll start crying. I dig through my purse, looking for my keys and cannot find them. Leaning against the wall, she finally speaks up, "He took them, your keys. He's waiting out front for you."

I pull my purse onto my shoulder, and take a deep breath. I hold up the wet swimsuit. "I'll wash it and get it back to you ASAP. Thanks for letting me borrow it." I turn and walk quickly to the front door. I'm embarrassed Lindsay witnessed my temper tantrum.

"Reagan," she says just as I step outside. "I'm sorry. I heard you guys arguing—and you're right, he won't let you in, but you don't know his story. Please be patient and don't give up on him. Not yet. I know he cares about you..." She offers me a small, sad smile.

"You can't give up on something that doesn't want you," I say as I close the door tightly behind me and walk to my car. Landon is sitting in the driver's seat and the engine is running. I've never had such a myriad of emotions running through me as I jog to the driver's side door and yank it open.

"Get out!" My voice is loud and my entire body is shaking. He looks at me like I've lost my mind. And I have—almost twice today. "Now, Landon," I bark at him.

"You're not driving. So you can stand here on the street and yell at me all you want, but I'm not fucking moving from this seat."

"I'm not drunk, so get out of my car—now."

"Not happening. You've been drinking and you're emotional—you're not driving."

"Then Lindsay can drive me; *you're* not taking me

anywhere." I see him flinch when I say that.

"Reagan, from how I see it, you have two fucking choices. One. Get in the fucking car now, and I will drive you home, or two, I will get out of this car, pick your ass up, and make you get in this car, then drive you home. Those are your two choices, so you pick which one you want—either way, *I'm* driving you home." His voice is loud, full of anger, and I can see the muscles in his forearms twitch as he grips the steering wheel.

This man infuriates me. Anger and hurt boil just beneath the surface and I know with one more word, I will crack. All hell will break loose. Without a word, I walk to the passenger side of the car and jerk the door open. Stepping up into the seat, I sit down and slam my door shut. Before I can change my mind, he puts the car in drive and weaves carefully through the streets, headed to my condo. The radio is off, and the car is silent as I rest my head on the window and close my eyes as I try to calm myself down.

I wake up and the room is black except for the tiny hints of moonlight seeping through the shutters. I have no memory of lying down, but I can see a small stream of light from underneath my bedroom door and realize that the kitchen light must be on. My head throbs as I scold myself for almost driving home. As angry as I am with Landon, I'm appreciative he drove me. The large throw blanket that I keep draped over the end of my chaise lounge is lying across me, and I push it off, throwing my legs over the side of the bed.

My head continues to pound as I sit up and remember the

three large glasses of sangria I drank. I do not handle red wine well, and my head is proof I should have stopped after one glass. I shuffle to my bathroom, flicking on the bright lights. Squinting, I open the medicine cabinet and pull out the small bottle of ibuprofen. As I slowly move to the door, I see it out of the corner of my eye. The small box sitting on my nightstand, all closed up. Everything that was scattered on my bed is gone. I presume it's tucked away safely in the small box, but my heart stops when I realize it wasn't me who packed it up.

The small pill bottle in my hand rattles as my hand shakes, reminding me to go get water. Opening the door, I walk the long hallway toward the kitchen. Rounding the corner, I stop dead in my tracks as I see Landon sitting at the kitchen island, his head buried in his hands with a cup of coffee sitting in front of him.

"What are you doing here?" I ask quietly as I walk around him and open the cupboard, pulling down a small glass.

"Wanted to make sure you were okay."

"I'm fine, just tired and the sangria didn't help." I realize my tone is less than friendly, but I'm not in the mood to make small talk right now.

"You were passed out in the car. I carried you to your bed and you didn't even know it."

"I was sleeping, Landon." My voice snarls when I say his name. Setting the bottle of pills on the island, I push the glass into the water dispenser, filling it with cold water. Landon picks up the bottle of ibuprofen and opens it, dumping the pills into his hand.

"Here." He hands me two small pills, returning the rest back into the bottle. I take them from his hand and swallow them along with the cool water. "Drink some more water," he says, taking the glass from my hand and refilling it.

"I think I can handle this. I'm a doctor, for God's sake," I say quietly, taking the glass of water from his hands.

"I know you can," he says quietly. "But maybe I want to take care of you."

God, I want that, more than anything. Care for me, love me—choose me. I want nothing more than to lay my head against his chest and have him hug me, hold me—but my temper gets the better of me.

"Seems to me that the only person you need to take care of is yourself—go figure your shit out," I say bitterly and toss back the glass of water he handed to me.

"Thanks for driving me home." I turn and walk toward the hallway. "You know how to let yourself out."

"Doc," he says as I'm walking down the hallway. "This isn't done." I stop, but don't turn around to look at him. I can't.

"Yeah, it is. You said it yourself; you can't be what I want or need. As far as I see it, it's done. Go home, Champ." I walk as quickly as I can to my room, shutting the door behind me, before throwing myself onto the bed and crying into my pillow. I now know it's possible to love and hate someone in the same breath. Landon is everything I do not need, but he is everything I want.

CHAPTER 11

LANDON

Her words sting—but she's right. Pushing the stool away from the island, I pull my phone out of my pocket. Debating on whether to call Lindsay or Matt to pick me up, I pause when I hear her muffled cries. I stand momentarily listening to her ragged breaths and gentle cries—and I feel helpless. Turning the doorknob, I press the door open and see her body wound into a tight ball huddled in the center of her bed with a pillow pressed against her chest. The room is dark, but the bathroom connected to her bedroom has a light on, allowing me to see her. Her long hair lies on the pillow beside her, and her entire body shakes as she tries to settle her crying.

"Reagan," I say quietly. "I'm not leaving until I know you're okay." Her breaths are still ragged and she grips the pillow pressed to her chest tighter. Leaning against the doorframe, I stand and watch her. She remains curled in a ball, never bothering to look at me, or to acknowledge I'm standing here.

"I'm sorry," I whisper just loud enough so that I know she can hear me. "I never wanted to hurt you or upset you." Her crying has subsided, but her body remains still. I step away from the doorway and into her room. I stand at the foot of her bed, watching her, wanting her.

"Reagan, I'm not leaving until I know you're okay," I repeat myself. She continues to lie still. I can see her eyes are open and she stares straight ahead, making no attempt to look at me when I talk to her, or seek answers from her.

Moving from the end of the bed to the side where she's facing, I kneel on the floor, bringing us to eye-level. Her blue eyes glisten as pools of unshed tears have collected, waiting to spill over.

"Talk to me, Doc." I whisper. "Where did all of this come from today?" She watches me carefully, studying me as I do the same in return. She relaxes her hand and slides it from the pillow she is gripping and lays it flat on the bed, as if she is reaching out to me. I set my hand on top of hers and watch her as she looks at me—willing her to talk to me.

Her hand shifts slightly under mine and I tighten my hold on it. I don't want her pulling away again.

"Let me start, okay?" I push myself up from kneeling and sit on the side of her bed. Her head shifts slightly to follow me and I pull her hand into mine, linking our fingers together.

"You were right when you told me to figure my shit out, Reagan, and I have a lot of it I need to figure out." I swallow hard and run my thumb over her hand. Her eyes are attentive and focused on me as she watches and listens to me. "I have so much baggage and I don't ever want that coming back to hurt…"

"What baggage?" Her voice is raspy and quiet, and it catches me off guard. I'm not at a stage where this is open for discussion with anyone—even her.

"Just secrets from a long time ago, Doc. Secrets I'm not ready to share."

"We all have secrets," she says quietly, her chin quivering and her lip twitching. Tears leak from the corners of her eyes, spilling onto the satin pillowcase on which her head is resting. I release her hand and reach out to wipe her tears. Her eyes close, but her tears don't stop.

"My secrets are in that box," she says, gesturing to the nightstand. My stomach turns when she says that, since I packed up the contents that were spread across her bed. My heart hurts for her. "You know everything about me, and I know nothing about you." I wipe the tears from her cheeks, but as fast as I wipe them, more take their place.

"Landon," she says, her voice breaking, "we can't keep doing this."

I know what she's talking about, but I want to hear her say it. "Do what, Doc?"

"Pretending that we can be strictly friends, when I want more," she admits. I stare into the most perfect blue eyes I've ever seen and, for half a second, I think I might be able to make her happy, that I can try to be what she deserves and expects in a man—but then every insecurity I have beats those thoughts away.

"I can't..." I begin, when she interrupts me.

"No, you can," she snaps at me. "You could try, but you won't." Her words are full of venom, and she rolls over so her back is to me. I see her shoulders shaking gently as I move closer to her and lie down next to her, pulling her into me. I wrap my arms around her and kiss the back of her head.

She's right. I could try, I should try, but I'm so fucking afraid that when I fuck this up, because I will... I will lose her, and I'm not sure I could handle that. I hold her tight against my chest. I can feel her tears slide from her cheeks and onto my hand.

"Shh," I whisper and press my lips to her head. Pulling her closer to me, I can actually feel her heart beating.

"This is what I want," I hear her whisper. "This." And I want this more than anything in the world. I do, but I'm too fucking afraid to admit it. So instead of saying anything, I hold her—comfort her and kiss her.

"Landon," she asks, tearing my thoughts away from her.

"Yeah, baby."

"You know we all have secrets, right?" She turns to face me. "We all have scars; some scars can be seen and others cannot. Every scar has a story and every story needs to be told. When you're ready, I'll be here to listen to your story." She runs her hand across my chin, letting it come to rest on the side of my neck. Laying her head on my chest, she whispers to me, "You may never love me the way I need to be loved—but don't deny yourself the opportunity. Let me love *you*. You deserve that."

My heart hurts, it actually aches when I hear those words. The most amazing woman I've met is lying here next to me, opening her heart, telling me to accept her love, knowing I may never be able to return that love to her. My stomach churns and I feel nauseous. Pressing a soft kiss to her lips, I know I need to leave.

"God, Reagan," I sigh. "Tell me what to say and I'll say it. Tell me what to do and I'll do it, I'll try—I promise I'll try—for you."

"Stay." Her fingers dig into my arm as she clings to me. "Stay," she whispers against my lips as she bites at my bottom lip.

"I can't, Reagan."

"You can." She kisses her way from my lips to my neck. "Please," she says, nipping at my neck. Pushing me gently onto my back, she crawls on top of me, positioning herself across my hips. Sitting on top of me, she rests both of her hands on my chest.

Her eyes search mine, and I so badly want to tell her what I'm thinking, what I'm feeling—but I can't. Where she is strong, I am weak. Where she has words, I have none. I can see a million thoughts flash through her eyes, but she doesn't need to speak the words I feel coming from her at this moment—I know them as if they were my own.

From her position of lying down on my chest, she slowly slides off of me. Weaving her legs through mine, her arm drapes across my waist and her head rests on my shoulder.

"I don't know what it will take for you to open up to me, but I will wait. I will fight for you," she breathes against my neck. Those words, while startling, might be the sexiest words a woman has ever spoken to me. I pull her closer to me, if that's even possible, and hold her. Her breathing settles and I can hear the steady purr of her breaths telling me she's fallen asleep. Pressing a gentle kiss to her forehead, I disassemble our tangled bodies and slide out of her bed. Setting a blanket across her, I watch her sleep—not sure that I've ever seen such a beautiful sight. Leaning over her, I whisper words I never thought I was capable of saying, "I'll fight for you too, baby. I promise." As the words roll off my tongue, my stomach turns at the thought that I may not be capable of loving her the way she wants me to, the way she needs me to.

I pace the dark wooden floor in Reagan's living room, as I wrestle with everything I learned and shared today. I stop to study the pictures that stand perfectly organized in frames on top of the fireplace mantle, pictures of Reagan and her family from past and present. She is equally as stunning in photographs as she is in person.

"What'cha looking at?" I hear from behind me, startling me. "Sorry, didn't mean to scare you." She walks over and stands next to me, looking at the pictures.

"This is Rob, my brother with me when I graduated from medical school." She points to a picture of her with her cap and gown.

"This is my family last Christmas," she says, picking up a glass frame of her and her family in front of a large pine tree, all of them bundled up in jackets and scarves, standing in the snow. "We always cut our own Christmas tree," she says, recalling the memory.

"You and your brother look alike," I remark.

"Everyone says that. They think we're twins, except he's actually three years older than I am."

"He's in Germany you said, correct?"

"You were listening to me at breakfast the other day." She bumps into me with her shoulder.

"I've never missed anything you've told me, Reagan," I turn and look at her. Considering that it's four o'clock in the morning, it's no wonder she looks exhausted. "What are you doing up?" I reach out and tuck a strand of her long hair behind her ear.

"I thought you left," she whispers. I don't know how to respond to her, because part of me did want to leave—to flee where I don't have to deal with these unknown feelings. Feelings that leave me scared to death. So instead of saying anything, I pull her into a hug. I love that she's so tall. Her head fits right into the crook of my neck.

"You need to sleep," I say quietly. "You have to be at work in a few hours. Go rest; I'll be here when you wake up—I promise."

She pulls away and looks at me skeptically, but nods her head and shuffles down the hallway toward her bedroom. Stopping just outside her door, she looks back over her shoulder at me, then turns around slowly, walking back to me. Without a word, she weaves her fingers through mine and walks us back to her bedroom. I don't hesitate. In fact, I long for her touch and grip her hand tighter.

"Just lie with me," she whispers, pressing her finger to my lips so I can't argue or refuse. Pulling me toward the large bed, she pulls the covers back and slides in, moving to the center. I hesitate as I watch her, wondering if it will ever be possible to "just lie with" her and not touch her. Her long body stretches from the pillows to the end of the bed, and her fair skin is begging me to touch it.

Sliding in next to her, she pulls me to her. Wrapping her arm across my waist, she rests her head on my shoulder. She settles in as if she's done it a thousand times—and it feels natural, right.

"Thank you, Landon," she mumbles sleepily.

"For what?" I ask, confused.

"Trying. Thank you for trying."

CHAPTER 12

Reagan

I could seriously get used to waking up to his soft, warm kisses against my lips every morning. "Wake up, sleepy head," *kiss, kiss, kiss*. "You have to get ready for work," *kiss, kiss, kiss*.

"What if I don't want to go to work today?" I grumble against his mouth.

"C'mon, go get in the shower. I'll make some coffee for you." He pushes himself off the bed, and I watch his perfectly inked skin disappear from my bedroom. Gathering what little energy I have, I pull myself out from under the warm covers of my bed that smell like Landon.

"Hurry up, Doc, you're going to be late," I hear him say from the kitchen.

"I know, I know," I yell back as I strip out of my clothes and toss them in my wicker hamper. Grabbing clean scrubs from my closet, I turn on the shower and let it warm up for a minute before getting in. The large glass shower door almost immediately covers in steam and I step in, closing the door behind me. My body is tired and achy, a combination of the after

121

effects of the sangria and lack of consistent sleep last night.

I let the hot water carry away the tension as I quickly wash my body and shampoo my hair. Rinsing my body, I condition my hair quickly as I wash my face. Rinsing the final bit of conditioner from my hair and face cleaner from my face, I shut the water off and grab a towel. Drying myself swiftly, I twist the towel onto my hair and step out of the shower. I slip into my short silk robe and quickly brush my teeth. Tossing the towel from my head into the laundry hamper, I run a comb through my long hair, sorting through the tangles.

"Doc." He peeks his head in the door. "Coffee is ready." He steps into the room, carrying a large mug. "Extra hot with a dash of vanilla creamer." He hands me the mug.

"You know this is going to be the only thing that keeps me alive today, right?" I blow across the top of the mug, hoping to cool it down enough to take a small sip. He stands there, watching me press the mug to my lips and crinkle my nose when the coffee is still too hot to drink.

"What?" I ask as he continues to watch me.

"You're beautiful," he says as he plays with a piece of my wet hair, running it between his thumb and his finger.

"I'm wet, and late—and hardly beautiful, but thank you," I say, leaning in to press a kiss to his cheek.

I set the coffee down on the marble counter and pull my make-up bag out from a large drawer. Landon stays behind me, leaning up against the wall, just watching me. I quickly apply some powder to my face, mascara to my lashes, and lip-gloss to my lips; his eyes study every movement I make.

"Why are you watching me?" I laugh as he takes me in.

"I like watching you and I like you in that robe," he says, moving toward me slowly like a cat moves toward its prey.

Wrapping his arms around me from behind, he plays with the silk belt that holds my robe closed. Rubbing the soft fabric belt between his fingers, he tugs at it gently and the belt unties.

I still as my robe barely opens, showing just a hint of skin from my chest down to my thighs. Still positioned behind me, his hand settles around my neck, tugging my neck back against his shoulder. I can feel every muscle from his chest down to his calves tense as his forefinger rubs small circles around my neck. Goose bumps prick my skin as his finger trails the small line of skin down from my neck, through the hollow of my breasts, to the center of my body. Stopping at my waist, he inhales sharply and steps back from me.

"Finish getting ready for work or you won't be making it in today." His voice is low, and there is a hunger in his tone. I watch him from the mirror as he rakes his hand over his mouth before turning and leaving the bathroom. He grabs his t-shirt from the floor and shuts the bedroom door as he disappears down the hall.

I change into light blue scrubs and run the blow dryer through my hair, wrapping a ponytail binder around my wrist for later. Grabbing my coffee off the counter, I open the door and find Landon sitting at the kitchen island, drinking coffee and scrolling through his phone.

"Ready?" I ask as I slip into my shoes and gather my purse and phone.

"Yeah." He slides off the stool and pulls my keys from his pocket. Holding out my hand, he walks past me and opens the door. "After you." He smiles.

"Are you going to give me my keys?" I step through the door and he shuts it behind him, locking it.

"Nope. I'm driving." He's direct and to the point. I can see where many people would have a tough time dealing with his strong personality.

"It's my car. I'll drive." I stand in the garage with my arms folded across my chest.

"You're going to be late. Get your ass in the car, and drink this. I'll be driving you to work today." He shoves a travel mug of coffee at me. There is no point in arguing. One of the most important things I've learned in my thirty-one years of life is "pick your battles." This isn't a battle worth fighting over, plus I kind of like the thought of him driving me to work.

Shaking my head, I get in the passenger seat and sip on my coffee while Landon navigates the morning rush hour through the streets of Wilmington.

"What time should I pick you up?" he asks me with a smile on his face as he turns into the parking lot of the small office building adjacent to the hospital.

"I'll text you, but we're usually wrapped up around six o'clock." I open the door and step out of the car. Grabbing my coffee and purse, I can't help but feel happy today even though I'm exhausted—mentally and physically.

"Have a good day, Doc." He smiles at me as I shut the door and he slowly drives away.

"Who the hell was that?" I jump, startled by the voice so close to me.

"Jesus, Adam, you scared me." I press my hand to my chest in reaction.

"Who's in your car?" I want so badly to tell him that it's none of his business, but I have to work with this man, and it's best just to keep things civil.

"A guy. I mean a friend. I really need more coffee," I say,

laughing as I wave my empty travel mug in front of me, trying to change the subject.

"Why does he have your car?"

"Because he doesn't have his car." My voice is tinged with just a hint of annoyance. "I'm sorry, I didn't mean to sound rude, but I'm really tired, and need to get settled, and I need more coffee before patients start showing up. We'll catch up later, okay?" I smile at him as I walk toward the glass door that leads into the back part of our office. I can hear Adam's footsteps catch up behind me.

"Here, let me get the door," he juggles keys in his hand and unlocks the door, holding it open for me. I offer him a brief smile and head down the dimly lit hallway toward my small office. Settling in, I check e-mails and voice mails and get more coffee. Office staff is arriving and reps begin showing up—a typical Thursday.

Hours pass in what seems like minutes. I can't even remember how many patients I've seen when I finally sit down at the large desk to enter some notes in a patient's chart. As I click away on my small laptop, Melissa rolls her chair over to mine.

"So are you going to tell me about that hottie that brought you flowers on Tuesday?"

Without looking up from my computer, I answer her with a simple, "No."

"Why not? Is that your boyfriend? Because if it's not, I want you to introduce me to him. Did you see those tattoos? I wanted to lick…"

"Melissa," Adam calls out her name. "That's enough."

That is twice today that he's scared the shit out of me. "I'm sorry, Dr. Gerard." Melissa jumps up from her chair and quickly makes herself busy grabbing a box of pharmaceutical samples and walking toward the sample closet.

"What was that for?" I say, standing up and closing the screen on my laptop. "Melissa is my medical assistant and she was joking around with me."

He stands with his arms resting on the tall counter, clicking away at his pen. "Because that kind of talk should be reserved for outside of the office."

"There is no one here but us, Adam. It was harmless conversation," I say, picking up my laptop as I head to my office. That man is hot or cold. From the day I started working here, he is either over friendly or a giant asshole. He is the only other doctor in this practice that is relatively close to my age, so naturally, in the beginning, I gravitated toward him.

There is a light knock on my door. "Come in," I say, and the door creaks open slowly. Melissa peeks her head through the door and offers me an apologetic smile.

"I'm so sorry, Dr. Sinclair. I didn't mean to…"

"Melissa, it's fine, seriously. Just be careful what you say and who is around when you say it. I've already taken care of Dr. Gerard. But let me know if he says anything to you, okay?"

"Okay. Your four o'clock appointment is here," she says quietly, closing the door behind her. I know she feels terrible, but how Adam handled that was inappropriate. I make a mental note to remind myself to tell him he needs to apologize to her.

Tending to my last two appointments of the day, I check on the front office staff, the lab, and all the assistants, and it looks like everything is in order and we should be out of here on time, or early tonight. I shoot a quick text to Landon and head to my office.

Just as I'm finishing up the last of my charting, my phone rings and Landon's name flashes on my screen.

"Hey, you—are you already here?"

"Yeah, I'm right outside."

"Perfect. I'll be right out."

After shutting down my laptop, I arrange the papers on my desk and grab my purse. Most of the office lights are off, telling me everyone has already gone home. I'm usually the last one to leave; today is no different. Locking the door behind me, Landon waits for me in my SUV just a few feet away. Opening the car door, I step up into the car and am greeted with his soft lips pressed to mine.

"I missed you, Doc," he says against my lips.

"I missed you too," I admit, and it's true. Thoughts of him crossed my mind all day, a pleasant distraction. As I'm getting buckled in, I notice Adam sitting in his car, watching us. "Let's go."

"What's wrong?" he asks me, his tone serious.

"Nothing. Adam, I mean Dr. Gerard, has just been acting weird lately. He's over there." I motion with my head. "In his car, watching us."

"Where?"

"Don't look now; it's the black BMW. Let's just go. I plan to talk to him tomorrow."

"What did you say his name was?" He pulls forward and blatantly stares Adam down, not trying to hide the fact that he knows Adam is watching us.

"Dr. Adam Gerard."

"I went to high school with that asshole. He was a few years older, but he went out of his way to make my life miserable."

"Landon, let's go," I say, hoping he'll just let this go.

"What? I want that fucker to know I'm watching him."

"Well, he surely knows now." I chuckle.

"Good. Let me know if he keeps bothering you."

"I'm not sure I'd say he was bothering me. He's just acting strangely."

"Same thing, Reagan."

I roll my eyes. I haven't had anyone telling me what to do, or what to worry about since I graduated and went to college. I'm not used to it.

"So what did you do today?" I ask, changing the subject.

"Nothing exciting, just stuff." He shrugs.

"Just stuff, huh?"

He turns and smiles at me. His upper lip curls just a little higher on one side and I melt a little every time he smiles at me like that. I feel that through his smile, he speaks the words he cannot say.

"Where are we going?" I say, noticing that we are not heading in the direction of my house.

"To my house for dinner."

"No way. I need to go home and shower and sleep. I'm exhausted."

"I know, Doc. Just a quick dinner and I'll take you home. You can shower up at my place while I get dinner ready."

"But I don't have clothes to change into."

"Between me and Lindsay, there are plenty of clothes you can borrow." We pull up to a red light and he leans over to me. "Let me make you dinner, then I'll take you home." He presses a long kiss to my lips. "Promise."

How can I say no to that?

"Okay," I say against his lips, taking another kiss. The remainder of the drive to his house is quick, and our conversation is light—comfortable.

"What's for dinner?" I ask as I get out of the car.

"Grilled chicken and vegetables."

"Do you like to cook?"

"I guess. I always have. From the time I was eight, I made every meal for Lindsay and me." His voice is quiet and I notice his demeanor shift slightly. Reaching out, I slide my hand into his, and pull his hand into my lap. After pulling into his driveway, he meets me at my door, opening it for me as I gather my belongings. Sliding out of the passenger seat, he pulls me into a warm hug. I rest my head on his chest and hug him back. We stand like this for minutes… almost a dance, but more an embrace. Sometimes there are no words to be said, and in this moment, I need him to know that. When he holds me back, I feel like there is nothing in the world that could make me feel any safer. Pulling out of his arms, we walk hand in hand into the house.

"Go, get in the shower," he whispers against my head. "I'm going to get dinner started."

Standing in the bathroom with a large towel draped around me, I silently curse myself for not asking to borrow clothes before I got in the shower. I tiptoe over to the large chest of drawers in Landon's room and open the top drawer. The large drawer is full of boxer briefs and socks.

I feel somewhat guilty as I open the next drawer, feeling like I'm snooping through someone's personal belongings without permission; however, he did offer me clothes to wear on the way over here. This drawer is full of t-shirts in every color, folded perfectly and divided by color. Figures. Eyeing a navy t-shirt at the bottom of the stack, I reach in and shimmy it out from the pile. Unfolding it, a picture drops from the neatly folded shirt and flutters to the ground.

Bending down, I pick up the old picture that has long since yellowed and is torn at one of the edges. The picture is of a young blonde woman with a little boy and a little girl. There is no mistaking the children are Landon and Lindsay. I flip the back of the picture over and see that it's dated December 1991. Running a quick calculation, that puts Landon at roughly seven years old and Lindsay at three.

The three of them are huddled close together in front of a Christmas tree, Landon holding Lindsay in his lap—with her arms wrapped around him. Even when they were young, he was fiercely protective of her, and my heart warms. I notice the lack of emotion on all of their faces. For Christmas being such a happy time of year, their expressions are void of happiness—peace. There is no mistaking that the beautiful blonde woman in the picture is their mother, as all three have identical blue eyes.

"What are you doing?" His tone is harsh and loud. The picture falls from my fingers, floating to the floor as he walks toward me. I was so absorbed in looking at the picture, studying the details, I didn't hear him open the door.

I'm momentarily stunned as he picks up the picture and shoves it back into the drawer. "I was getting a t-shirt. You said I could borrow some clothes and that picture fell out of the drawer," I stutter and hold up the blue t-shirt so he could see what I was doing. Feeling uncomfortable, I pull the towel that is loosely wrapped around me a little tighter, and take a step back, increasing the distance between us.

He breathes heavily as he watches me, and I take another small step backward. "Stop," he mutters, taking two steps toward me, closing any distance there once was. My heart beats violently in my chest, not because I'm afraid of him... I'm not, but because I'm afraid *for* him. The look on his face scares me; it's the same face that was in the picture. Lost, void of emotion.

"Landon," I whisper and set my hand on his chest. He grabs my wrist, holding me firmly in place. "Talk to me." He shakes his head slowly from side to side, as if clearing his head. He stands silent, watching me, holding me by the wrist. "Let go." I try to wiggle my wrist out of his firm grasp, but his grip tightens.

"Don't leave," he breathes against my face. Dropping the t-shirt to the floor, I bring my other hand to his chest.

"I'm not going anywhere, I promise. Just let go of my hand." His grip loosens a bit and I wiggle my hand away, rubbing it.

"Did I hurt you?" he asks, running his fingers over my inner wrist, gently caressing it.

"No. You didn't hurt me. I know you wouldn't hurt me." His eyes quickly find mine, searching for something.

"Never. I would never," he says quietly.

"I know."

With deep breaths, his breathing finally begins to settle, and he appears calmer. I bend down and pick up the t-shirt I had dropped.

"Don't." He pulls the t-shirt from my hands, tossing it onto an oversized chair that sits next to his dresser. His fingers trail up both of my arms where he finds the edge of the towel that I have wrapped around me. Slipping his finger under the edge, he pulls the end of the towel out. The only thing keeping the towel in place is my arms. With both of his hands placed on my upper arms, he gently pulls them away from my body and the towel falls into a pile at my feet.

He inhales sharply as he takes in the sight of me standing before him completely naked. I've never felt more vulnerable, more on display. Shifting, I try to pull my arms out from his gasp, but he won't release them.

"Landon, please…"

"Lie down," he orders, gesturing to the bed behind me. My heart races as he gently guides me backwards, the edge of the bed hitting the backs of my knees. Sitting on the end of the bed, he stands in front of me, still holding the tops of my arms. His thumbs strum the fronts of my shoulders as I wait for him to tell me what to do next.

"Scoot back to the middle of the bed." My mind races in anticipation of what's next and my arms shake as I push myself backward to the center of the bed, my legs extended straight out in front of me. Wasting no time, he kneels on the foot of the bed, straddling me at my feet. "Lie down," he says, and I do. My heart beats erratically as he sits at my feet.

He runs his hands up the front of my legs, stopping just above my knees. His eyes inspect every inch of me as they follow his hands up my body. "So soft," he whispers as his hands begin moving upward again and I catch my breath as his touch ignites goose bumps on my skin.

"Are you okay?" he asks.

"Yeah." I nod my head. His thumbs hover at the junction of my hips and groin, gently rubbing small circles.

"Gorgeous," he mumbles against my hip as he kisses a trail from my hip to my stomach. I close my eyes and grip the comforter beneath me, wanting to feel his every touch, every kiss. His arms snake along the side of my body as he nudges my legs apart, settling between them. His warm breath presses against my stomach before his lips trace the six-inch scar across my lower abdomen—my secret. I flinch when I feel his lips hover, over the scar, pressing kisses against it.

"Landon," I whisper, urging him to stop. My fingers find their way to his forearms, pulling him upward to me. He takes his time, again trailing kisses all the way from my stomach to my chest, neck, then lips.

"Let me touch you," he whispers as his hands explore me. His calloused fingers running across my sensitive breasts send a shiver through me. He notices, and does it again. He kisses his way back down my naked core, stopping at the scar. He runs his fingers over it and kisses it again.

"You okay, Doc?" he asks me again. I nod, trying to swallow against my dry throat.

"My secret." My voice creaks. He crawls his way up me and settles in the bed next to me. Pulling my face into his hands, he cups my cheeks and kisses me. Intense, deep, passionate kisses. Resting his forehead on mine, he peppers my cheeks with soft, gentle kisses.

"Talk to me," he says quietly, pulling a blanket over me, covering me. I almost find humor in the fact that he wants me to talk to him, trust him with my innermost secrets, yet he's so closed off and unwilling to share even some of the simplest parts of himself. I inhale deeply, and close my eyes as the words shakily fall from my lips.

"I was sixteen years old and a sophomore in high school." I pause when I hear a sharp inhale from him, but he kisses the corner of my mouth, urging me to continue. "I was dating Nathan; we'd been together since I was fifteen and a freshman and he was a junior. He was the captain of the football team, captain of the hockey team, and his dad was the mayor. Everyone in my small hometown knew of and loved his family."

My heart races as I pull the buried memories to the surface. "He was everything to me; I guess you can say he was my first love. Everyone wanted to be 'us.' I was the honor student and he was the star athlete, until I found out I was pregnant."

I play with the little hairs at the base of Landon's neck as I swallow the small lump that has suddenly formed in my throat.

"I knew the day I missed my period that I was pregnant. You just know your body. I was so scared, so afraid—but I was raised that you own your mistakes, you take responsibility for your actions, and I knew without a doubt that I was keeping my baby."

The muscles in Landon's jaws flex as he stares at me and I continue. "It was early May, and Nathan was within weeks of graduating. He had accepted a scholarship to play football at the University of Minnesota about four hours away in the Twin Cities. I didn't know what he was going to say, but I knew we were strong, solid—so I wasn't all that worried. I just assumed we'd figure it out as we went along." I actually choke on those words. "Let's just say, that's not exactly how it went."

"What happened, Reagan?" He pulls me closer to him while his hand rests on top of my stomach. His fingers gently trace the scar as I speak.

"He told me to get rid of it. He wasn't ready for a kid or a serious relationship, and he questioned whether the baby was his. He had the audacity to imply that I was sleeping with someone else." My voice is still shaking, but now with anger. "We'd been together for a year and I'd never been with anyone else. Of course, the baby was his. He left my house that day, and I never saw him again. He must have told his parents because his parents offered me money for an abortion, but when I declined, the rumors started running rampant about how I was a whore and had been cheating on Nathan while we were together."

I bite at my lip as I recall the feelings, the emotions of those days—fifteen years ago. "Instead of dispelling the rumors, I packed a bag and spent the summer here in Wilmington with Mac and Gemma. Gemma talked me through some of the worst days of my life, or so I thought at the time."

"What do you mean?" He brushes the hair off my forehead and tucks it behind my ear.

"When I moved back home for school in August, the rumors hadn't died down. Every friend I thought I had didn't want anything to do with me. Nathan had left for college. He walked away from me and his unborn baby—yet everyone believed his lies. The comments, the snickers, the bullying were horrible." I pause for a second to calm myself.

"Obviously, being pregnant changed everything for me. I couldn't play tennis in the fall like I used to, and I went from being one of the most popular girls in school to one of the most loathed, so I basically buried myself in schoolwork. I was a straight A student prior to getting pregnant, but being alone with no friends and no activities just forced me to throw myself even more into my school work."

Landon buries his face in my neck and I can feel him breathing me in. "Go on," he urges me.

"So it was September sixth, Labor Day Weekend. My parents drove up to our lake cabin for one night to get it winterized and to pull the boat in from the lake. I decided to stay at home, since they'd be gone for just one day. I wasn't feeling great when I woke up that morning, so I was glad I didn't go with them. Throughout the day, I had minor cramping and I felt anxious, but I just thought I was over exaggerating and just nervous being home alone. I had laid down for a nap and, when

I woke up, I was covered in blood. So much blood that my bed looked like a crime scene. I knew something was wrong, I just didn't know how serious it was. I was dizzy and nauseous, and when I tried to call my mom and dad, it went straight to voicemail. There is little to no cellular service at our lake cabin and no one has landlines."

I feel Landon's hand flex over my stomach and he presses a gentle kiss to my cheek before I continue.

"I had no one to call, not one person. My friends were no longer my friends, and we had no family that lived near us. I was too scared to call 911 because I was afraid. Everyone in that town vilified me and I didn't want the added attention of an ambulance or police at my house. For the next hour, I laid in bed, crying, praying, not knowing what to do."

"What did you do?" His hand flexes gently over my stomach.

"I got in the shower and cleaned myself up and then drove myself to the hospital. I don't even know how I made it there. I was in so much pain and I honestly don't remember driving there. There was so much confusion once I got to the hospital. I was a minor and they wanted my parents' permission to treat me, because they didn't know or didn't think it was anything serious. Once it became an emergency, it was basically too late. My blood pressure had risen so high they immediately took me in for a C-section. Everyone knew it was too early to deliver a baby. I was barely nineteen weeks pregnant, but to save my life, they had to deliver my baby." I choke back a sob as I relive that day. "I remember every detail as if it happened yesterday, the sounds, the smells—Hailey."

"That was her name?" he whispers.

I nod. "Hailey was born at 6:51pm. Hours later, after I was

stabilized, they explained to me that I had a placental abruption. That means the placenta separates from the wall of the uterus. Both of us were in extreme danger, which is why they had to deliver her."

Tears roll from the corners of my eyes and into my hair as I try to tell the rest of the story. "She was so little, so frail, and they flew her to the children's hospital in the Twin Cities. I didn't even get to see her before she left. They were able to notify my parents via the sheriff's department and they were on their way home to me." I pause, inhaling deeply. "I called Nathan, since he was in the Cities. I explained what happened and that our baby was minutes away from him, and I needed him to be there—for her."

Landon wipes the tears from my cheeks as they continue to fall, never loosening his firm hold on me. "He never went to her," I continue. "He hung up on me when I told him what happened. She died twelve hours after she arrived there. Her little body was just too frail; her organs weren't developed enough. She died alone." A sob breaks free. "I never got to hold her." Landon pulls me into his arms and holds me while I cry. And I cry again, for the second time this week for my little girl, that I never saw, never touched, and never held.

"I hate him," I cry into his chest. "He was so close and he should have been there for her."

"It's okay," he comforts me. Holding me in his arms again, it's the one place I feel safe. Silence fills the air around us, and it's peaceful, calm, content. Pulling myself together, I'm able to finish the story without crying, feeling a little stronger.

"The little box you saw, the pictures, the little hat, and the socks... that's all I have of her. I still cry and hurt for her, and for me. For years, I harbored the blame for her death. But I finally realized, not so long ago, that to move forward, I had to forgive myself, and not place the blame on myself. I was so young."

"It's not your fault, Reagan," he whispers against my temple.

"I know that now." I sit up and pull the blanket around me tighter. Landon remains lying down, and I pick up his hand, playing with each finger and rubbing his palm. "So Hailey is buried at home in the little cemetery across town." I drop my eyes to our hands, which are linked together. "I guess if there is one thing I took away from losing her, it's that life isn't fair. Life sucks serious ass sometimes, and I miss her. I miss her more than anything in this world, but I choose to be happy. I choose to know that it wasn't my time to be a mom, but it will be when the time is right."

"Thank you for trusting me enough to share this with me," he says, squeezing my hand.

"Thank you for listening," I say, lying back down next to him. He wraps his arms around me, pulling me to him.

CHAPTER 13

LANDON

Yesterday was the first day I haven't seen her since I met her. It was hell. Everyone agreed that we'd go to Mac's tonight to celebrate my new position, but I don't want to wait another thirteen hours to see her. She's quickly becoming a narcotic I need to have, a craving I can't shake.

Throwing on some shorts and a t-shirt, I grab my phone, keys, and wallet with a plan in mind. Pulling into a visitor parking spot at her condominium complex, what I once thought was a brilliant idea has me second-guessing myself. Opening the car door, I juggle the two large cups of coffee while trying to use my body to contain a wild beagle in the car. "Jesus Christ, Ollie, hold on."

Setting both cups of coffee on top of the car, I untangle the leash that is now twisted around the gearshift in my car. With Ollie out of the car and wagging so wildly he looks like he's having mild convulsions, I grab the two coffees and head for the front door.

"Now behave," I tell Ollie, "and don't piss on anything." I can't believe I'm talking to a fucking dog. I use my knuckle to press the doorbell and wait patiently in hopes that she answers. The door cracks open and there she stands in a black tank top and little white pajama shorts.

"Was hoping maybe you'd be up for a couple of visitors." I shrug as Ollie bounds forward, jumping at her feet.

"Ollie," she squeals, bending down to accept dog kisses all over her cheeks as she rubs his head. She stands up and sends me the most genuine smile I've ever seen. "Kiss me," she says, leaning in and pressing a kiss to my lips.

"I like surprises like this," she mumbles against my lips. "But what's with Ollie?"

I laugh, and hand her a coffee. "Oh, Ollie and I decided to hang out for a little while together this morning... so we mutually decided that we'd swing by and bring you a coffee." I laugh again. She reaches down and unhooks the leash from Ollie's collar. He sniffs his way around the kitchen and living room while we both sit down on the stools at the kitchen island. "I love that dog," she says. "I'd adopt him if I had more time at home with him."

"I figured you'd like to see him." I wink at her.

"Mmm... white chocolate mocha. How did you know that was my favorite?"

"Let's just say I'm a damn good detective." She studies the writing on the side of the cup, setting it down on the island as she narrows her eyes at me.

"This is exactly how I take my coffee. Non-fat, no whipped cream, extra hot... how did you know that?" I chuckle at her as she looks between her cup and me.

"You left an empty cup in your cup holder in the car the

other day. When I went to toss it, I made a mental note of how you liked your coffee."

She shakes her head and lets out a little laugh. "You're going to make an excellent detective. I can't even believe you're real," she mutters under her breath in between sips of her coffee. Her hair is piled on top of her head in some sort of messy ponytail, and she doesn't have a speck of make-up on; however, I don't think I've ever seen her as beautiful as she looks right now.

"I hope it's okay that we swung by unannounced?" That reminds me to look for Ollie. I spy him curled into a little ball, lying on the floor in the sun that has found its way in through a large skylight in the living room.

"You don't ever have to ask to come by. I was just going to clean the house."

"There's nothing to clean," I remark. "This house is immaculate."

She lets out another laugh. "Hardly, but thank you."

"Well, we didn't mean to interrupt your cleaning, but we wanted to stop by and bring you some coffee... and selfishly, I didn't want to wait until tonight to see you." She leans in from her stool and presses a kiss to my lips.

"I'm glad you stopped by," she whispers against my lips.

"I should probably get Ollie back to Mrs. Fitzpatrick anyway." I say each word in between little kisses.

Pulling back from me, she says, "Let him stay. I'll bring him back to her later. I hate that he's cooped up over there and he seems to be comfortable here." She smiles at Ollie, who is snoring on the floor.

"Are you sure? I didn't mean to bring you more work."

"Yeah, it's fine. I like the company."

"It's a dog, Reagan." I laugh at her.

"It's a dog I happen to like, and it's lonesome here alone." She shrugs.

"Okay, we'll be by to get you at eight tonight." I stand up and collect my coffee.

"I'll be ready," she says, her voice husky.

"Shot gun!" Lindsay yells as we file out the front door to pick up Reagan. I offered to drive, but Matt insisted that tonight was to celebrate, and I was to enjoy myself. I didn't argue.

Matt navigates the Wilmington streets just like he does when on patrol, with ease. He knows every short cut and every back road. There is no need for a navigation system when you have Matt Kennedy behind the wheel.

"Holy shit! This is where she lives?" Lindsay exclaims as we pull into Reagan's upscale condominium complex. "I bet these cost a small fortune," she says, looking out the window at the large townhouse-style condos.

"Her place is nice. I'm sure she'd love for you to see it— another time," I emphasize. "I'll be right back." I jump out of the SUV and jog up the small sidewalk to the front door. Reagan greets me at the front door, shutting the door and locking it as I approach.

"You look amazing... and tall." I admire her. She's wearing a short black dress that make her long legs carry on for miles with wedged sandals that put her at almost my height.

"Thank you." She tugs at the hem of her dress, trying to cover her thighs. Lacing her fingers through mine, I walk her to Matt's car and open the door, helping her up into the back seat.

Reassuming my seat in the back next to her, Matt heads towards Mac's as Lindsay and Reagan make small talk.

I can't take my eyes off of her long legs. My eyes burn a trail from her upper thigh down to her ankle and back up again. She pinches me when she catches me looking at her legs, and she rests her hand on my leg, just above my knee. The drive to Mac's is short, but every minute it takes us to get there is a minute that I want to turn around and be alone with her. As we pull into the crowded parking lot, Reagan's eyes light up when she sees all the cars.

"Mac is holding a table for us," she says, grabbing her small purse. "The band is really good tonight, so I knew it would be busy." She opens the car door and slides down onto the concrete below. Reagan takes the lead, guiding us to the front door, while Lindsay and Matt follow behind us.

Entering the bar, we're instantly greeted by Sam, who pulls Reagan into a hug and presses a kiss to her cheek. I don't like it at all, so I move closer to her, hoping that Sam sees that she's here with me. The music is loud, so I can't hear what they're saying, but I see her nod, then lean over to whisper something into Lindsay's ear. Lindsay grabs Reagan's hand and drags them through the crowd to a round table tucked away in a darkened corner.

"Hope this table is okay. I wanted to be out of the way." Reagan smiles as she sets her purse on the table.

"It's perfect," Lindsay says, sliding into one of the chairs. Matt sits next to Lindsay and I sit on the other side of Reagan. The two girls are whispering to each other and Matt looks at me, shaking his head. Sam shows up with a pitcher of beer and two mugs, just as another waiter slides two pink drinks on the table and walks away.

"Beer for you two," he says, looking at Matt and me, "and vodka cranberry for the ladies, and I hear congratulations are in order." He reaches out to shake my hand.

"Thanks." I accept his handshake. I still don't want him kissing Reagan on the cheek, but I'll be civil, for now.

"Drinks are on the house tonight, Mac's orders. Enjoy yourselves and let me know if you need anything."

"Thanks, Sam," the girls say in unison and start laughing.

Lindsay raises her glass. "Let's toast! To new beginnings." She smiles, looking between Reagan and me. "Oh, and new jobs too." Reagan blushes, but raises her glass.

"To everything Linds just said," Matt echoes, raising his glass. We all toast and set our drinks on the table. Lindsay leans in and whispers something to Matt, and they both stand up and walk to the dance floor.

"Want to dance?" I ask Reagan as she twirls her straw in her drink, hoping she says no.

"Yes, but not yet. Maybe in a little bit."

Feeling like she's too far away, I pull her chair closer to me. I immediately feel better as her leg brushes against mine, and I can drink in the smell of her sweet perfume.

"How was the rest of your day?" I ask, curious as to what she did after I left her house.

"It was good. Finished cleaning, took Ollie to the beach for a quick run, then back to Gemma's. Oh, and I went and got my nails done." She wiggles her fingers in front of my face. Reaching out, I take her hand and study her fingers. They are long and dainty—just like the rest of her. I press a kiss to her palm and lace her fingers though mine.

She leans in and presses a light kiss on my lips, and I'm thankful that we're tucked away in this dimly lit corner.

"If we weren't celebrating your promotion, I'd rather be at home with you," she says, her voice low and seductive. The hair on my arms raises as her warm breath touches my ear.

"Let's go." I reach for her hand and stand up.

"Go where?" Lindsay asks, sliding four shot glasses on the table. "Sit your ass back down; no one is going anywhere. We just got here and there is some partying to do." She winks at Reagan.

"What the hell are those?" I ask, looking at the large shot glasses rimmed with either sugar or salt.

"Hell if I know." Matt shrugs. "All I know is that they're pink."

"Raspberry Kamikazes," Lindsay says, passing out the shot glasses.

"No shots for me; I'm driving," Matt informs her and shoves the shot glass back at Lindsay. "Drink up, buttercup." He smiles at her.

"Did you just call her 'buttercup'?" I ask. Lindsay just shrugs and giggles before lifting the shot glass to her mouth.

Lindsay, Reagan, and I take our shot and Lindsay looks at Reagan. "These are going to be dangerous—they're delicious." She takes the shot Matt left on the table and downs it.

"Take it easy tonight, Linds. We'd like to make it past eleven o'clock," Matt teases her.

"I'd like to leave now," I whisper in Reagan's ear as she rests her hand on my thigh, giving it a little squeeze. She moves her hand a little higher to my upper thigh, and I can't help but put my hand on top of hers to stop her.

"What would we do if we left right now?" she asks quietly, her breath warm and fruity from the shot.

"Use your imagination, Doc. You're a smart girl." I wink as

I tip back the tall glass of beer and finish it. There is no way I will last another thirty minutes in this bar with her, sitting this close, touching me and kissing me.

"Let's all dance," Lindsay squeals, pulling poor Matt from his chair. "C'mon guys," she says to Reagan and me.

"Dance with me, Champ," Reagan murmurs in my ear as she tugs at my hand, pulling me off the tall barstool. Weaving through the mass of people standing alongside the dance floor, she wraps her arms around my neck, pressing herself against me. Her skin is soft and warm, and there is too much of it showing for a place like this.

I can feel the curve of her breasts and hips and I want nothing more than to run my hands up and down her perfect body. Resting her head on my shoulder, I can feel her press her lips against my neck, lightly sucking and nipping.

"Reagan," I warn her. "Don't fucking start something that I won't be able to stop."

"Oooohhhhh." She giggles.

"I'm serious."

"So am I," she whispers as she pulls at the hair at the nape of my neck. I'm fucking hard as a rock as I think about pulling her from this crowded bar and taking her home to make love to her for hours.

"Mind if I cut in?" Sam stands, waiting for me to hand over my girl. That isn't happening tonight—or ever.

"Not right now, man. She's mine tonight." He shakes his head and laughs, but doesn't argue as he backs away.

"What was that about?" Lindsay asks as she and Matt dance up next to us.

"Sam wanted to dance with Reagan, I said no. End of story." Reagan drops her forehead to my chest and laughs at me.

"You know you have nothing to worry about with Sam, right?"

"I wasn't worried, sweetheart."

"Yeah, right," she scoffs. "You know he's gay."

"He. Is. Gay?" Lindsay bellows. "Why? Why are the good ones gay?" Matt narrows his eyes at her and his body stiffens. "What?" she says as Matt drags her off the dance floor and back to the table.

"I've known Sam since I was seventeen. He's the only other person who knows about Hailey," she says quietly. "He grew up down the road from Mac and Gemma and has kind of been the son they never had. He's going to buy this bar from Mac when Mac's ready to let it go." We step from side to side slowly to the music. "Mac has cancer."

"What?" I say, shocked to hear this news.

"He was diagnosed this spring. It's in his pancreas. Sam is fully prepared to purchase the bar, but Mac isn't ready to let it go yet." She shrugs.

"I'm sorry to hear about Mac."

"So am I," she responds. The songs ends, but I don't let her go. I hate dancing, but I could stand here and hold her forever. The band is taking a break and everyone clears the dance floor except for us. When I unwrap my arms from around her, she stops me.

"Kiss me," she quietly demands, her blue eyes sparkling in the bar lights.

"Gladly." I press my needy lips to hers. She breaks the kiss with a laugh when the catcalls and whistles get louder and she gives a little curtsy as she walks back to the table. Sam meets us with another four shots, and Matt shakes his head and points at my sister.

"What? We're enjoying ourselves." She rolls her eyes and slides a shot over to Reagan.

"Last one," Reagan says, holding up the shot. She wets her lips before taking the little glass, tipping it back and emptying it. Lindsay takes another shot, and then another, leaving the last one for me. Fixing my eyes on hers, I lift the shot glass and dump the contents down my throat. There is a gentle burn, but the aftertaste is sweet.

"So what's the deal with you guys, anyway?" Lindsay asks, giggling as she takes a seat. She hooks her arm through Matt's, I presume to balance herself, but Matt seems unfazed.

"What do you mean?" Reagan questions her.

"Are you guys dating? Are you a couple? More importantly, inquiring minds want to know, are you screwing?"

"Jesus, Lindsay," I bark.

"Right there. See. He's cranky. You're clearly not having sex yet." She waves her hand in the direction of us. "In fact, I bet Reagan has seen more pussy in the last week than you have."

Matt elbows Lindsay, while Reagan spits her drink across the table. She's laughing. She fucking thought that was funny.

"That. Was. Awesome." She high fives Lindsay and the two of them laugh. Matt drops his head and I can tell he's doing his best not to laugh either, and she's right. I've not thought about another woman since I met Reagan.

"I'm glad you find this amusing, girls." I slide into my seat next to Reagan. I place my hand on her thigh at the hem of her dress, and slowly slide it under. The girls continue giggling, but Reagan stops, her back straightening when she feels my hand travel higher.

"Ahem," she clears her throat.

"What's wrong, Doc? You suddenly seem so quiet," I smirk.

My hand snakes up her leg higher as I let it fall between her thighs. Pushing herself away from the table, she quickly stands up and my hand falls to my side. She winks at me as she squeezes behind me to free herself from the table.

"I'll be right back," she says as she walks away. I see her greeting people, most likely regulars here at Mac's, as she heads toward the bar. Her long hair in perfect waves falls down the middle of her back and, in those shoes, her long, lean legs are perfection. I want every inch of those legs wrapped around me.

Our eyes meet as she saunters back to the table, holding four glasses of water. "Thought everyone could use some ice water," she says, handing out the glasses. Lindsay hiccups, but pulls the small straw into her mouth and empties her glass.

"Here, drink some more." Matt hands his glass of water to Lindsay.

"It's hot in here," she complains and drinks the water Matt just gave her.

Reagan eyes the growing crowd and turns to me. "I've never seen it this packed. Maybe we should go before the band starts again."

Matt nods in agreement and Lindsay rolls her eyes. "I'm fine, you guys!" she says, linking her arms through Reagan's. They waddle through the packed bar in their high heels, arm in arm, brunette and blonde. Matt and I a few steps behind them.

"Hey, I'll make sure Lindsay gets home safely, if you were planning to stay at Reagan's," he smirks.

"Yeah, thanks, man. I'd really appreciate that. But let's not assume she wants me there." I smack his back.

"Looking at you two tonight, I don't think that's going to be the issue." He laughs as we both wave goodbye to Sam and Mac from across the bar.

The ride to Reagan's house is fast, but not fast enough for me to keep my hands off of her. I run my fingers through the back of her long hair as we listen to Lindsay giggle and try to tell jokes, but she keeps giving away the punch line. When we pull up to Reagan's house, I open the door and let Reagan slide out. She walks around to the passenger side of the car and leans in Lindsay's window. They're whispering and giggling again, like two twelve-year-old girls.

Meeting Reagan, I wrap my arms around her waist from behind and lean in and press a kiss to Lindsay's cheek. "Behave, and don't give him too much trouble," I tell her and nod to Matt.

"I like trouble, though," she says sarcastically.

"Behave."

"I should be telling *you* to behave." She winks at me while Reagan laughs. Finding my hand, Reagan tugs at me and pulls me towards the front door. The porch light illuminates the small patio as she fumbles with getting her key into the lock.

"Here, let me do it," I offer, reaching for the keys.

"I can do it." She nudges me out of the way, finally turning the lock and pushing the door open. The house is dark except for a small overhead light that is above her kitchen sink. It provides just enough light to see the kitchen and into the attached living room.

"Help me," she grunts as she hops on one foot, trying to unbuckle her shoe. I steady her, then kneel to unbuckle both of her shoes.

"It feels so good to be out of those damn shoes. I hate them," she whines, wiggling her toes. I run my hands up her calves, behind her knees, and up the outside of her thighs. I hear her gasp as I move higher, palming her ass.

Placing her hands in my hair, she tugs gently, getting my

attention. "Come on," she urges me to stand up. Walking down the hallway to her room, she moves gracefully and full of confidence. I follow her, knowing that every rule I've put in place, every concrete wall I've built, will crumble with just one taste of her.

I stand in the doorway to her room, watching her. She pulls the earrings from her ears and her bracelet from her wrist, setting them on her nightstand. She reaches behind her and unzips the black dress she's wearing and it slowly falls from each shoulder, eventually sliding off of her completely, pooling at her feet.

She stands before me in nothing but a pair of black lace thong panties and a barely there black lace bra. The sight of her is breathtaking. "Can you unclasp me?" She turns around and lifts her hair. In a matter of steps, I'm standing next to the most beautiful woman I've ever laid eyes on. I reach for the clasp of her necklace and unhook it, setting it on the nightstand next to the earrings and bracelet.

"One more," she whispers, her back still to me. She drops her hair, but pulls it forward over one shoulder. Glancing over her shoulder at me, she smiles as I rest my palms on her shoulders. I slide them down her upper back, feeling her soft skin just beneath them. I reach the clasp of her bra and unhook it as she pulls the straps off of each shoulder.

I inhale fast and deep at the sight of her standing in nothing but a little black thong. The curve of her hips, her ass, and the sight of her pale skin against the little piece of black fabric has my body coursing with need.

"So fucking beautiful," I say, running my hand from the back of her neck, trailing all the way down her spine down to the small of her back. Her head falls forward at my touch and I press my chest against her back. I wrap my fingers in her hair at the nape of her neck, pulling her head back.

"Don't move," I say, releasing her hair. Her arms fall to her side and she stands still. I pull off my shirt and unbutton my pants, leaving them on.

"Where is your robe?"

"Hanging on the back of the bathroom door. Why?"

"Don't move."

"If you want me to put my clothes back on, just tell me."

"Reagan. Be quiet."

I find her robe hanging on the back of the door just as she said. I pull the long satin belt from the two loops in each side of the robe and find her standing exactly where I left her.

"Good girl. Don't move," I whisper. Standing behind her, I press my erection against her backside. "See what you do to me, Reagan." She swallows hard and nods her head. "Walk to the bed." I nudge her and she moves slowly. "To the middle and lie down on your back." She follows my directions and takes her place in the center of the bed.

"Put both hands in front of you and clasp them together." Her fingers are trembling, but she does exactly as she's told. I take the soft belt and wrap it around her wrists, weaving it around and in between, leaving the ends dangling. She watches me intently, and wiggles her wrists. She can't get out, yet I don't want this to hurt her.

"You okay?" I ask in a hushed tone.

"Yes," she whispers and her voice cracks. Pulling her hands above her head, I tie the loose ends to one of the slats on her bed, securing her arms. I run my thumb across her lip, and she instinctively licks it, pulling it into her mouth, causing my erection to become harder. I run my hand across her cheek, down her neck, finding the curve of her bare breasts. Spending

152

my time on each one, I move between her breasts and down to the edge of her panties.

I run my finger just under the edge, across her stomach, teasing her. I leave them on, for now, and run my finger under the edge just inside her thigh. This time, I move to her center and brush against her opening. She's wet, as I knew she would be.

"Is that for me?" I run my finger up and down her warm folds, spreading her wetness. She gasps as my fingers roam. Standing up, I pull her panties down her long legs and stand at the foot of her bed. Tossing them to the floor, I let her feet dangle just off the end of the bed as I spread her legs. Her chest rises and falls with each shallow breath she's taking. A little moan escapes her as she wiggles on the bed, pulling at the belt that holds her hands above her head. I unzip my pants and pull them off along with my boxer briefs. Kneeling between her legs, I can see how ready she is.

"Do you want me to fuck you, Reagan?" She closes her eyes and her breathing becomes more rapid. "Answer me. Do you want me to fuck you?" She shakes her head from side to side. "No? Your body is telling me otherwise." I run my finger through her wet lips again, finding her swollen clit. I rub it lightly and she bucks her hips.

"Tell me you want me to fuck you, Reagan," I breathe against her mouth. My cock is pressing against her as I tease her.

Her body shudders, and she opens her eyes, "I want you to fuck me," she pants.

"Condom?"

"Nightstand," she says.

Rolling off of her, I open the drawer and find two condoms sitting next to her vibrator. Pulling it out of the drawer along with one of the condoms, I hold it up.

"Is this what you've been getting off with?" I push the little button at the end of the rubber vibrator and it hums to life. Setting the condom on the bed, I turn the vibrator off and hold it up again.

"Answer me; is this what you've been using to get off?" She nods her head. Positioning myself between her legs, I turn the vibrator on and click it twice, turning it to its highest setting. I twirl the buzzing tip around each of her nipples, causing them to harden into stiff little peaks.

"Do you like that?" I ask as she smiles. Running it down her stomach, I slowly lower it and press it into her wet center. She gasps as I pull it in and out of her slowly. Moving it to her clit, I circle her and her thighs begin shaking violently.

"Landon," she screams.

"More?" I continue circling her clit and watch as every muscle in her lower half tightens. Sliding two fingers into her, I continue circling her clit with the vibrator as she bucks wildly beneath me.

"Come baby," I encourage her. I slide my fingers in and out gently as I feel her wet release as she lets go. Pulling my fingers from her, I click the vibrator off and put the condom on. Her breathing is heavy and her thighs continue to shake. "Did you like that?" I ask as I roll the condom over my length. She doesn't answer me, but concentrates on regulating her breathing.

"Answer me. Did you like that?"

"Y… y… yes," she stutters.

"Good. Because that's the last time you're going to use a fucking vibrator to get you off. Do you understand?"

"Yes." Her voice shakes.

"As long as I'm here, you will never use that piece of shit

154

again. I will give you pleasure."

"Okay." She nods and wiggles her arms, which are still secured to the bed slats. Positioning myself between her legs, I rub her swollen clit between my thumb and forefinger. She's tender and ready. Pressing myself to her center, I slowly inch my way inside of her. She gasps with each inch I take.

"Jesus, you're so tight."

"It's been a long time," she says as she lifts her ass off the bed and accepts me fully into her. I rock gently, letting her adjust. Her legs fall further apart and I lean forward and press a kiss to her mouth.

"Do you want me to fuck you, Reagan?"

"Yes," she whispers.

CHAPTER 14

Reagan

I let myself feel him, breathe him, and love him. I said it—I love him. I am fully aware that he is incapable of telling me how he feels, but I know he is showing me. He's not fucking me; I've been fucked before. He's making love to me.

"Untie my hands, please," I ask quietly.

"Not yet." He rocks himself in and out, taking his time. His touch is warm and gentle, yet full of need—want. His warm breath against my neck causes goose bumps to prick my skin. His lips pull at the soft skin of my neck and he presses light kisses just behind my ear. His hands move over every inch of me.

"I need to touch you," I muster between breaths. He takes his time moving in and out of me.

"Every day, Reagan. I want to fuck you like this every single day," he mutters between breaths. Eventually, he reaches above and pulls at the tie and my hands fall from the slats to the pillow above my head. He never stops moving, but with one hand is able to release the robe belt from around my hands and wrists. My shoulders ache as I bring my arms down and hold onto his muscular biceps.

Our bodies move together as if we've made love every day for years. "You feel so fucking good," he mutters against my neck. My legs are wrapped around his waist, holding him exactly where I want him.

"I'm so close," I whisper and he picks up his pace. Reaching up, I take his face in my hands. "Look at me," I tell him quietly. Even through the darkness of the room, I can see his light blue eyes.

"What's wrong?" he asks.

"Nothing. I'm perfect. I just want to see your face." He presses a kiss to my lips and I feel him harden inside me, a sign he's just as close as I am.

"Come with me," I say as I rock my hips with his. A low growl escapes from his throat as he plunges into me one last time. Collapsing on top of me, his fingers brush gently through my damp hair.

"You're amazing," he whispers against my neck.

"So are you," I say under my breath. Pulling himself from me, he saunters to the bathroom. I wrap the sheet around me and wait for him, wondering if he will leave me and go home. Returning to the bedroom, he slides into bed, and my heart breathes a sigh of relief. Pulling me to him, he spoons me and strokes my arm with his finger. As we settle into the comfortable silence, I roll over to face him.

"You okay, Doc?" he asks, cupping my cheek with his hand. I nod and clear my throat.

"Do something for me, please." My voice is hoarse with emotion. He pulls me closer so we're lying face to face on the same pillow.

"Sure." He sounds confused.

"Break your rules for me."

"What do you mean, Doc?"

"Don't leave me with just one night. Break your rules. Give me more than tonight." He pulls me into a tight embrace. "Just try," I whisper as I see him shake his head from side to side a little bit. My heart breaks a little as minutes go by and he never answers me—I've now just become another one of his "fuck them and leave them" girls, except that he's with me right now, and maybe he'll stay.

Waking in the pitch-black room, my heart falls when I reach for him and he's not there. Glancing at the alarm clock on the nightstand, I see that it reads 3:21a.m., and my stomach turns at the thought that I was just another fuck to him. He got what he wanted, so I'm not sure why I'm surprised by his absence.

"I'm right here." I hear his low voice coming from the corner of the room. He's sitting on the end of the chaise lounge, and I'm just able to make out his shadow.

"What are you doing?" I ask as I sit up and push the sheet off of me.

"Couldn't sleep, and I didn't want to wake you." His voice is raspy and dry.

"Come here." I can see the outline of him in the dark room as he walks to the bed and sits down. "Lie with me." I pat the empty space on the bed next to me. He lies down on his back and raises his arms above his head.

"Talk to me," I whisper and lay my hand across his chest, resting it over his heart. "Why can't you sleep?"

He pulls one hand out from underneath his head and lays it over my hand on his chest. "I rarely sleep. Or I should say, I fall asleep, but seldom stay asleep."

"Nightmares?"

"No, not really. Just memories I can't shake." I roll toward him and slide my leg in between his, nuzzling up to him. I want him to be comfortable talking to me, sharing with me, but I know I cannot force it.

"You need to sleep."

With a short laugh, he presses a kiss to my forehead. "You need to stop worrying."

"Let me worry about you, let me care for you—let me love *you*," I whisper and I notice him visibly tense at the sound of those words. I know I've pushed it. "Sorry, I didn't mean to..."

"No, it's fine. It's just been a really long time since anyone, actually, I'm not sure if anyone..." His voice trails off.

"Let me," I whisper as I close my eyes and drift off to the peaceful sounds of his breathing, wrapped in the arms of the man I love.

I wake to the sounds of pans clattering and a barrage of curse words from the kitchen. Pulling on my robe, I look for the belt that has been discarded on the floor next to the bed and I pick it up and tie it around my waist, closing the robe.

I pad down the hallway in my bare feet to see Landon standing over the stove, preparing to make breakfast.

"I woke you up." He looks disappointed as he walks over and places a kiss to the side of my head. "I wanted to bring you breakfast in bed." Pouring coffee into a large ceramic mug, he hands it to me and leans against the kitchen island, wearing nothing but the dark grey dress pants he wore out last night. His chest is bare, but my eyes follow the sprinkling of light brown hair that trails down his abdomen and beneath the waistband of his grey pants. My eyes fall to the floor and I notice he isn't wearing socks either, and his feet are perfect. Everything about this man is perfection.

Setting down my mug, I place both hands on his chest and kiss his neck. "I was hoping I'd wake up next to you." I run my hands down his chest, over his abs, and back up again.

"Oh yeah? Why?" He tugs at my robe and it falls off one shoulder. His blue eyes darken and he bites his bottom lip as he takes me in. Pinning me between himself and the kitchen island, he tugs at the belt, watching it fall to the tile floor below. The robe opens, covering just my breasts and he inhales sharply as he runs a finger through the skin between my breasts down to my navel. Moving my coffee mug to the counter behind him, he lifts me by the waist and sets me on the kitchen island.

"Because I wanted a repeat of last night," I say with a sharp inhale when he pushes the robe aside and pulls my nipple into his mouth, sucking it hard. He cups the other breast, teasing it as he continues sucking.

"Because what, baby?" He forces my knees apart and positions himself between my thighs.

"I wanted you to… oh my God," I scream as his fingers rub and pull at my clit.

"Is that for me?" he asks, rubbing the wetness around. "Are you wet for me?"

"Yes," I mutter between gasps.

"Lie down." He guides me so that I'm lying on the cold

granite counter. I shudder when my back hits the freezing cold granite. My legs dangle off the edge of the island, still spread, and I hear his pants hit the floor.

He guides himself into me with one gentle thrust. "God," I moan as he moves, and I flinch when I feel how sore I am from last night, but not enough to make him stop.

"You okay?" he asks, noticing my reaction. I nod and move my hips slowly, meeting his rhythm.

"Sore?"

"Mmm hmm."

"Good." He chuckles. "Then I know I've done my job." His thrusts become harder, faster, and I can feel my climax building already. "So wet," he says as his hands hold my hips in place. I move my hips faster to meet him and he lets out a groan.

"Fuck me, Reagan."

"God I'm so close," I mumble in between my jagged breaths. My hands grip at the cold granite counter top as he pushes himself in and out of me. "Landon," I moan.

"Not yet, baby." I know he isn't close yet. "We go together," he says as he squeezes both of my breasts and bites at my neck.

"Please," I hiss through my teeth. Grabbing his hands, I lace my fingers over the top of his and close my eyes.

"Ready." He gives my hands a little squeeze and I feel his body tighten. Every muscle in his arms and chest become rigid and his head drops back slightly.

"Yes," I groan. And in that moment, we both release. Leaning forward, he scoops me up from the island and I wrap my legs around his waist.

"Shower," he stutters through his still ragged breaths.

"Bath," I tell him as he carries me down the hallway, my entire body wrapped around his. We're still connected, a single being as he walks carefully. Entering the bathroom, he holds me for a minute and I can still feel him pulsing inside of me—there is no better feeling than him inside of me. Pulling out of me slowly, he sets me down in the bathroom and turns the knob to turn on the bath in the huge garden-style tub. Pulling off the robe that's hanging off my shoulders, I kick it to the floor when I feel the warm liquid on my inner thigh.

"Landon," I gasp as I freeze.

"What? What's wrong?" He runs his hands through the water as he pours bubble bath under the streaming water.

"You didn't use a condom." His head snaps around and he meets my eyes. I'm mumbling numbers as I count the days since I think was my last period.

"You're not on birth control?" He sucks in a quick breath.

"No. Why would I be?"

"Because you're a fucking doctor," he snaps.

"I was a fucking doctor that wasn't fucking anyone—so there was no need," I snap back at him, losing count of the days I was counting.

"Okay, let's not panic," he says, reaching for my arm. I continue counting until I'm confident that I've added correctly.

"We should be fine," I announce. "But I'll take some emergency contraception to be safe."

"God, don't scare me like that." He pulls at me gently, stepping into the tub, and I follow him. I gasp at how hot the water is as I lower my body into the bubbles. He wraps his arms around me, guiding me backwards so that I'm leaning against his chest.

He palms water over my chest and plays with the coconut-scented bubbles that have pooled around us, and every muscle begins to relax.

"You sure we're okay?"

"Yeah," I reassure him. "We're good." A deep sigh of relief escapes from him. He holds me as we soak in the hot water and relax. I study the tattoos on his arms that are wrapped around me, holding me firmly against him.

"What do all of these mean?" I ask, running my hand around the skull with a snake.

"Lots of things. This is my newest one." He brushes my hand, pointing to the skull tattoo. "The skull, in many cultures, is a positive symbol. It means rebirth. I guess, for me, it was about new beginnings." I study the black ink and trace the outlines of the other tattoos that mark his arms.

"What about the snake? What is the meaning behind the snake?"

"Again, many cultures view the snake differently. The Greeks view the snake as a sign of healing. The Romans view the snake as a source of protection, a protector."

"So what do these mean to you?" I ask, hoping he'll bite and share with me a bit more about himself.

"A lot of it is personal."

"I can see that. Healing, protector, rebirth… and then this," I trace the two words etched along the front of his wrist. "Strong survivor," I whisper.

"I know what you're doing, Doc, and when I'm ready to share with you, I will. I'm not ready yet, okay?" I don't say anything in return; I just lie against him and let the warm water work at relaxing my sore body.

"You're wrinkled," he says, pressing his hand against mine, palm to palm.

"Go ahead and get out. I'm going to relax in here for a while longer," I say, scooting forward so he can get out. When he stands up, I realize it's the first time I've really seen him fully naked. Every perfect, muscled inch of him is standing within inches of me. "What's this?" I ask, running my hand across a large jagged scar on his side.

"Just a scar." His voice is clipped. He steps out of the tub and pulls a towel down from the shelf. Wrapping the towel around his waist, he saunters away into the bedroom, collecting scraps of clothes off of the floor as he goes along.

"You know, someday you're going to have to talk to me."

"Maybe, maybe not," he mutters and walks out of the bedroom, slamming the door.

"Fuck," I grumble as I slide into the hot water. Closing my eyes, I replay every minute of last night and this morning and I kick myself for pushing him to talk to me. I know he will when he's ready. Even though it's across the house, I can't mistake the sound of the front door slamming shut. He's left.

CHAPTER 15

LANDON

"What happened?" Matt asks as I step up into his Tahoe.

"Nothing. Thanks for picking me up." He knows when to shut the fuck up and not ask questions, and he knows that time is right now. He pulls out of the condo complex and drives the few miles to my house. The ride is silent and the air filled with tension. I stare out the passenger window while my heart beats rapidly.

"She's asking too many questions," I say quietly. "She saw my scar and she wants to know things—things I'm not ready to share." Matt is quiet as he turns onto my street. Pulling into the driveway, he puts the truck in park.

"Maybe you could tell her. I mean Lindsay and I are the only ones that know." He pauses. "I've never seen you like this with anyone, not even..."

"I'm not ready to tell her anything." I open the car door and get down. "Thanks for the ride home." I shut the door and walk briskly toward the front door of my house. I can hear Matt's window roll down and his words shoot through me, stopping me in my tracks.

"You know, she might be the one to save you."

Turning around quickly, my eyes shoot daggers at him and my words fire back at him, "Save me? Save me from what?"

"From yourself, you stupid asshole." He rolls his window up and backs out of the driveway, leaving me contemplating his words.

Sprawled on my large sectional, I flip through hundreds of channels on the TV, not finding anything that I want to watch. Agitated, I kick the throw pillow off the end of the couch and toss the remote control on the coffee table.

"I have two questions for you," Lindsay says, leaning against the wall. "First, what the hell happened? I haven't see you in a mood like this in a long time."

"Nothing," I bark, ignoring her and turning my attention to a pre-season football game on the TV that I honestly don't give a shit about.

"Whatever," she mumbles under her breath. "Oh, and the second question. Why the fuck is there a broken vibrator in the trash can?" I turn my head to look at her, but she has already started walking away. "Never mind, there are some questions I would rather not know the answers to," she says over her shoulder as she disappears down the hallway. The front door opens and I sit up to see Reagan step inside and I can tell she's pissed.

"Ever heard of knocking?" I spit out.

"Ever heard of saying goodbye?" She tosses her purse onto the coffee table and stands before me with her arms crossed over her chest.

"I was pissed, so I left."

"Well, I'm pissed now, so I'm here." She taps her foot on the wood floor as she scowls at me.

"What do you want, Reagan?" I breathe out the words.

"I want you to talk to me. I want you to tell me what you're thinking, tell me what you're feeling." I actually laugh. Not because it's funny, but because everything she just asked me to do, I can't.

"What's so funny?"

"I told you I can't be what you want. It's probably best if you just leave." Her arms fall to her sides and the visible anger that was on her face turns to sadness. I know I'm a dick, but it's better if I push her away now, before either of us becomes too attached.

"So I am just like the other women. Fuck me and leave me, just like them. Way to *try*, Champ," she says quietly, her chin quivering and her hands trembling. "I'll go," she whispers, reaching down to pick up her purse from the table. Walking to the door, she stops with her hand resting on the doorknob. Turning around, she looks back at me as she swats at the tear that rolls down her cheek. "Someday, you're going to find someone and, when that day comes, I hope you're able to talk to them about whatever it is you're keeping pent up inside you."

My fists clench as I look at her, and guilt rolls through me. I struggle with wanting her and never wanting to see her again.

"Just. Leave."

"... and when you find her and trust her, tell her... don't be a coward..." And like that, I fly off the couch and grab her. I can feel my hands gripping her upper arms. She whimpers as I push her backward slightly.

"Trust her? Why? So I can tell her what? Tell her how my dad used to beat the shit out of me every single day? Every. Fucking. Single. Day," I yell in her face. She reaches for my forearms as I grab onto her shoulders.

"My arms have been broken seven times, I've had three skull fractures, a broken foot, two broken hands, and I can't even count the number of times I've had black eyes or a broken nose. Is that what you fucking want to hear, Reagan? Is it? Do you want to hear all the gory details of how my mom got the shit beat out of her nearly every fucking day, and how I was the one who had to clean up the blood?"

My body is shaking with pure rage. I can feel her warm skin beneath my fingers, but I cannot see her at all; I can only see the memories of my mom curled in a protective ball while my dad kicked her, punched her, and spit on her.

"Did you also want to hear how she fucking packed up her bags when I was eight fucking years old, and walked out on Lindsay and me, and left us with that monster?" I snap at her. "Because that's what Lindsay and I lived through every goddamn day of our lives, and no one, not one single person, ever tried to help us." My heart feels like it's going to explode, and anger continues to roil through me. "I never knew when I woke up in the morning if this would be the day he killed me or not, so I learned to live as if it was. Why should I bother getting attached to anything, or anyone? Who the fuck was there to trust?" I growl at her.

"Stop!" I hear Lindsay scream just like she did when we were younger. Only this time, she's telling *me* to stop and not my father. I can feel her shaking hands pulling at me, clawing at my arms just like she used to pull at my dad, trying to get him off of me.

"Landon," she cries, pushing herself between Reagan and me. "Are you okay? Oh my God," I hear her cry out as Reagan takes the loudest breath I've ever heard. My vision is back in time for me to see her sink to the floor on her knees while Lindsay kneels next to her, looking up at me. The look of fear on Lindsay's face, but most importantly seeing Reagan huddled over, scares the shit out of me. Reagan swats at Lindsay's hands as Lindsay tries to push her hair back from her neck. Loud panting breaths fill the quiet space as Reagan tries to recapture her breath.

"Reagan, talk to me," Lindsay whispers, her voice cracking. Reagan looks so small huddled into a ball on the floor with her arms wrapped around her waist. She's leaning forward, and her long hair covers her face so I can't see her.

"Reagan..." I stutter as I move towards her. She holds up a trembling hand to stop me from coming any closer and Lindsay reaches out and touches her arm, just as it falls back into place around her waist. A million memories flash through my mind as I stand here, looking at her kneeling on the floor. So many times, I remember my mom huddled into a little ball on the floor as she tried to deflect punches and kicks from my father. My stomach roils when I realize I have become the very animal my father was.

"Fuck," I murmur as I run both hands through my short hair. "Reagan, I'm so sorry. So, so, sorry," I repeat over and over. Her breathing finally settles and her hands move from her waist to her lap, and finally to her neck. She rubs the front of her neck along her throat and when she finally raises her head, I get a glimpse of her tear-stained cheeks covered in mascara and I can see the rise and fall of her chest and she continues to take deep breaths as she tries to calm herself.

Lindsay sits next to her, crying, huddled as close to her as she possibly can. Just like she did with me when I was the one taking the beatings. "I need to go," Reagan whispers as she tries to push herself to her feet. Her legs are noticeably shaking as she walks toward the front door. She pauses for a second before turning around. "Do you think you could drive me? I'm not sure I should drive right now," she asks Lindsay, who is wiping tears from her face.

"Of course. Let me grab my purse. You'll be okay here, right?" she asks, looking between Reagan and me. Reagan nods her head and I notice her one hand is still holding her neck.

"I didn't mean to hurt you. I would never purposely hurt you," I say, moving toward her. I have the overwhelming urge to scoop her into my arms and hold her; comfort her.

"I know," she says as she swallows hard.

"God, Reagan, please tell me I didn't hit you?" My heart falls and my stomach clenches. "I would never hit a woman, especially one I…"

"You didn't hit me," she cuts me off.

"Here, sit down." I motion toward the couch. I hesitate to reach out and help her as she sits down. "I'm going to go get a bag of ice. Just lie down." She rubs at her upper arms, and I can see red marks where my hands were squeezing her.

She sits on the couch while I walk to the kitchen and pull an ice pack out of the freezer. Walking back to the living room, I freeze when I see her elbows resting on her knees, her head bowed, and her shoulders shaking lightly.

"Here's some ice," I say from behind her to let her know I'm approaching.

"Thanks," she whispers as she wipes the fresh tears from

her cheeks. She presses the ice pack to her neck and leans forward again as she tries to hide her face behind her long hair.

"Please look at me," I say, and she shakes her head back and forth. "Reagan?" She raises her head and finally meets my eyes. She's wiped the mascara from her cheeks and her tears have dried, but she's afraid of me. I can see it in her eyes—the trepidation, the fear.

"Set the ice down on the table, please." She stares at me with somber eyes. Her bright blue eyes have turned to grey, and her lips tremble as she watches me move toward her slowly. I can actually hear her swallow as I sit down next to her and brush her hair back over her shoulder.

"Set the ice down, please," I tell her again, waiting to see what she's hiding. With shaking hands, she lowers the ice pack to her lap and I close my eyes and curse myself when I see the large red mark across her throat.

"I did that? I fucking did that to you?"

"It's fine," she whispers. "It's just tender."

"It's not fine. It's not fucking okay that I did that to you. Your arms, your throat." My voice wavers as I try not to scare her any more than I already have. I stand up and walk down the hall to my room, slamming the door behind me.

Pressing my forehead against my bedroom wall, I close my eyes and struggle to remember what happened. In my mind, I know I didn't mean to hurt her, but in my heart, I know I did. Turning, I reach for the first object in sight, the lamp on my bedside table and toss it against the wall, smashing it into a million pieces. Reaching back, I throw my fist into the wall, and again punch two large holes through the sheet rock. The pain soaring through my hand feels good—a painful release.

"Stop. Please." I hear her voice from behind me; soft, yet full of fear.

"It would probably be best if you left," I say, wiping the sweat from my forehead with the back of my hand.

"No." Her voice is weak, yet strong.

"Why can't you ever do what I ask of you, Reagan? Goddammit, listen to me. I told you before I was going to hurt you and look at you," I say with a strained voice. She watches me intently as I walk in circles around the room.

"Sit down," she orders me as she points to the bed. "Please." She shuts the bedroom door, walks over to the edge of the bed, and sits next to me. Rubbing her temples with her fingers, she lets out a deep sigh before she begins.

"I know you didn't mean to hurt me."

"But," I interrupt.

"Stop." She reaches out and touches my arm. "Let me finish."

"I know you didn't mean to hurt me," she pauses for a second before she continues. "And I didn't mean to push you, to ask so many questions. But if for one goddamn minute, you think anything you said out there in that living room changes how I feel about you or what I think about you, you're mistaken." She slides off the bed and kneels before me, positioning herself between my legs. She rests her hands on my thighs and looks up at me.

"None of that was your fault," she says quietly. "None of it." I nod my head slowly in agreement. "And if you push me away because of that, then you're really not the man I thought you were." And there is the punch to the gut I deserve, "But you have to let someone in, Landon. If not me, someone."

"I'm sorry," I whisper and rest my hands on top of hers.

Leaning forward, I kiss the top of her dark hair lightly, inhaling her scent for what may be the last time. "But I need you to leave." Her hands flinch when I ask her to go. She stands slowly as she pulls her hands from my thighs, letting them fall to her sides. With no other words, she walks to the door.

"I'm sorry," I say loud enough that I know she heard me. The click of the door and the quiet footsteps that fade down the hall tell me she's gone, and for the first time since my mom left twenty-two years ago, my heart breaks.

CHAPTER 16

Reagan

The sound of the alarm for the fourth time this morning only indicates one thing—I'm really fucking late. I don't think I slept for more than twenty minutes last night and now I have a full day of work ahead of me.

Pulling myself from the bed, I drag my exhausted body into the bathroom. Between the bloodshot eyes, the dark circles from lack of sleep, and the giant red mark that is still visible across my throat, I look like a zombie.

"Coffee," I mutter and shuffle down the hallway to the kitchen to make a pot of the strongest coffee ever. In record time, I've washed my face, brushed my teeth, and fixed my hair, leaving it loose so that it hangs around my neck to cover the pink mark that stretches across my neck.

The ride to work is short and quiet. I'm left with nothing but my thoughts and my exhaustion. Pulling into my covered parking spot, I don't even recall driving here. There is no way I'm going to make it through this day. Pulling my cellphone from my purse, I check to see if I have any missed calls or text messages, but I have nothing. I toss it back into my purse and gather my belongings.

It's early, so the office is dark and empty and I settle into my small office, powering up my laptop. Leaning back in the oversized leather chair behind my desk, I lay my head back and take a deep, cleansing breath. Closing my eyes, I relax and take another deep breath, focusing on clearing my head and preparing for the day ahead.

"So are you going to let him get away with that?" The husky voice fills the small, quiet space of my office, startling me.

"Excuse me?" I ask as I open my eyes to find Adam leaning against the doorframe of my open office door.

"Your neck." He nods. "I hope you're not going to let him get away with it like his father did."

"What are you talking about?" I question him, as I scramble to figure out how he knows Landon's father.

"Christianson," he says, walking into my office.

"What about him?"

"He's the one that did that to your neck, right? I saw him driving your car the other day, Reagan. I know it was him that did that to your neck, right?" I don't answer him, but search for any excuse I can to end this conversation, but I'm so exhausted, I can't even think straight.

"No."

"Don't fucking lie for him, Reagan. Like father, like son," he snarls.

"I don't understand what you're talking about, Adam." I sit up straighter in my chair.

"His old man used to beat the shit out of his mom. From what I heard, she was a cheating whore and he almost killed her the night she finally left. When she finally left, he used to beat the shit out of Landon."

"How do you know this?" A wave of nausea runs through me.

"Wilmington today isn't as small as it used to be, sweetheart." I hate that he calls me that. "Twenty years ago, everyone knew everyone else's business. It wasn't a secret what his old man used to do to them, but he got away with it because of who he was."

"Who was he?"

"He was the chief of police and a lousy drunk. He was killed in a car crash on duty about seven years ago. That was probably the best thing that ever happened to that family." He pauses for a few moments as he considers what to say. "Look, Landon's always been a loose cannon. We went to high school together and I never liked the kid. I have to say, though; I used to feel bad for him when I'd see him at school. I swear he was always in a different cast, or bandaged up." He chuckles.

"What about his mother? What ever happened to her?" Adam visibly tenses when I ask this question, which I find odd.

"Last I heard, she set up house with another family. Got to play 'mommy' to some step kids. She left and never went back for them," he says, backing towards the door. "I'm serious, Reagan. Don't take that shit from him, do you understand?" He points to my neck. "The last thing this office needs is a dead doctor all over the news because her loser boyfriend beat the shit out of her, or worse, has killed her."

"He didn't do this." I'm confident with my answer, but inside, I'm shaking.

"Don't fucking lie and cover it up like his mom tried to do. You'll end up almost dead like her," he says as he turns to leave the office.

"He's not his father," I announce loudly.

"First stage is denial," he mumbles over his shoulder.

"Such a fucking dick hole," I say under my breath as he walks away, shutting the door behind him. Dropping my head in my hands, I rub my temples and think that Landon's behaviors all make perfect sense now that I understand the abuse he went through. Seconds later, there is a knock on my door, "What now?" I bark, assuming it's Adam again.

"Hey." The voice is calming as the door opens slowly. Matt pokes his head in. "Mind if I come in?"

"No, please, come in," I offer.

"Lindsay asked me to stop by." He offers me a half smile. "Mind if I sit down for a minute?" He motions to the chair that sits in front of my desk.

"Of course," I say politely. Matt is tall and handsome with dark brown hair, hazel eyes, and a calming demeanor. He's average build, very all-American boy next door. He takes a seat in the chair and steeples his hands. I know he's uncomfortable coming here, and I'm positive it's because of last night.

"So Lindsay told me what happened last night," he starts. "She's really worried about you."

"I'm fine, really," I sigh as I try to dismiss his concern. "I think everything got a little blown out of proportion," I add.

"Lindsay didn't see what happened in the beginning, only what she saw when she came in the room. Did he…"

"Hit me? No, he didn't. And I'm not saying that to protect him, Matt. He didn't hit me."

"Then what happened, Reagan? The truth." His voice is calm and soothing.

"He left my house yesterday rather abruptly after I was pushing him to talk to me."

"About?"

"About everything? Why he's so closed off, why he can't talk about things, why he can't commit."

He chuckles. "You really went for the jugular, didn't you?"

"Well, how was I supposed to know? He doesn't tell me *anything*, which is why I was pressing him. Anyway, he left my house angry; he didn't even say goodbye. He just got up and left. I was so hurt and angry." My voice cracks slightly.

"That's when I came to get him," Matt recalls. "Continue."

"After I cleaned up, I went over to confront him about leaving. To finally force some answers out of him, and he snapped. He jumped up from the couch and ran over to me. He didn't hit me, I swear. He was holding me by the shoulders and I backed myself up against the wall. He was just yelling at me and he moved his arm so that it was pressing against my neck, but I don't even think he knew he was doing it. You should have seen him, the look in his eyes; it was like he wasn't even there."

"I've seen it before," Matt acknowledges.

"Anyway, Lindsay comes around the corner and immediately starts screaming at him and pushes her way in between us. It took me a few minutes to catch my breath, but I'm okay. Really, I am."

"Do you mind if I take a look at your neck?" He points at my neck. I ponder his question, but I know if I tell him no, he'll think it's more serious than it really is.

"Sure," I say as he stands up from the chair in front of my desk. Sitting on the edge of my desk, he tilts my head back just a little. His fingers brush over the mark across my neck.

"Does that hurt?" he asks, his touch gentle.

"Not really. It feels more like a burn. I don't think it will even bruise."

"Reagan, I don't know what answers you got, or what answers you'll ever get from him. Just know that he would never intentionally hurt you. I know him, probably better than anyone."

"I know," I say as I nod. Matt still sits on my desk, lost in thought.

"Matt?"

"Yeah?"

"He told me what happened to him, last night when he was yelling at me."

"What did he tell you?"

"About the abuse, his dad, the beatings." He nods his head. "If I had known, I wouldn't have pushed for answers like I did."

"Don't blame yourself, Reagan." He pauses. "He's just never cared about anyone like this before. These feelings are new, and I'm sure he feels vulnerable, exposed, and honestly—I can guarantee he's fucking scared to death."

"Why?"

"That you'll leave him. That's his biggest fear—rejection."

"Is that why he does what he does? The sex? The women?"

Matt sighs and his head drops back a little. "Yeah, better to leave than to be left. Better not to get attached," he admits quietly. "That's Landon's motto in life." I let the information he's just shared with me about his best friend settle in.

"Would he kill you if he knew you were talking to me and telling me this personal stuff?"

"Yes. But I know you need to know this, or he's going to lose you, and Reagan—he needs you," he says, raking his hand across his chin. "But this conversation never happened, got it?" He smiles at me.

"You're a good friend to him, Matt."

179

"And he's a good friend to me. Lindsay and Landon are my family. I'd do anything for either of them."

"Speaking of Lindsay, will you let her know I'm okay and thank her for me? Tell her I'll call her later."

"Of course," he says, standing up from the edge of my desk. I stand up from my desk chair so I can walk him out.

"Thank you for coming by, Matt. It means a lot."

"Give him some time, but not too much time. He won't come for you," he says. "If I know him, he hates himself right now, but he won't come for you."

"So what do I do?"

"Fight for him."

"I've been fighting, Matt."

"I know, but fight harder."

I let out a frustrated sigh and roll my neck. "I don't have much fight left in me," I mutter as he offers me a tight smile.

"Bye, Reagan," he says as he exits my office. I follow him out and the office is buzzing with employees. Checking the time on my watch, I see that it's almost nine o'clock and patients will be arriving shortly. I grab my cell phone from my pocket and send a quick text message to Landon, wishing him well on his first day as a detective.

The morning drags on at a snail's pace. By noon, my body is shutting down from lack of sleep. "Melissa, can you rearrange my afternoon clients? Split them between the two nurse practitioners, or reschedule them for tomorrow, if you could?"

"Sure, is everything okay?" she asks, concerned.

"Yeah, I'm just not feeling well. I need to go home and get some rest."

After a quick nap, I drive myself to the WXZI studio. Pressing the call button on the side of the building. I offer my name and I announce that I'm here to see Lindsay Christianson. With a long buzz, the automatic door lock clicks and I enter the stark lobby. I hear her heels click down the travertine tile hallway as I hear her announce my name. "Reagan."

"Thanks for letting me stop by," I say as she reaches out to hug me as she approaches.

"Are you okay?" she asks, pulling away while she looks me over—honing in on my neck.

"I'm fine. Tired but fine. But I have a couple of questions for you. Do you have just a couple of minutes to talk privately?"

"Sure, but just a few. I'm about to go shoot a segment for tonight's newscast," she says as she leads us into a small glass-walled conference room that sits just off the lobby. It feels like a fishbowl where everyone can watch us.

"Please sit down." She gestures to a chair at the large rectangle conference table. "So what's going on? Is this about last night?" she questions as she takes a seat across from me at the table.

"No, it's not about last night. Do you happen to know Adam Gerard?"

"Never heard of him. Why?"

"He works with me. He's a partner in the practice. He went to high school with Landon, and is aware of everything you two went through," I inform her and she gasps quietly.

"What do you mean, 'aware'?"

181

"Let me back up for a minute. Landon dropped me off at work the other day and Adam saw him leave in my car. He questioned me as to who was driving my car, but I ignored him. I blew it off as him being a concerned co-worker. I mentioned Adam to your brother and he admitted that they went to school together and they never liked each other." I pause for a moment to make sure I'm not leaving out any important details.

"This morning, Adam saw my neck and immediately starting spouting off shit about your family. About your dad and what he did." I find myself gently rubbing over the sore spot across my neck as I mention it. "He mentioned that I had better be careful, that Landon was just like his father."

"Fucker," she mutters under her breath. "He's not."

"Lindsay, I know he's not. I'm just curious... does everyone know about your dad? What he did?"

"No." She startles. "At least no one ever said anything before." She wraps her arms around her waist. "And if they did, no one helped us." She pauses.

"Lindsay, I'm so sorry," I whisper. She nods at me with a sad smile on her face.

"So what about this Adam Gerard has you concerned?"

"He knows so much. He knew about Landon, your mom leaving and playing 'stepmom' to a new family. He even knew about your dad. He mentioned him being an alcoholic, and that he was killed seven years ago. It just seemed odd how much he knew."

"Back up. What about my mom?"

"That she left, and played stepmom, but never went back for you," I mumble quietly.

"How would he know that?"

"I don't know, Lindsay. That's why I'm asking you."

"We never heard from her after she left. She literally packed her suitcase, walked out, and disappeared from our lives. She hasn't been seen from or heard from since." Lindsay looks out through the glass conference room and stares straight ahead at the small cubicles that circle the room.

"You have no idea where she went?"

"No," she whispers. "Look, hey, I have to get back to work. But if I can place Adam Gerard, I'll be sure to let you know." She stands up quickly and walks to the door. Holding it open, she waits for me as I gather my purse and stand to leave.

"Sorry to bother you about this at work, Lindsay," I say sympathetically as I follow her out of the conference room and into the main lobby.

"Don't apologize. I'm glad that you know now," she says as she hugs me. "Don't let him push you away," she says quietly as she pulls out of our hug and walks down the hallway, leaving me with more questions than answers.

CHAPTER 17

LANDON

My first day as a detective has been anything but exciting. I perused the local online classifieds, looking for anything suspiciously criminal. I searched online ads for guns, drugs, and stolen goods, or sex for sale. Today, I've come up empty handed. While I'm excited for this new position, my thoughts are never far from Reagan. I ache inside, a foreign feeling for me. I hate myself for the way I treated her last night, for scaring her, for pushing her away—but it's for her own good.

My first day comes and goes with little fanfare. Detective Weston, another narcotics detective, passes by my desk on his way home. "How was the first day?"

"Everything I thought it would be," I joke with him.

"That exciting, huh?" He laughs. "Trust me, there are very few days like this. Enjoy it now. See ya tomorrow, buddy." He waves on his way out.

I sit at my new desk and look at the stark walls that surround it. My desk holds nothing but a note pad, a grey phone, and a computer. That's it. There is nothing personal here. I don't have a dog, a wife, kids, or even a fucking hobby to display proudly. What does that say about me? I scan the rows of desks in the room and directly across from me sits Weston's cube. His desk and cube walls are full of family pictures and drawings from his kids—and, for the first time ever, a pang of envy runs through me. *I want that.*

Pulling my cell phone from my pocket, I swipe the locked screen to check for any missed calls or texts. I see a text message from Reagan and tap it. *"**Hope you have a great first day**,"* it reads. I close the message. Grabbing my keys, I zigzag through the rows of cubes and out the door of the police station to my car. Minutes later, I sit in her driveway, staring at her front door, my heart racing. Never in my life have I been so afraid of losing anything, or anyone. I used to fear the physical pain my father would inflict on me, but the pain of loving her and losing her because I was too fucking selfish to admit it hurts more than any punch, kick, or broken bone.

Opening the car door, I step onto the concrete driveway and contemplate what to say. I run through every possible scenario in my head, except for the one that unfolds in front of me. There she stands, staring at me, her headphones in her ears and her body covered in sweat. I watch the beads of sweat roll from her temples and down her cheeks to her neck. I cringe when I see the pink mark spread across her throat.

"Landon," she says quietly, pulling the ear buds from her ears.

"Hey."

"I'm surprised to see you here." Her voice is quiet. She walks around me toward the front door and pulls a key out from under her doormat. She unlocks the door and looks back at me, waiting for me to say something.

"Can we talk?"

"About?" she says quietly as she unlocks the front door.

"Everything." I mean it; I will answer any question she has. I will apologize a million times. I just need to talk to her—I just need *her*. She nods and holds the door open for me as I step into her house. Kicking off her shoes, she walks to the fridge and pulls out two bottles of water, handing one of them to me.

"Thanks," I mumble and follow her into the living room, where we each take a seat on her couch. She pulls her long legs and feet up onto the couch and curls them underneath her. She plays with the bottle of water, twisting and untwisting the lid on the bottle nervously.

"Where do I even start?" I say with a sigh as I set my water bottle on her coffee table. "Bear with me; I'm not used to talking about what I'm thinking, or how I'm feeling," I admit. She offers me a small, reassuring smile.

"I know last night I told you some of the things that happened to me." All of her attention is focused on me, and she nods, encouraging me to continue. "Please don't think that I'm using that as an excuse for my behavior; it's not an excuse as much as it is an explanation. I guess I never learned to express my feelings correctly. I truly only ever understood what it was like to feel scared and angry, and when I'm feeling vulnerable, I react by shutting people out, or never letting them in, in the first place." Her eyes hold their gaze on me and I see the muscles in her neck, underneath the mark I left, tighten as she swallows.

"What I'm trying to say is, I don't know how to do 'this.'" I motion between the two of us. "There is no denying I feel something for you, but my head is telling me not to let you in, that when you get too close, you'll realize just how fucked up I am and you'll leave."

"That's a risk in any relationship," she whispers. "It's a very real feeling for anyone, Landon. You're not different for having those fears."

"Maybe. But that's why I don't do relationships. It's easier for me not to feel— not to care."

"But you just said you feel something for me," she says nervously.

"I do."

"Then let go of the fear. Trust *me*." Her voice pleads with me as she pushes herself forward on the couch, moving just a little closer to me.

"Trust *me*," she whispers again. "I won't hurt you. I won't leave you." She reaches out and wraps her fingers around my wrist, giving it a squeeze. Everything about her is comforting. Her words, her presence, her touch. "But we have to be honest with each other, we have to communicate, we have to *trust* each other."

We sit in silence for a few moments as I let her words sink in. *Trust her.* My heart wants to, but my head says *trust nobody*. She scoots closer to me, resting her head against my shoulder. "Talk to me. Tell me everything," she says quietly as she laces her fingers through mine and pulls our tangled hands into her lap.

My head is flooded with memories from so long ago, most of which I've buried into the depths of me, in hopes that I'd never have to relive them either physically or emotionally, yet here I am, ready to pull them to the forefront and share them with Reagan. I struggle with where to actually begin and how much I should tell her. Then I hear her words echo inside my head: *trust me.*

I take a deep breath and begin. "For as far back as I can remember, my dad was an asshole. I honestly don't remember a time where I liked him, or enjoyed being around him, even as a very young boy. It was always my mom, Lindsay, and me. I remember my mom baking cookies, and taking us to the park, and walking me to the school bus every morning." I pick at the side of my thumb as the dusty memories become clearer, more vivid.

"My dad was the chief of police and he was never around. Work was his priority. I'm not sure what happened or exactly when, but it was when I was around six years old, he started drinking heavily, to the point where he stopped coming home after work. He'd end up at a bar, drinking himself into a stupor. Most nights, my mom would feed us, and get us to bed before he got home. I used to see the bruises on her arms, or the occasional black eye, but I didn't really know what was happening."

"Once I figured out what he was doing, I learned he was really good about hitting her where the bruises could be easily covered. I will never forget the bruise on her back that matched the outline of his shoe." I close my eyes at the memory of that bruise. I clear my throat and Reagan squeezes my hand tighter before I continue.

"Anyway, he used to come home and, damn near every night, he'd beat her. I used to hide in my room and just listen to it happen, listen to her cry. He tormented her." I shudder when I think of her voice, her pleas begging him to stop. I can still hear her as if it was happening right now.

"One night, I finally got brave enough to open my bedroom door and peek out into the living room where he was yelling at her. She was huddled in the corner in a protective ball, and he'd just kick her over and over in the ribs and on her back. I ran over to her and wrapped myself around her as best I could, and he just laughed at me trying to protect her. He pulled me off of her with one hand, and flung me across the room where I landed against another wall. It was the first time I believe I had a concussion."

"First time?" she whispers, and scrunches her eyebrows.

"There were so many times, I lost count, but I remember my head hitting that wall, and I'll never forget how bad it hurt. I blacked out for a while, and had a headache for days." I see her physically shudder when I say that.

"That was the night he started hitting me. It was a game to him. He'd come home, and start in on my mom—he'd taunt me by hurting her. He'd see how long it took to get me to try and stop him, and then he'd turn the beatings on to me. When he was done beating the shit out of us, he'd make me clean up any blood, or pick up anything that had gotten broken during the beating. He'd sit and laugh at me as I cleaned up the mess he made." I take a drink of water to help ease the dryness in my throat.

"To this day, what haunts me the most is how he'd make my mom sit in the corner and watch me clean up our blood. If I missed any, or if my mom made a sound, he'd continue hitting us, usually with blows to the back of the head. That was his favorite place to hit. There was no visible bruising through our hair." She gasps quietly.

"This went on for well over a year. Each night, I'd wonder if this was going to be the night he'd finally kill one of us. The beatings got progressively worse over time, much more aggressive."

"Why didn't she take you and Lindsay and leave, or get help?" Her voice breaks when she asks.

"She claimed no one would help us because of his position.

Who's going to charge the Chief of Police with child abuse and domestic violence?" I sigh. "This is exactly why I decided to go into law enforcement, because of this—because of him. I want to help those that have no one else to help them."

She rubs my arms gently and sits quietly, patiently, as I sort through my thoughts. "The night my mom finally left, he had come home from work. Lindsay and I were already in bed, but I was wide awake, waiting for him to get home, just like every other night. It was December, the week of Christmas. I heard the front door slam, and I instantly jumped out of bed. It got to the point where he didn't even talk to my mom, or yell at her, or argue with her. He used to just hit her, beat her for the pure enjoyment factor in it." I close my eyes as I recall the worst day of my life.

"I stood inside my bedroom with the door shut and my ear pressed against the door. His heavy footsteps echoed down the hallway, stopping just outside of their bedroom. I cracked my door open to peek across the hallway just in time to see him take three long strides toward the bed and pull my mom off the bed by her hair. She landed on the floor like a rag doll and he starting kicking her. This time was the first time I heard him call her names, though. I'll never forget the venom in his voice as he called her a dirty whore and a slut."

I swallow hard and realize how dry my mouth is and how rapidly my heart is beating. I take another drink of the water and set it back on the table. "With closed fists, he punched her face repeatedly, and that's when I entered their room. I had finally summoned up the courage to try to help her. She was huddled on the floor, trying to cover her face with her arms and hands as he kept delivering punch after punch, all while still calling her names." I rake my hands over my face as I recall vividly the sounds of his voice yelling at her, and hers screaming for help.

"I could hear the sound of his hands hitting her face with each punch. Blood was everywhere; he had landed a punch to her nose and there was a large gash under her eye that was also bleeding heavily. I had a matter of seconds to help her, or I knew he would kill her. I jumped in between his fist and my mom and I began taking the blows. He always liked to punch my ribs and chest. I felt ribs crack and break with each punch he threw at me. I couldn't breathe as the wind had been knocked out of me, but I remember a sense of relief, for just a moment, that my mom wasn't being hit. She slid out from underneath me and crawled to the corner of the room. It wasn't until Lindsay, who was only four at the time, was screaming from the doorway that my Dad hesitated to throw another punch."

My voice is hoarse as I continue. "My dad spit on my mom as he walked past her and out of the bedroom. He yelled at us to clean up the mess before he got home, the door slamming behind him. My mom scrambled to her feet and pulled a large suitcase from the closet and began tossing her clothes in it. A sense of relief washed over me, knowing that we were leaving this hell. She told me to go get a bowl and scrub brush and to start cleaning up the blood before my dad returned. I didn't question her; I just figured she'd continue packing for us while I cleaned up."

"So what happened?" she asks as she loops her arm through mine, holding me against her.

"She packed her shit and walked out. She left Lindsay and me and never looked back. Not once did she come for us, or call us, or anything. She left us with that piece of shit who continued to beat me for years."

"My God, Landon," she whispers and wipes a tear that slips

from the corner of her eye.

"We didn't celebrate birthdays or holidays after my mom left, but I always hoped; every night, I'd say a prayer that she would come and get us for one of our birthdays, or for Christmas. In my head, I assumed she needed some time to figure out her game plan, but I never doubted she'd come back for us." I clear my throat of the noticeable lump that has formed.

"About six years after she left, I gave up hope. She wasn't coming back for us. Yet every time my dad hit me, broke a bone, bruised me—I was so thankful it wasn't her."

"Did he hit Lindsay?" she asks timidly.

"No. It was always me. I would never have let him hurt her." We sit in silence and her thumb rubs the top of my hand. I can tell it's a nervous habit of hers.

"When did it stop?" she whispers.

"When I was fifteen. I think the alcohol finally wore him down enough that he knew I'd fight back and win. The day I turned fifteen was the first day I hadn't been beaten in seven years. He never said a word to me, or Lindsay; he just rotted away until he finally was killed in a car accident seven years ago. Is it wrong of me to say that was the happiest day of my life?"

She shakes her head, but doesn't speak. "This is why I'm so fucked up, Reagan. All of this baggage."

"You're not fucked up, Landon. You just need to talk about it. You have to let it go to move forward," she says, wrapping her arms around me.

"I miss her and hate her all in the same breath. She just left us." My voice trails off.

"I won't leave you—ever," she whispers. "I promise."

I find it oddly refreshing that reliving the darkest days and years of my life and sharing them with Reagan has lifted the proverbial weight from my shoulders. As vulnerable as it feels to talk about the most painful parts of my existence, it feels good that someone else knows and isn't judging me.

"I'm sorry for everything, Reagan. For pushing you away, and pulling you back in, for pushing you away again. You deserve better than that. But mostly, I'm sorry for last night, for scaring you. The look in your eyes will haunt me forever."

"Thank you for trusting me," she says, pressing a kiss to the side of my mouth.

"Thank you for not giving up on me."

"Never," she whispers.

CHAPTER 18

Reagan

Hours turn into days, days into weeks, and weeks into months. We fall into a comfortable pattern, a familiar routine. We're learning to navigate the unknown territory of *us*, as the term, or rather the label "relationship" seems to send Landon running in the other direction. There is no term, no name that describes what we are or what we have.

We see each other nearly every night—to the point that the nights that we are apart, there is an emptiness that surrounds me. It's been nearly thirty-five hours since I've seen him. The case he's working on has him working insane amounts of hours, but I know there is no other job he'd rather be doing. As I drive to work, I remind myself to tell him about my annual trip home every September. I've booked my flight and as much as I don't want to go without him, I need to do this—for me.

After I park in the same parking spot as I do every day, I grab my purse and coffee and head into the office, ready to start my day. As usual, the day flies by as I juggle scheduled patients and emergency appointments. There is never a dull moment at work. Four o'clock and I'm finally sitting down for the first time today when Melissa notifies me that my last appointment has cancelled. I'm grateful for the down time, and finally take a moment to check my phone. Two text messages, one from Landon and one from Lindsay. I open Landon's first.

"Still out of town. Won't be home again tonight. Will call when I can."

His message puts a damper on my already solemn mood. Opening the second message from Lindsay, I can't help but smile.

"Me and You. Date tonight. 7pm. I'll bring Chinese, you supply the wine." As tired as I am, I actually look forward to spending some time with Lindsay.

"It's a date. See you at 7," I reply.

Wrapping up my day, I finish charting and returning patient calls. Remembering that I have to stop and purchase wine on the way home, I shut down my laptop and gather my belongings to leave.

"You're leaving early." His voice startles me.

"Jesus, Adam, you're always sneaking up on me."

"I'm not sneaking up on you; you're always distracted or lost in thought." I roll my eyes when he says that.

"I'm not feeling that great, so I'm leaving a little early. See you tomorrow." I offer him a tight smile as I pull my purse strap over my shoulder and walk to the back door. Adam has kept his distance from me for a couple of months. The only time he talks to me, it's strictly business, just the way I like to keep it with him—strictly business. Something about him is off. I shouldn't feel that way about my business partner, but I do.

"See you tomorrow," he says from behind me as the door closes. Getting settled in my car, I shoot Lindsay a quick text asking her what kind of wine she likes and I head toward the liquor store. I walk the aisles in search of multiple varieties of wine, since I have not heard back from Lindsay. I settle on a Pinot Grigio, a Riesling, a Cabernet Sauvignon, and a Merlot. Lindsay isn't due to arrive for another thirty minutes, so I shower quickly and change into some comfortable clothes, just in time to hear her come bounding through my front door.

"Honey, I'm home." She laughs as she juggles her purse and three large bags of Chinese food.

"Jesus, Linds, it's just us… we're not feeding an army!" I rush over to help her by taking two of the bags of food from her hands.

"I know, but I didn't know what I was in the mood for, so I got a little of everything." She kicks off her four-inch heels and wiggles her toes.

"Kitchen table or coffee table?" I gesture to the short table that sits on a plush rug surrounded by the couches in the living room.

"Definitely coffee table," she says, walking over to the table and sets down the bag of food. I follow with the other two bags. She sits on the floor and starts pulling the little white cartons out of the bags, arranging them in the center of the table.

"What kind of wine?" I ask as I pull plates down from the cupboard. "I picked up Pinot Grigio, Riesling…"

"Pinot," she hollers, cutting me off. Grabbing two white wine glasses, plates, napkins, and the chilled bottle of Pinot Grigio, I meet her at the coffee table.

"I picked up lo mein, broccoli with beef, kung pao shrimp, sweet and sour chicken, sesame chicken, egg rolls, and pot stickers."

"All of it sounds good," I say as I open the bottle of wine and pour two glasses. Lindsay fills up both of our plates and we sit around the short table like I used to do in college when I didn't have a kitchen table to sit at.

"I feel like I haven't seen you in forever," Lindsay says as she tries to pick up chicken with her chopsticks.

"It has been a while."

"Things are good, though?"

"Yeah, really good." I smile as I think of Landon and how comfortable things have been recently.

"Good. He's happy, you know," she says, setting down her chopsticks.

"I'm happy too," I admit. "Really, really happy."

"Have you heard from him?" she asks, looking a little concerned.

"He sent a text this afternoon saying that he wouldn't be home tonight. Why, is everything okay?"

"No, I mean, yeah. I don't know, Reagan." She sighs and finishes her glass of wine.

"Talk to me, Linds, I don't like the look on your face."

"Remember when you came to my work asking me about Adam Gerard?"

"Yeah, of course. Did you find something out?"

"I don't know," she says as she runs her finger around the rim of her wine glass, clearly deep in thought. "I mean, yeah, I found out something. But I don't know..."

"What is it, Lindsay? Tell me. I work with him, and he's been acting so strange for months now, ever since he saw me with Landon."

"So let me back up a minute." She clears her throat and takes another sip of wine. "After you left that day, I was so bothered that someone other than Landon, Matt, and me knew anything about our past, about my dad—and my mom." She pauses. "I started spending every minute of my free time looking into him. For the last eight weeks, it's been a fucking obsession of mine. I can't stop trying to figure out who he is and what he knows—but most importantly, *how* he knows anything."

"What did you find out?" The hair on my arm raises and I get the chills as I wait for Lindsay to continue.

"I spent every free minute I had and resources at work, trying to dig up any information on him. It's what consumed me every waking moment. I hit dead ends, though, everywhere I looked, so I hired a private investigator, Reagan," she mumbles. "At first, all he gave me was the basic shit, that he graduated three years ahead of Landon; you already knew that because Landon told you. That he played football, and so did Landon. I thought it was just some stupid guy who was jealous of my brother, that still harbors some old shit from high school."

"Is that what it is?"

"No. It's so much more."

"Spit it out, Lindsay." My stomach is in knots as she stumbles over words.

"Be patient… I hadn't heard from the investigator in over a week and I was pressuring him for information, anything that would help me figure out who Adam Gerard is. The P.I. claimed he was continuing to look into things and that he was onto something, but needed a few more days."

"And…" I break out in a light sweat and my knee bounces nervously.

"Well, he pieced everything together and sat me down this morning to lay it all out in front of me."

"Okay... Jesus, Lindsay, just tell me." My heart feels like it's about to jump out of my chest.

"So Adam is my stepbrother." That's all she says. Drops a bomb and doesn't say another word.

"What?" I spit out. "I don't understand."

"Neither did I, until he laid it all out in front of me. In 1988, Adam's mother, Kathryn, passed away from cancer. He was eight years old. In 1992, Adam's father, a prominent local banker, Louis Gerard, suddenly packed up his new girlfriend, Josie, and twelve-year-old twin sons, Adam and Aaron. He quietly moved them across the country to Tucson, Arizona, with little explanation to friends or family."

"Okay, I still don't understand," I say, confused.

"Josie is my mom." And my heart literally stops beating. The look on Lindsay's face is pure disgust.

"She left us, and moved away with Adam, his brother, and his dad. She fucking left us for another family."

It all makes sense, what Adam was saying. *Last I heard, she set up house with another family. Got to play 'mommy' to some step kids. She left and never went back for them.*

"The private investigator talked to some old friends of Mr. Gerard's and, apparently, my mom met him at a charity event. He was a very generous supporter of some of the local law enforcement charities, and apparently took an interest in my mom. Louis Gerard was trying to help her divorce my dad. He didn't go into greater detail about my mom specifically because I asked him for information on Adam, not her. The report gave me information on Adam and where he went to college, his girlfriends, where he attended medical school, and other shit I don't care about. He found my mom."

"Will you excuse me for a second?" I push myself up and

move quickly toward the bathroom. I feel nauseous. Pushing my way through the bathroom door, I empty my stomach of the dinner I just ate. How in the hell are we going to tell Landon this? Will she tell him? I can't keep this from him. The bathroom door opens behind me, and Lindsay pushes her way in.

"Ah, you had the same reaction I had this afternoon." She laughs and pulls my hair back, holding it while I pull toilet paper from the roll and wipe my nose and mouth. Leaning back against the bathroom wall, I look up at her.

"What are we going to do?"

"We're not going to do anything. I need to digest this information, get everything straight before I take this to Landon."

"I can't go to work and pretend that I don't know this about Adam, Lindsay."

"Yes, you can. And you will. Let me figure this shit out, and decide how and when to tell Landon. This will destroy him."

"We're not going to let that happen."

"No, we're not. I even toyed with not telling you. Ripping up the report and pretending I didn't even know."

"Why?"

"She's been gone for so long, and to know that she's been living under our noses for as long as she has without trying to get a hold of us." She pauses. "It's disgusting, and it will destroy Landon."

"Are you going to try to get a hold of her? I mean, now that we know Adam's connection, I can essentially lead you to her front door."

"I don't know," she whispers and stares dead ahead at the wall, a blank expression on her face. "I don't know what to do about her."

"Is this really happening?" I ask as I gently bang the back of my head against the bathroom wall.

"Yeah. Yeah, it fucking is."

CHAPTER 19

LANDON

I know that it's four in the morning and it's ridiculously early, but selfishly, I've missed her. I need to see her, taste her—feel her. I slip into her dark condo using the backlight from my phone to see as I quietly move down the hallway to her room. I've been gone for nearly two days, working on this investigation and, as much as I love my job, the difficult part is that there are no set hours, no nine to five days.

I strip off my clothes and slide into bed beside her. She's bundled under the comforter, hugging a large pillow. I notice how she smells like flowers as I press myself against her warm body. She startles as my hand snakes around her waist.

"Hey, baby," I whisper, pressing kisses to the soft, warm skin behind her ear. She releases the pillow she was holding and twists her soft body toward me, wrapping long arms and legs around me. There is no other feeling like the feeling of her supple body in my arms.

"I missed you," she says sleepily, pressing a kiss to my lips. "What time is it?"

"Just after four, Doc. Go back to sleep."

"No way. How was work?" She yawns.

"Just work. Can't really talk about it yet. How were things here?" She doesn't say anything, but just studies me, running her fingers up and down my scruffy cheeks. I haven't shaved in almost three days, and she always likes to play with the rough hair. Moonlight spills in from her skylight, providing just enough light to see her features perfectly.

"They were good, quiet. I had dinner with Lindsay last night. Work was non-eventful. That's about it," she says, her voice quiet.

She trails her fingers from my cheeks, to my neck, and down to my arms. She traces the tattoos on my arm as she has always done. Her gentle touch never gets old. She pushes me to my back, and moves herself on top of me, straddling me.

"I missed you," she tells me again as she leans forward, kissing her way from my chest up to my lips.

"I missed you too, baby."

"Show me how much you missed me," she says against my lips with a little giggle. In one fluid motion, I have her beneath me. She wiggles out of her tank top while I remove her panties.

"I hate that you wear these," I grumble and toss them to the floor before settling in between her long legs.

"Landon," she whispers, and I pause when there is hesitation in her voice. "Just make love to me. Nothing kinky, please—just be gentle with me." Her request is distant, quiet.

"Is everything okay?"

"Yeah, I just need this from you." She's never requested this before and I'm caught off guard. I sink into her warmth; she's ready, wet. A soft mewl escapes her as I settle all the way into her.

"You feel so fucking good," I moan as I move in and out of her slowly. She hitches her legs up around my hips, allowing me deeper. "So. Good." I kiss her between each word. Our fingers are laced together and placed on either side of her head. She rocks her hips slowly with mine in perfect rhythm.

I've missed this, but I've missed her more. My pace remains slow and gentle, and I take in every breath, every moan that escapes her. Her hands move from my shoulders to my face, and when she opens her eyes, she holds my gaze. So many emotions lie behind those blue eyes of hers.

"I love you," she whispers as I move slowly within her. My stomach clenches at the sound of those words, and my heart aches when I can't return them. The feelings are there, I think... but I won't lie to her. I won't tell her I love her if I'm not sure. I drop my forehead to hers and we ride out our climaxes together. No other words are said between us as she rolls over, pulling the pillow to her stomach again before falling into a peaceful slumber, leaving me with the words she offered, words that I don't think I'll ever be able to return.

When I awaken, I find her already gone. The clock reads just after nine. "Shit," I mumble to myself as I stumble from the bed. Dressing quickly, I make a quick stop for coffee and muffins on the way to her office. I don't give a shit if she has patients this morning. I need to see her.

I enter the double glass doors and flash a smile to the girl at the front desk, raising up the bag of muffins and the cup of coffee in my hand. She smiles back politely and waves me through the door to the back. I see Reagan standing at the tall counter at the end of the hall as I sneak up behind her.

"I missed you this morning, Doc," I breathe into her hair, just behind her ear. She turns quickly, a smug smile on her face.

"I didn't want to wake you. You didn't even move when my alarm went off."

"Always wake me up. I want to see you before you leave." I lean in and press a kiss to her lips. She pulls back and looks around the office area.

"What's that?" she asks, looking at the bag in my hand.

"Breakfast. I brought you some coffee and muffins." She wrinkles her nose a little.

"I'm not feeling great this morning." She rubs her stomach. "I tried to drink some coffee earlier and just the smell upset me." She shivers.

"You didn't have coffee this morning?" I ask sarcastically. "I thought you'd spontaneously combust if you didn't get your coffee." She laughs at me.

"Me too. I hope it's not the flu. I'm just really tired and my body aches."

I notice that douche Adam Gerard has taken a seat at the horseshoe-shaped desk just a few feet away from us and keeps eyeing us. Reagan visibly tenses when she sees him. Tugging at my arm, she leads me toward the front office. "I have a patient that I have to see, but thank you for bringing me coffee and muffins." She places a kiss on my cheek.

"Anything for you, Doc."

"See you tonight," she says as she turns around and grabs a chart off the wall before entering an exam room.

My next stop is to swing by and see Lindsay. I have not seen her in over a week, and she rarely stays at the house anymore. I have no idea who she's dating or where she is most of the time. I'm buzzed into the WXZI studios and wait for her to meet me in the lobby.

"Hey," she says as she rounds the corner into the lobby. She plants a kiss on my cheek and pulls me into a hug. "I'm glad to finally see you. How's the job?"

"It's great. I really love it, the hours suck… but I knew that going into it."

"Yeah, you've been gone for a few days. I think Reagan was starting to get worried—so was I." She purses her lips.

"Hey, speaking of Reagan, is everything okay with her?"

"Why are you asking me?" She pulls away and folds her arms across her chest.

"Because she said she had dinner with you last night. She said she's not feeling well, and she's just acting different. Did she say anything to you?"

"Different?" she questions. "You've been home all of how many hours?" She raises her eyebrow at me. "Let the girl be sick without you questioning every little thing. She's fine."

I chuckle at my sister. She always puts me in my place. "I'm just worried about her," I admit.

"She's not feeling well. Take care of her. Feed her some fucking chicken noodle soup and watch movies in bed. I have to go. I have to go tape a story." She leans in to kiss me on the cheek again before she pulls away and starts walking back down the hallway.

"Hey, where have you been staying?" I ask her as she all but runs down the hallway away from me.

"Here and there." She waves me off with a flick of her wrist and a sly smile over her shoulder. "Bye, Landon."

Why are all the women in my life such pains in the ass? The rest of my day flies by. Between briefing my sergeant, hitting the gym, and picking up soup, crackers, ginger ale, and French bread, Reagan beats me home. Her car is parked in the garage, and I park behind her in the driveway.

Stepping through the front door, I find her asleep on the couch, a blanket pulled over her. I instantly feel guilty for getting upset this morning, thinking that she was giving me the brush off. I've never seen her asleep before six thirty. I begin warming the soup and slicing the French bread when she begins to stir on the couch.

"Hey," I say as I walk over to check on her.

"Hey," she says back as she stretches her long body on the leather couch. "When did you get here?" she asks as she blinks her eyes so they can adjust to the light in the room.

"Just a few minutes ago. How long have you been asleep?"

"A couple of hours. I left work early again. I just can't shake this."

I press my palm to her forehead and then against her cheek.

"You don't have a fever," I proclaim as I press my lips to her forehead to double check.

"Thanks, Doc." She giggles.

"Smart ass. Go lie in bed. I'll bring you something to eat, and I picked up some movies. Action or romantic comedy?"

"Action. Please tell me it's something with Channing Tatum." She smiles.

"*White House Down*. It's your lucky night," I exclaim with an eye roll. I reach out and help her to her feet. "Now go lie down. I'll be in, in just a minute." She shuffles down the hallway toward the bedroom as I head back to the kitchen. Juggling a tray with a bowl of soup, bread, a glass of ginger ale, and the movie, I find her lying in bed, curled up in a little ball in the center. She offers me a lazy smile when I sit down on the edge next to her.

"You look miserable," I observe.

"I feel miserable."

"Maybe you should see a doctor tomorrow," I suggest.

"I am a doctor."

"You're a vagina doctor. Your vagina is not making you tired or look like shit." She busts out laughing at my observation.

"I just need some rest. It's been a busy few weeks," she says as I set the tray on the bed next to her. Grabbing the movie, I turn on the TV that is attached to the wall above her tall chest of drawers.

"Speaking of busy," she says as she sips from the glass of ginger ale, "I'm heading back to Minnesota next weekend."

"For what?" I insert the DVD into the player and walk to the bed. I slide in carefully next to her.

"My annual trip home, to visit Hailey," she whispers.

"How long will you be gone?" I ask, hoping I don't sound insensitive.

"Just a long weekend. I leave Friday morning and will be back Monday afternoon." I brush the hair away from her face, tucking it behind her ears.

"I'm glad you're going," I tell her, wanting to support her. I can't imagine what it would feel like to relive that year after year. "But you're not going anywhere if you're sick—so let's get you better." I pick up the bowl of soup and hand it to her. Sipping on some of the hot broth, she cringes as she swallows it.

"Too hot?"

"No, I just have a really upset stomach," she says, putting the bowl back on the tray. "I'll try to eat something later. I just want to rest." She curls up next to me, wrapping herself around me. I push the play button on the remote control to start the movie and, within minutes, she's sound asleep. Her breathing sounds like little purrs, with each inhale and exhale.

I keep the volume low so as not to wake her, but her sleep is restless. Finally, she wakes and rushes off to the bathroom. I follow behind her when I hear her getting sick.

"Babe, are you okay?" I ask through the door.

"Water," she replies before she continues gagging. I hustle to the kitchen to bring her back a glass of ice water just as she's brushing her teeth at the sink.

"Stomach flu?" I ask, handing her the glass of water. She nods her head and spits.

"Looks like it. You should probably stay at your house tonight so you don't get it," she says before sticking the toothbrush back in her mouth.

"No way. I'll be staying here to take care of you."

She puts her toothbrush in the holder before turning around and leaning back against the vanity.

"I appreciate you wanting to take care of me, but I don't want you to get sick too."

While she washes her face, I clean up the bedroom, shutting off the movie and removing the tray of soup and soda. Reagan crawls into bed and pulls the covers over her. I feel helpless, and wish I could do something to make her feel better.

"I will sleep on the couch, but I'm staying," I announce.

"Go home. Sleep," she mumbles at me from under the covers.

"I'll check in on you later," I say from the doorway.

"Landon?"

"Yeah, babe?"

"I love you." There they are again. I walk to the side of the bed and pull the covers away from her face. I press a kiss to her forehead—I hope my kiss will tell her what I'm unable to.

"Call me if you need me," I whisper as I cover her again.

CHAPTER 20

Reagan

My text message to Lindsay is frantic, and her response is equally as dramatic. Within minutes of Landon leaving, she is busting through my door with a brown paper bag.

"You're overreacting," she says, tossing the bag on my bed. "Go piss on the stick and get your sick ass back in bed. You have the flu. Tis the season." She giggles. "I have to be at the station for the eleven o'clock news, and I'm going to be late—so text me if you have any news."

"We're all late, Lindsay," I mumble as I hear the front door shut behind her.

I grab the bag and head to the bathroom. Lindsay came prepared with three different tests, all different brands, including one for early detection. Finishing up, I toss all three of them in the drawer on my vanity. I don't need a test to tell me what my body already knows. I pull the covers over me and try to fall asleep.

"Still no fever." He presses his lips to my forehead and pulls the comforter off of me. "Are you going into work today?"

"No. I feel like shit," I grumble. "Why are you here so early?" The alarm clock flashes six o'clock.

"I tried texting you last night and you never responded. I was worried about you." He runs his fingers up and down my arms, giving me goose bumps.

"Let me draw you a bath," he offers, pressing kisses to both of my cheeks. He walks to the bathroom and turns on the water. I pull myself out of bed and walk to the kitchen to get a glass of orange juice. It's the only thing that sounds good. I pour two glasses and put the carton back in the fridge. Tucking the most recent *People* magazine under my arm, I pick up the two glasses of juice, in time to drop one of them when Landon's voice startles me from behind. Bouncing off the granite counter and onto the tile floor, the glass shatters all around my bare feet.

"Dammit," I bark, deciding if I should try to step around the glass.

"Don't move," he orders as he rounds the island and picks me up, carrying me down the hall to the bedroom. "Get undressed and in the bathtub. I'll clean up the kitchen." He kisses my forehead and disappears down the hallway.

Before I forget, I send a quick text message to both Melissa and Adam, letting them know I'm sick and won't be in today. I toss my t-shirt and pajama bottoms in the hamper, and pull my hair into a messy bun before stepping into the tub full of warm water and bubbles. Closing my eyes, I enjoy the quiet while I rest my head on the back of the tub and soak in the warm water.

"Hey." Landon sits on the edge of the tub.

"Hi."

"Feeling better?"

"Yes, a lot."

He reaches under the bubbles and finds my leg, pulling it out of the water. He starts massaging my foot and I can't help but groan.

"That feels so good." My words are drawn out as I speak them.

"Hey, you don't say that when I'm doing other things to you." He laughs.

"You've never massaged me like that." I raise my eyebrows and splash him with some water from the bath.

"Say, I'm going to run a quick errand and stop by the house and grab a few things. Is there anything you need while I'm out?"

"A strawberry shake."

"A strawberry shake?" he asks.

"Yep. I'm craving a strawberry shake." I smile at him and bat my eyes.

He laughs and shakes his head at me. "A strawberry shake it is. I'll be back in just a little bit. Rest until I get back."

"Bye," I say as he leaves me soaking in the tub. I wash my hair and pull myself out of the tub, wrapping myself in an oversized bath towel. I pull open my vanity drawer to pull out my hairbrush and there lie the three white sticks. A plus sign, two dark pink lines, and the word "pregnant." I feel nauseous as I brush through my tangled hair and find myself sprinting for the toilet yet again.

I haven't been able to keep any food down in almost three days, and I know that may be why I feel so weak and achy. I wash my face and brush my teeth before I call myself in a prescription of Zofran to help with the nausea. I need to be able to eat something and keep it down.

I lie down in bed and my mind races with questions, with unknown answers, with fear. I let the stress and exhaustion carry me off to sleep as I wait for Landon to return. I have to tell him—today. A soft tongue and wet nose wake me up from my deep sleep. Ollie is on the bed and licking my face frantically. I can hear Landon's heavy footsteps getting closer as Ollie continues to lick my face.

"Goddammit, Ollie. I said to leave her alone." He walks in the bedroom and sets down my shake and a bag. He walks to the bed to pick up Ollie and sets him on the floor. "And no dogs on the bed, either."

"Aww, you're no fun," I mock him. "I'm glad you went and got him," I say as Landon sits on the edge of the bed.

"I figured since we were going to be here all day, he might as well join us." My heart warms just a little to know that there is a little bit of compassion behind that rough façade. I smile and stretch as I kick the covers off of me.

"How are you feeling?"

"So much better. I'm not sure it's the flu," I say, knowing the truth.

"What time is it?"

"Almost noon. I brought you your strawberry shake and I picked up a few more movies. Oh, and I even brought Scrabble over." He grins. "I always win at Scrabble. I figure we can order some pizza later, and just lay low today." My stomach turns when he mentions pizza, and I rub my stomach. "You need to eat," he mentions when he sees me react to his mention of food. "You're getting too skinny, and I like your ass." He leans in and pinches my bottom.

"Ow," I say, pushing his hand away. I sit up as he gathers all the pillows from the bed and props them up. He sits next to me on the bed and hands me my shake.

"Thank you for taking care of me," I say as I sip on the milkshake. He watches me intently, tracing my cheekbone with his thumb. He finds my lip and wipes it when I pull the straw from my mouth.

"You had a little bit, right there…" He wipes my lip again and sticks his thumb in his mouth, licking the strawberry shake from his thumb. Reaching for the shake, he sets it on the nightstand. "Good?"

I nod and swallow. I've seen that look in his eyes before. "Raise your arms," he says, sliding over next to me. He pulls the tank top off of me and tosses it to the floor. He pulls my legs and I slide down the satin sheets so that I'm lying flat on my back. "Lift," he orders and taps my hip. I raise my hips and he discards my shorts and panties.

"Gorgeous," he says as his fingers trace small circles on my stomach. "Don't move." He gets up from the bed and pulls the comforter off, tossing it onto the chaise lounge. He begins digging through the bag he set on the floor just minutes ago, when I hear the metal clank, and my breath hitches. I don't need to see them, to know what they are. He stands next to the bed with the handcuffs dangling from his finger as he searches for any sign of hesitation from me.

"Do you trust me?" he asks, maintaining constant eye contact with me.

"With my life," I whisper.

"You tell me to stop, and we stop. Understand?" I nod as he leans over me, attaching the first cuff to my left wrist. Looping the last cuff through the wooden slat on my headboard, he raises my right arm and cuffs it. Both arms are raised above my head and attached to my bed. I wiggle my wrists to find there is no slack; there is no getting out of the metal cuffs unless I ask him. He is in complete control.

"You okay?" he asks as he pulls his t-shirt off over his head and pulls his athletic shorts down, kicking them onto the pile of my clothes. His erection hangs heavy and I catch my breath as he joins me on the bed. Running a single finger from my pelvis up to my neck, his erection presses against me. My legs fall apart, inviting him, but he stays at my side. He pulls my nipple into his mouth, sucking it into a hard little peak. "Beautiful," he says as he moves to the other breast.

While his tongue works my nipples, his hand snakes its way down my stomach and in between my legs. My hips buck wildly as his finger slides its way between my labia, teasing—stroking. He groans against my breast as he finds my entrance and inserts a finger, causing me to clench around it.

My breathing is rapid and my chest rises and falls quickly with the myriad of sensations assaulting my body. "Close your eyes," he says, his voice husky and low. He pulls his finger out and leans across me as I close my eyes. He moves himself between my legs and spreads them, bending me at my knees. I'm wide open to him and a wave of anxiety courses through me.

"Keep your eyes closed," he says again. "Breathe." I take long, cleansing breaths and gasp suddenly when I feel the cold drops start at my chest and move down my stomach to my pelvis. I can smell the sweetness of the shake before he begins to rub it across my chest, massaging it around my breasts. He licks and rubs and rolls my nipples between his teeth and my back arches off the bed. He holds my legs open with his hands on my knees as he licks his way down my stomach, licking the shake from my belly button. The sensation of his tongue circling and licking me has me aroused and wanting more.

"Fuck me," I growl at him, causing him to chuckle. "Now."

"Not yet, baby." He continues licking and kissing his way down as his fingers push at my labia, exposing my clitoris. I feel his warm breath hover just above as I throb in anticipation. My hips buck, inviting him to touch me, lick me, do anything to me.

"Landon," I whimper as he takes his time teasing me. I finally feel his soft lips pull my clit into his mouth as his tongue works circles around it. The pressure of his sucking has me damn near close to losing it. My hips begin rocking steadily as he continues to lick, suck, and pull. He easily slides a finger inside, then two curling them to hit the spot that only he can find. My hips begin to buck wildly as he inserts a third finger and gently guides them inside and out.

"Oh God," I moan, not sure I'm going to be able to last much longer. My arms instinctively pull downward, wanting to touch him, reach for him, but I'm immediately stopped by the metal cuffs.

"Keep your eyes closed," he whispers again. "Just feel." His fingers slide out of me and I feel his other hand pressing on my thigh, holding my legs open. Pulling his fingers from me, he settles between my legs and I can feel his erection pressing at my entrance—teasing me. He inserts the head and pulls back out, repeating it again.

"Please," I beg him as he pushes himself inside me, finally all the way. He groans as I raise my hips, accepting him as far as he can go.

"Fuck," he says as his pace becomes steady. My arms are becoming tired from fighting the cuffs.

"Oh, God," I cry out as I feel myself release for the first time.

"Good girl," he says, his pace quickening. "But you're not done yet," he growls. His thumb finds my already swollen and sensitive clitoris, and he rubs small circles around it, pulling it between his thumb and forefinger. With each touch and pull, my back arches off the bed and I'm closer to climaxing again. A warmth invades my abdomen and the tingling sensation takes over again. My thighs shake uncontrollably and I feel Landon harden inside of me.

With two hard thrusts, he finds his release, filling me. He gently pulls himself from me and pulls my legs together. My eyes fall open and find his blue eyes peering into mine. "Think you can take these off of me?" I ask, jingling the cuffs.

"I like having you tied up," he says.

"Why?"

"Because then I can do whatever I want to you." He smiles at me.

He pushes himself up from the bed and digs through the bag, bringing a small key over, and inserts it into the center of the cuffs. Each arm falls when the clasp is opened and I notice how sore my shoulders are. He tosses the cuffs and keys onto the nightstand and lies down beside me, pulling me to him so the fronts of our bodies are touching.

We lie in silence, studying each other, reading the words in each other's eyes that neither of us is willing to speak. "I love you," I finally whisper, knowing he won't repeat the words I want so badly to hear. I've grown used to saying them and getting nothing in return. I will never miss an opportunity to tell him what he means to me. He closes his eyes and pulls me closer to him, tightening his grip on me. "I love you, Landon," I say again, pressing a soft kiss to his lips. "Always."

I hang my head as the warm water washes away the sticky ice cream from my body. I squirt some body wash onto the sponge and begin rubbing small circles across my body. "Let me do that," he says as he steps into my shower and shuts the glass door behind him. Taking the sponge from my hands, he gently cleans my entire body, removing any trace of strawberry shake residue.

"I'll never look at a strawberry milkshake the same way again." I laugh. He sets the sponge in the shower rack and pulls me closer to him. I wrap my arms around him as we stand in the warm water, wrapped in each other's embrace. There is nothing more comforting than his arms—they are my personal heaven.

"Landon," I say, getting his attention. I back away from him just a bit so that I can look him in the eyes. "Remember when we were talking and I said we needed to be honest with each other and communicate?"

"Yeah."

"I have to tell you something, but I'm afraid."

"Afraid of what?" Both of his hands find mine and he laces our fingers together.

"Afraid of your reaction. Afraid you're going to leave," I admit and swallow hard.

"What is it, babe?" he asks, pulling me out of the water. He lets go of one of my hands and brushes the wet hair away from my face. I pause and suddenly feel nauseous again. *Tell him.*

"I don't have the flu." The words fall from my mouth so easily and so quickly. He immediately laughs at me.

"Good, because I'm not sleeping another night without you." He presses his lips to mine and pulls me into him under the warm water. My heart races as he nips and sucks at my lips.

"I'm pregnant," I confess quietly. My lips pressed against his collarbone, my arms wrapped around him tightly, hoping he won't flee. His body stills. Not a movement, not a breath— nothing. The sound of the water beating against our skin is the only sound I hear. He pulls himself away from me, his eyes inspecting me from head to toe while he grips my upper arms.

"Say something." My voice shakes as I beg him to talk to me.

"What do you want me to say?" His voice is hoarse.

"Tell me you're not angry. Tell me it's going to be okay— just tell me something," I beg of him. His hands release me and he pulls them over his face, running them up through his hair. His face has drained of color and his look is distressed.

"Please," I whisper and I reach out to touch his chest. He pulls away from me and opens the shower door, stepping out of the shower.

"Dry off. We need to talk." He wraps a towel around his waist and disappears from the bathroom. I stand under the warm stream of water and wish the water could wash me away. I'm close to hyperventilating when I shut off the water and dry myself quickly before wrapping myself in my robe. I find Landon sitting on the end of the bed in a pair of jeans, no shirt on, with his elbows resting on his knees. He's lost in his own thoughts as I walk over and sit down next to him.

"We're not ready for this," he states, but then corrects

himself. "I'm not ready for this." He looks at me, and I see a man so confused, so lost.

"I don't want to do this alone," I admit, a lump forming in my throat. "But I will if I have to." My voice finally breaks. The fear I felt sixteen years ago floods me once again. *Alone.* I'm going to have to do this alone. His eyes are fixed on the floor as tension swirls around us. Finally, raising his head, he stands up and looks down on me.

"I have to go." His voice is gentle, quiet... not angry as I expected it.

"Go where?" Panic sets in.

"Just give me some time, okay?" He pulls on his t-shirt and walks toward the bedroom door, anxious to flee as he always does.

"I know you're scared," I sputter, "but so am I. I don't want to lose you. I need you—*we* need you." My voice breaks and my chin quivers so badly I can't continue speaking. He stands in the doorway with his hands in his front pockets, watching me.

"Don't go, please," I beg him. My stomach is in knots and I can hardly breathe. "Choose me. Choose *us.*"

"I have to go," he mumbles with a weak voice.

I don't know how many times he's said those words to me, but this time it feels like it might be the last.

CHAPTER 21

LANDON

My life has been anything but planned. In fact, it's always been a series of *what ifs*. I've lived life like it doesn't matter because, until *her*—it didn't. The three-mile drive home feels like three thousand miles. The weight of a million bricks is on my shoulders and I know I'm standing at the crossroads in my life. I need to pick a road and follow it; it should be an easy decision, right? For me it's not. I can choose the road I've always known—comfortable and mind numbing. Easy sex, careless days and nights, and no plans—no commitments. Or, I can choose the difficult road—the one where I will have to fight my old ways to be what she needs me to be—the man that won't hurt her, but will love her. To be what our baby needs—a father, a protector. That road is not comfortable, or easy—or planned, but something inside of me aches to choose that road, to choose her.

Two loud knocks pull me from my thoughts, as I see Lindsay standing outside my car window. I kill the engine and open the door.

"You've been sitting here for twenty minutes. I thought you were on the phone, so I didn't want to bother you, but I need to talk you." Her voice is almost frantic and she rubs her upper arms as if she's cold.

"What's wrong? You've been crying."

"Inside." She motions to the house. She scans the street as if she's looking for someone.

"What's going on, Lindsay?" I ask as she locks the door behind us.

"Sit down." She pats the cushion next to her on the couch. I toss my keys on the coffee table and sit down. Her pale face has red splotches all over it, and her blue eyes are rimmed with pink. "I have to tell you something, but you can't be mad. You have to listen to everything I tell you, okay?" God, why does this sound so familiar? I rake my hands over my face and release a deep sigh.

"Sure, my day can't possibly get any worse," I mumble under my breath.

"I bet it can," Lindsay says, running her hands up and down her thighs anxiously.

"Just spill it, Linds. I'm tired and have a fuck-ton on my mind right now."

"Well, be ready to add another fuck-ton or two," she snorts. I shoot her a death glare, suggesting she hurry up with her news. "Lan." She hesitates. "I found Mom. I talked to her. She lives here—in Wilmington." Her sentences are short, to the point, full of emotion. Her eyes fill with tears as I sit in complete shock. "She wants to talk to both of us."

"Fuck her." I stand up and walk down the hall toward my bedroom, slamming the door behind me. In a matter of two hours, my entire world has shifted on its axis. As quickly as I shut my door to leave my reality behind, it flies open and Lindsay barges into my room.

"Listen, Landon. I understand you're pissed off. So am I. But we need answers."

"We," I motion between her and me, "don't need anything. I'm perfectly fine without her—you know, as it's been for the last twenty-two years."

"Why are you always so stubborn? You never give anyone a chance," she screams at me. Anger courses through my veins and, for the first time ever, I get in Lindsay's face.

"She doesn't deserve a chance. She lost her chance when she walked out on us. I have nothing to say to her, and I have nothing to hear from her—especially her petty excuses for leaving us with that psychopath."

"Then what excuse do you have for Reagan?" she snarls at me.

"This isn't about Reagan. Leave her out of this."

"You push everyone away. You never let anyone close—all I'm asking is that you hear Mom out."

"Stop calling her that."

"What?"

"Mom. She's not our mother; she left us. Mother's don't do what she did."

"Jesus Christ, Landon. I know. I get it. I'm angry and hurt too. But we need to talk to her."

"Sounds like you already have. I'm good with that. Can you shut my door behind you, please?" I know I sound like an asshole, but I'm done with this conversation.

"No."

"Lindsay, I'm not fucking around. I've had a really shitty day. This conversation is over."

"No, it's not. Not until you agree to give her fifteen minutes." I sit on the edge of my bed and drop my head into my hands. I've never had a nervous breakdown before, but I imagine it's close to what I'm feeling. "Don't hate her," Lindsay says quietly.

I release a loud sigh and rub my eyes. "It's hard not to," I mumble.

"Just fifteen minutes, Landon. Not a minute more, please." I know she won't leave until I agree to this.

"Fine. Fifteen minutes."

"Yes. Thank you," she whispers, a sign of her victory. "Now are you going to tell me what else is bothering you?"

"No."

"Landon, you know I'm always here if you need somebody to talk to you, right?"

"I know, but this is about me. I have to work through this on my own."

"You don't ever have to work through anything alone," she says, sitting down next to me on the bed.

"You always have me, and Matt… and Reagan." She pauses. "This is about Reagan, isn't it?" I nod my head and try to swallow past my dry throat. "I can't tell you what to do—but can I offer you a piece of advice?"

"Yeah."

"I told her not to give up on you multiple times, and she never did. Now it's your turn. Don't give up on her. She's a strong woman, but she will need you now more than ever."

"How do you know?" I give her a questioning glance.

She gives me half a smile and punches my arm. "I had to make an unexpected pit stop at CVS last night." She shrugs. "But I do know that I'm going to be the fucking coolest aunt on the planet." The mood is still heavy, but for some reason, my sister knowing makes me feel better.

"I told her I needed time to think."

"Think about what? What is there to think about?"

"A whole hell of a lot of stuff," I bark at her.

"It's not that hard, Landon. You man up. You adjust. You have a great job; she has a great job. You make this shit work."

"It's not always that easy, Linds."

"Do you love her?"

Those words gut me. I know I do, but something about saying them—admitting my feelings—makes me feel sick to my stomach.

"Did you hear me? Do you love her?"

"Yeah, I do."

"Then it's easy. Love her. That's all you need to do." She leans against me and rests her head on my shoulder. "You always took care of me, and I know you will do the same for Reagan and your baby."

I awake to the smell of coffee and something baking. Lindsay can't cook for shit, so I'm immediately on alert. I reach for my cell phone and realize I must have left it in my car after I left Reagan's yesterday. My alarm clock flashes just after seven o'clock a.m. and I realize that I have been asleep for almost fourteen hours. Tossing on some athletic shorts, I move toward the kitchen to get some coffee. I can hear soft voices talking and my heart skips a beat when I envision Reagan in the kitchen with Lindsay.

When I turn the corner, two sets of eyes meet mine and my stomach sinks. Twenty-two years and she looks nearly the same. Her blue eyes, the same eyes that Lindsay and I have, search mine as I find myself lost in the past and in the present. The little boy in me wants to run to my mother and pull her into my arms, but the man that I've become knows better. She has aged—not that I expected her to look exactly the same, but small wrinkles meet the outer corners of her eyes. Her light blond hair is now streaked with grey.

She sits on a stool at my kitchen island, next to Lindsay, who watches me closely—a sympathetic look in her eye.

"Landon." Her voice cracks, full of emotion. A small smile pulls at her lips as she waits for me to react. Lindsay jumps up from the stool and meets me with a kiss on the cheek. She grasps my forearm to keep me from fleeing, giving me a slight tug toward the island.

"Sit down. I'll get you some coffee," she says, guiding me toward a stool on the opposite side of the island.

"This isn't exactly how I expected this to go down," I tell Lindsay, loud enough so that my mom can hear.

"I know. It just kind of happened," she says apologetically.

"If now's not a good time, I can leave. I understand," my mom says quietly. Her hands are folded in her lap. They are marked with wrinkles as well, but they are still my mother's hands. There are few things I remember of my mom, but I remember her hands. Her fingers are long and perfectly manicured. A large diamond sits on her left ring finger, a sign she moved on—without us, and my blood boils.

"I've got to get to work," I mumble as Lindsay sets a large mug of coffee in front of me.

"I talked to Matt; he's talking to your sergeant, letting him know that you'll be a little late. If anything comes up, he said he'd call me." I flash her a look, letting her know I'm not happy.

"Well, then, looks like we have a little time," I say, stirring some creamer into my coffee. Lindsay sits back down on the stool next to my mom, across the island from me.

"Landon, let me explain a couple of things." Lindsay picks at a blueberry muffin as she stutters over her words. "I found Mom with the help of a private investigator." I choke on a sip of the hot coffee.

"Why would you do that?" I ask, knowing it sounds insensitive. My mom sits and watches me intently, showing no emotion to what I've just said.

"You remember Adam Gerard, the other partner in Reagan's practice, right?"

"What does this have to do with that douchebag?"

Lindsay sighs. "Reagan came to me, asking how you two knew each other. He had made a few remarks to her about you, about Dad, and mentioned some things about our family that no one knew, not even me. It raised some red flags, so I hired an investigator."

"Why wouldn't she say anything to me?" I question her.

"Do you really have to ask that question?" she says sarcastically.

"Continue. What does this have to do with him?"

"The investigator gave me a lot of info on him, the usual… stuff you could find out at work, or I could find out on the internet if I tried hard enough. Things like where he went to college, medical school, who he dated, and so on. What the report also told me was who his father is, his brother is, and his stepmother is." I glance at my mom, who hasn't so much as blinked since Lindsay started talking.

"You?" I raise my eyebrows and ask.

She nods her head and a quiet "yes" falls from her lips.

"Goddammit," I spit out, and slam my hand on the granite counter. The spoon inside Lindsay's coffee cup rattles, and both my mom and Lindsay startle at my outburst.

"Landon, let her explain."

"Explain what? That you left us." I glare at her. "That you moved in with another family, a family that has kids I went to school with, and never... not once... came back for Lindsay and me? Explain that!" I yell at her. "You know, I'd heard rumors that you were still in Wilmington, that you'd moved on and had a new family—but I never wanted to believe that you'd do that and not come back for Linds and I." I can feel my heart beating wildly and I ball my hands into tight fists to try to stop them from shaking.

She sits calmly, taking deep breaths as she gathers her thoughts. "You have every right to be angry with me. I don't blame you," she starts. She moves her hands to the island and plays with the coffee mug that sits in front of her. "Before I start, I need to ask you both to forgive me. Forgive me for not taking you with me that night. Forgive me for not trying harder to protect you both." Lindsay reaches out and places her hand on my mom's. Anger simmers to the surface as I listen to her ask for forgiveness when all I can remember are the beatings I endured after she left.

"You were both so young, so I'm not sure you fully understand how everything happened and progressively got worse. I met your dad when I was in college. He was already a police officer and had been for almost five years. I was graduating with my degree in elementary education. We fell hard and fast. Within a year of meeting and dating, we got married.

From the beginning, he was always a little controlling. At first I found it sweet, almost protective—but as time went on, it was anything but. He questioned where I was, who I was with all the time. Even when I was alone, he never believed me. He started showing up at the elementary school where I worked, just to check in on me." Her voice wavers.

"He quickly moved through the ranks at the police department and when he made assistant chief, he suggested I quit teaching. I was newly pregnant with you." She gestures to me. "He was doing well financially, and I always wanted to be a stay-at-home mom, so I didn't question him. I finished out that year teaching and never went back. I had you that spring, and things got worse. He was so jealous of you, a little baby," she says, her voice strained.

"Something changes inside of you when you become a parent. For most people, except your father, obviously, your life isn't about you anymore; it's about that precious baby." Lindsay raises her eyebrows at me and I glare at her in return.

"I was head over heels in love with you. Everything was about you," she says, pausing. I can tell she's trying to contain her emotions, and she takes a sip of her coffee before she continues. "I spent every minute of every day with you. Your father would question me if I took you to the park, to the library, even to the grocery store. He wanted to know where I was every minute. It became smothering—and I began to resent him. But, here I was with a little baby and no job. We depended on him, so I dealt with it." She twists her fingers and I notice them shaking as she continues.

"I figured that things would eventually change. That he wouldn't question everywhere I went, or everything I did—that he'd understand my life was about him and you. When you were three, I found out I was pregnant with Lindsay. As excited as I was, I was nervous and then things got worse at home. Your father became increasingly more abusive verbally. He hadn't started hitting me yet, but he was horribly mean. I could do nothing right. Dinner was never prepared the way he wanted, the house was never clean enough, and I was never a good enough mother. He hated that you," she looks at me, "would curl up in my lap every night to read a book. He was never around, yet he expected you to want to be with him." She takes a deep breath and swallows hard."

"After Lindsay was born, things got progressively worse. I wasn't allowed to grocery shop without him. I wasn't allowed to leave the house with you kids. He didn't even want me to walk you down the street to the park. I used to have to sneak out the back door immediately after he left for work so that I could take you down the street to put you on the swings for a few minutes." She smiles. "He would drive by the house multiple times a day and stop in at random times to make sure we were home.

"One day, I snuck you kids out of the house to the park, and there was my old friend from college, Louis Gerard, Adam's father," she explains. "We were good friends in college. His wife had recently died and he had a set of twin boys he was raising on his own. Your father knew Louis well; he was a prominent banker here in town and donated a lot of money to many of the local charities. I saw him at many of the local law enforcement fundraisers. Anyway, he was at the park with his boys and their new nanny. We reconnected that day, talking and catching up on old times. We quickly became confidants—nothing more than friends, though.

"It felt so good to laugh, and have someone to talk to. I confided in Louis about what was going on at home, and he promised to help me get out. There were never any feelings on my part for Louis, but he was always a good friend to me, offering me help and even giving me money to get us away from your father. One day, your father came home and confronted me about Louis. Someone had told him that they had seen us talking at the park. I swear everyone in this town told your father everything." Her voice is angry at the memory.

"That was the first time he hit me. He hit me so hard across the side of my face, I blacked out. He told me if I was going to act like a dirty little whore, that I'd be treated like one. Each day got worse. There was never a day he didn't come home and hit me. Louis would call and check in on me because I stopped going out in public at all. He was working to figure out how to get us away. He offered to call the Department of Children's Services, but I discouraged it because I knew that your father would think I did it, and my worst fear was that they'd take you both away from me." As my mother talks, I remember her on the phone many times, whispering quietly to whomever was on the other end of the line. I remember not being allowed to go to the park anymore—and I believe everything she is telling me, even though I want so badly not to believe her.

"Louis was arranging for us to escape to Arizona. He had a job lined up with a family member for himself and had a house in Tucson. He was working on gathering everything I needed to divorce your father, and gain custody of you kids. The problem was being able to take you kids out of the state. Here in North Carolina, judges don't like to allow parents to just uproot their children from the other parent in a divorce and I had never filed a police report against him for the abuse, so there was nothing to show that he didn't deserve custody or even visitation, and there was no way they were going to allow me to just pick up and move with you both." I sit and listen intently as her voice fluctuates and she relives those painful memories.

"You two were the one thing your dad dangled over my head time and again. He threatened to kill you both if I ever considered leaving him. The night I finally left, I had full intentions of coming back to get you the following day. I ran down the street to that gas station and called Louis from the pay phone. I truly believed that if I had stayed the night in that house, he would have killed me." She chokes up and stops speaking for a moment. "I hid behind the gas station in the dark for him to come and pick me up. We went back to his house and he gathered his boys and a few belongings, fully intending to get you two in the morning and leave for Arizona."

"Then why in the hell didn't you come back to get us?" I bite out.

"I tried. I came back the next morning. Louis parked down the street and I walked home to get you. I snuck in the back door, and he met me in the kitchen. He held a gun to my temple and told me if he ever saw my face again, he'd kill you both. He would have. He was certifiably insane. He told me to get the hell out and never come back. That I was an embarrassment to him and his family."

"Bullshit. If he wanted to kill us, he would have. He tortured me for years, damn near killing me a couple of times, but he never did," I snap, interrupting her. Her eyes look apologetic as she continues.

"So I left with Louis to Arizona. His plan was that we'd be away from North Carolina and we'd file reports to Child Protective Services about the abuse at home. Since I was out of the picture, I couldn't be blamed. So we did. We filed and filed and filed. Every case was either never investigated or dismissed.

How, I don't know. Landon, I heard the stories of how you'd show up at school covered in bruises. I'm so sorry." She apologizes and dabs tears at the corners of her eyes.

"We moved back to North Carolina and I finally filed divorce papers, but since I fled to Arizona previously, I was severed of any parental rights. If I had known that, I would not have left. I tried, God, did I try." Her voice cracks. "I ended up marrying Louis." She pauses. "He's a good man, and he tried so hard to help me get you back."

"So you married Louis and played mom to Adam and Aaron, while Dad was beating the shit out of me every night." I know I'm an asshole for rubbing it in her face, but she needs to hear it. She watches me as I rub my head, another headache brewing from this conversation, before she continues.

"By the time you were in your early teens, I'd been gone so long, I knew it was just better if I stayed away. There was not a day that went by that Louis and I didn't try to get you back. We did everything, even talked of kidnapping you. After your father died I struggled with whether I should contact you," she pauses with tears in her eyes.

"But you never did," I say quietly.

The room is silent as we sit and absorb everything she just said. Lindsay wipes tears from her cheeks and I just sit, looking at both of them seated across from me. It amazes me how much Lindsay looks like my mother. I try to pull from my memory the good times we had. The trips to the park, her reading to me, but those memories aren't what I remember.

"So what do you want?" I ask, short and to the point.

"I want you to forgive me." It's straight to the point. Matter of fact. I chuckle at her request. As if forgiveness is just something you hand out.

"What?" she asks after I'm done smirking.

"You want forgiveness and all Lindsay and I ever wanted was a fucking mother who loved us enough to not leave us in the hands of a monster." I stand up and push myself of the stool. "Do you see that?" I point to the scar along my side, the one that Reagan questioned me about. My mother nods her head. "Do you want to know how I got that?" She stares at me, her eyes opening wider.

"I was in eighth grade. I played baseball that year, and one night, when I got home, Dad was drunk as usual and waiting for me—waiting for a fight. I disappeared into my room as I usually did, but he wasn't having any of that. I sat down at my desk and pulled out my homework, hoping that if I didn't come out of my room or that if he found me studying, he'd just leave me alone." I shake my head at the memory. "He busts through my door, telling me what a fucking loser I was, that I was a worthless piece of shit, and that even my mother left because of me. He told me this family would be better off if I just killed myself." She gasps at that comment.

"Finally, he picks up the wooden bat that I had in the corner of my room and breaks it over my desk. The bat splinters, and he's left holding the handle with a long, sharp piece of wood sticking out. He wasted no time in stabbing me twice in the side. I was convinced that was the night he was going to kill me, and that was the first night I almost killed him. If I hadn't lost so much blood, and wasn't in so much pain, I would have. Lindsay is the only reason I survived that night. She walked in and stopped him."

Lindsay bursts into tears and my mom tries to comfort her, but even she pulls away slightly at her contact. "So forgive me if I'm not willing to hand out forgiveness like fucking candy on

Halloween, all right? I need to get to work. Glad we had this little chat. You can run home to your little family. Lindsay and I are just fine here by ourselves. I'll make sure nothing ever happens to her, even though, as a mother, that was something *you* should have done."

"I'm sorry," I hear her cry as I walk away to get myself ready for the day. Something stirs inside of me as I stand in the hot shower, trying to wash the stress and anxiety away. I will never let anything happen to my child. I will never let anyone hurt that baby, or Reagan. That is all it takes for me to make the decision I was struggling with.

CHAPTER 22

Reagan

"Hey, do you have a minute?" I ask nervously as I enter his small office. It's set up much like mine, except more masculine. Black and white abstract art hangs on his wall.

"Yeah, come in. I've been wanting to talk to you," he says. I sit down in the chair opposite him. It's uncomfortable, and my heart races.

"What about?" I ask curiously.

"You," he says dryly. He turns away from his computer to face me. "As the newest partner in the office, you've been gone a lot and leaving early... I'm just surprised by this."

"Let me explain," I interrupt him. I take a deep breath and slide my hands into the pockets of my lab coat. "I'm pregnant."

"Jesus, Reagan," he says, shaking his head. "As an OB/GYN, you should know better than anyone there are ways of preventing that."

"I don't need a safe sex speech, Adam. I need some time off."

"I think you've taken enough time off lately," he fires back.

"Look, I've been dealing with a really bad case of hyperemesis gravidarum. I've been on Zofran for a day now and it seems to be helping a bit, but I'm hoping if I give it another day or so that I should be feeling great. I already planned a trip back to Minnesota next weekend, so I just figured that I could take the rest of this week and next week off and be back to work when I get back. It'll give me some time to clear my head and, hopefully, start feeling better. I know I don't need to ask your permission, I'm partner here, but you'd be carrying the brunt of the load while I'm gone, so I'm asking as a courtesy. We need to work together, and I don't want to dump patients on you..."

"That's fine," he interrupts me. "Get your head on straight—and for Christ's sake, eat, and take the Zofran."

"I am," I respond sincerely. "I'm really sorry if I have come across as anything other than professional, Adam. I love my job. I love this office. It's just that this really took me by surprise." He nods his head, but doesn't say anything. "There is something else I wanted to talk to you about." He leans back in his chair and props his leg up on his knee.

"Sure," he says, tapping his fingers on his desk.

"I know about your connection to Landon." He stares at me and leans forward, scooting himself closer to the desk.

"What do you think you know?" he asks.

"I know that Josie is your stepmom, and I know that Josie is Landon's and Lindsay's real mother." I pause to gauge his reaction to this news. He doesn't say a word; he just narrows his eyes and purses his lips. "What I don't know and would like to understand is why you hate him so badly, when he didn't do a damn thing to you, and never even knew about Josie and your dad?"

"Quick question first. Is the baby his?"

238

"Yes."

He sighs. "It's a long and complicated story," he says, looking away from me.

"Give me the Cliff Notes version, but don't lie to me."

"Where should I start?"

"From the beginning," I state.

"I don't know all the gory details, but Josie was hardly a stepmother to me and Aaron," he says as he picks at a string on the hem of his pants. "Here's what I do know: Captain Christianson was an angry man, everyone knew that—but no one knew exactly how angry he was. From my understanding, my dad and Josie were good friends in college. After my mom died, they reconnected and continued their friendship. I remember being maybe eleven, almost twelve, when one night, my dad packed us up and moved us to Tucson. Josie was with us. I was scared to death, as she had clearly just been beaten—and badly." He exhales loudly before he continues.

"Aaron and I asked my father what was happening and he explained that he was good friends with Mrs. Christianson and she needed our help. I never even knew of Landon or Lindsay at this point. I was a few years older than Landon, so there was no reason we'd know each other," he states.

"Aaron and I were really upset about being moved across the country and we didn't even know why. As we later found out, my dad was helping her escape her abusive marriage. Over the course of the next year or so, there was not one conversation in our house that didn't involve Landon and Lindsay and how to get them away from Captain Christianson. Aaron and I became second to Landon and Lindsay, two kids we didn't even know— and we fucking hated it. My dad and Josie spent every minute discussing and planning how and what to do to get custody of them." Adam stops speaking and looks at me seriously.

"Do you know how hard it was to lose my mom to cancer, but then lose my dad to two kids we never knew? Josie and he became obsessed with them; it was like a fucking pastime for them. The notes, the discussions, the plans... it consumed them. Aaron and I grew up in the same house with them, yet we were complete strangers." My heart sinks as I listen to him admit how badly this hurt them, and right after losing their mother.

"Anyway, we moved back to North Carolina and Josie divorced. As the months and years passed, the talk of Landon and Lindsay died down, little by little—but Josie was always depressed and my dad always tended to her. I hated those kids, and I didn't even know them. I just hated that they were everything to Josie and Josie was everything to my dad—which meant Aaron and I were always last."

"I'm sorry," I say, acknowledging his pain. "Why didn't you tell me this when you first saw me with Landon?"

He shrugs. "What did you want me to say? Hey, you know that guy in your car, his mom is my stepmom and he doesn't know it, and his dad was an abusive dickhead and I think maybe you shouldn't see him." I laugh at Adam and he laughs back.

"Okay, I can see where you might not want to share what you know, but Adam... he's a great guy. He's not his dad." Adam stares at me and nods his head.

"Does Josie know you work with Landon's girlfriend?"

"Nah, we don't talk much—and even when we do, it's never about Landon or Lindsay anymore."

"Okay, good. I have a feeling she's about to hear from Lindsay and I just need to understand what everyone knows. This is crazy, you know that, right?"

He nods his head again slowly. "Hell, yeah, it is. Now go get some rest and I'll see you in a couple of weeks. If I hear anything while you're away, I'll let you know."

⁓❧❧⁓

I check my phone damn near every minute, hoping that there will be a text message, a missed call, or a voicemail from Landon. Since he left yesterday I haven't heard a word from him, and my heart is heavy at the thought that he was so easy to dismiss me and our baby. I fold a pair of jeans and place them in my suitcase, which is sitting at the end of my bed. The doorbell chimes and my heart skips a beat as I hope Landon stands on the other side of that door. Glancing through the peephole, I see Lindsay's blonde hair whipping around violently in the wind, and she tries to steady herself against the pillar on the patio. I unlock the deadbolt and she bursts through the door just as I open it.

"Shit, there is a bad storm coming," she says as she fights to untangle her long hair. I notice the dark clouds building in the sky as I shut the door.

"Why aren't you at work?" I ask Lindsay, noticing her workout attire. She hangs her purse from the back of one of the kitchen chairs and walks to the fridge in the kitchen.

"Took the day off," she says, leaning into the fridge and pulling out a bottle of water. "Shit hit the fan this morning," she announces as she twists off the cap from the water bottle and presses it to her lips.

"He told you?" I ask quietly.

"No, he didn't need to. I knew when I dropped off those tests the other night. Congratulations by the way, Mama." She chuckles.

241

"So what happened?"

"I met my mom." I watch her for signs that she's joking, a smirk, a crooked smile—anything. She's serious.

"What? When?"

"I talked to her on the phone yesterday for a few minutes, but I invited her to the house and she talked to Landon and me this morning."

"Holy. Shit," I sputter. "What did she say? Better yet, what did Landon say?" She fidgets with the water bottle in her hands as she gathers her thoughts. "Come here, sit down." I motion to the couches in the living room. She takes a seat and sinks into the large leather cushions.

"It was so surreal, Reagan. She told us everything," she sighs. "Everything, meaning she explained why she left, how she tried to get us numerous times, what she's been doing over the years, her relationship with Louis Gerard."

"Do you believe her?" I ask cautiously, not wanting to come across that I think she's lying.

"Yeah, I do, and I think Landon does too, which pisses him off. He wants a reason to hate her."

"How long did you talk?"

"Not long, just about a half hour. Landon had to leave for work. I really should have waited to have them meet. He is so stressed out..." Her voice wanders off.

"About the baby," I whisper.

"About everything," she says firmly. "He's got a lot going on in his life right now, but it's not just the baby."

"He left me you know—again."

"He didn't leave you, Reagan. He just needs some time to process all of this."

"Well, how do you think I feel as I process all of this—*alone*. It's not any less upsetting for me than it is for him—yet he seems to think it's perfectly acceptable that every time the going gets tough, he can bail—take all the time he needs to *think* about things." I realize I've raised my voice and I sound angry. Lindsay watches me carefully. "He doesn't even realize how much I need him right now." My voice cracks. "Just once, I need him to tell me this is going to be okay, that *we're* going to be okay. I can't always be the one to be strong, Lindsay."

"Have you told him this?"

"I tried. I sent him a text message this morning to call me, but he hasn't yet. Now I understand why, but I'm leaving for Minnesota in a couple of hours."

"I didn't think you were leaving until next weekend?"

"I wasn't. But I changed my plans. I need to go where I can clear my head—where people won't run from me when I drop a bomb on them. I need to go home."

"Reagan." Lindsay sits up and reaches out, placing her hand on my forearm. "I know this isn't home with your family, but Landon and I will always be your home, here—in North Carolina."

I snort sarcastically as I choke back tears. "Then why does he keep running from me? I'm done chasing him, Lindsay. I'm done." Her eyes plead with me, yet she says nothing. "I have to finish packing," I say quietly.

"What time is your flight?"

"Three thirty."

"Can I at least drive you to the airport?"

"I'd appreciate that." I smile at her.

"Good, go finish packing. I have to make some phone calls," she says, jumping up from the couch. "I'll be in your office; shout at me when you're ready," she says as she saunters down the hall to my home office.

***

"It has not rained like this in months," Lindsay says as she grips the steering wheel, her knuckles white from fighting the wind that is damn near blowing her small sports car off the road.

"Take your time. I guarantee my flight will be delayed because of this weather." She swerves hard to the left to avoid a tree limb that is lying in the road. The sudden shift causes my purse to fall from the back seat spilling its contents all over the floor of Lindsay's car.

"Shit," I mumble, unbuckling myself to reach around and pick up the scattered contents as I shove them back into my purse.

"Sorry," she says as she swerves back into our lane. "This weather is insane."

"You're doing great," I encourage her. I'm nearly all the way turned around, trying to get the remaining items that are rolling around the floor when I hear Lindsay gasp, then scream. The car swerves suddenly and then I'm not sure what happens, but I know we're rolling.

"Reagan." I can hear Lindsay moaning as she calls my name. "Answer me." Her voice is panicked, yet weak. "Reagan, oh God, please," she cries. "Talk to me."

My head hurts, my arm hurts, and my abdomen hurts. The pain is excruciating, so much so that all I can do is cry in pain.

"Reagan, please answer me." Her voice breaks and she sobs. I feel her hand on my arm, but I'm so disoriented, I can't tell where she is. It's dark and I can hear the rain beating down on the car and the wind howling around us.

"Lindsay," I mumble when her hand finds mine. She grasps onto my hand for dear life.

"I can't find my phone," she screams hysterically. Her voice is frantic. "I can't move my leg." I'm trying to process everything that is happening, and all I want to do is close my eyes and sleep. I fight the urge to do so as I try to remain calm and figure out what is happening.

"Breathe… try to calm yourself down," I instruct Lindsay slowly. My words sound slurred and I have to really focus on what I'm trying to say. I know I shouldn't close my eyes, but I have to.

CHAPTER 23

LANDON

My phone has been vibrating on and off in my pocket for the last ten minutes as I finish briefing everyone on the plans to serve a search warrant, and hopefully, take down one of Wilmington's drug suppliers. I've got several detectives, my sergeant, SWAT, and even patrol all gathered together as I inform them how we're going to do this. Everyone is in agreement about where they are supposed to be and when, and how this is going to go down.

"Thankfully, the weather is shitty, which hopefully means our guy will be home and not out and about," I say as I look around the room at everyone. "Any questions?" Everyone seems prepared and, if all goes well, this should be a pretty clean bust— in and out, and hopefully, we'll find the drugs we're looking for.

"Good, let's do this." Everyone gathers their belongings and heads out of the old warehouse where we met and briefed. It's just down the road from the house we're planning to serve. My sergeant is off in the corner on his cell phone as I pull mine from my pocket. Seven missed calls from Matt. Just as I'm ready to stuff the phone back in my pocket, it rings again… Matt.

"Matt," I answer. "Now's not a good time; just going to serve a warrant." I can hear his heavy breathing on the other end of the line.

"It's Lindsay," he says between sharp breaths. "And Reagan."

"What about them?" My pulse quickens and my stomach turns. Instinctively, I know something is wrong. "They've been in a car accident. It's bad, Landon."

"How bad? Where are they? What the fuck is happening?" I scream at Matt. My sergeant pulls my cell phone from my hand and guides me toward the large metal door where our cars are parked just outside. I hear him mumble some words to Matt as he pushes me towards his car.

"Get in," he says. Fear courses through me as we drive toward Memorial Hospital. My hands shake as a million things race through my mind. My sister, Reagan—my baby.

"What happened? What do you know?"

"I just got the call about the same time you did," my sergeant states. He's a no-nonsense kind of man. He always tells it like it is. "From what we know, it looks like the car lost control and flipped several times. It made impact with a tree. Both girls are alive, but it's serious."

Tears sting the backs of my eyes. My heart feels like it could jump out of my chest as we pull into the emergency department at the hospital. We pull right up to the doors where there is an ambulance parked and I jump out. Just inside the door sits a large circular admitting desk and nurses and doctors stand at the desk. I slap my badge on the counter and try to collect my thoughts.

"Lindsay Christianson and Reagan Sinclair," I say. "Where are they?"

"Sir." A young nurse steps towards me.

"I'm Lindsay's brother. Detective Christianson." I pound my badge on the desk. "And I'm Doctor Sinclair's…"

"Sir, please calm down," the nurse says. "We don't know anything yet. They just arrived a few minutes ago. They are both in the care of the best doctors and, as soon as we know anything, you'll be the first to know." I run my hands over my face as I rest my elbows on the tall countertop.

"There's a smaller private waiting room just down there." The nurse points. "You can wait in there and I'll send the doctors in as soon as we hear anything." Her eyes are sympathetic as she gives me a half smile. "Come on," she says, guiding me down the sterile corridor.

Opening the wooden door, which has a long glass panel down the middle of it, I take a seat in a hard chair. "I'll let them know you're in here," the nurse says as she closes the door behind her, leaving me alone with my thoughts. I rest my elbows on my knees and drop my head into my hands.

As I wait to hear from a doctor, a nurse, anyone at this point, my mind races to the last time I saw Lindsay. I left angry this morning because she brought our mom to the house. I didn't say goodbye to her and I was an asshole to her. However, unlike Reagan, I saw her today. I talked to her. Guilt washes over me as I think of how I left Reagan yesterday. I was abrupt and cold, and she was scared. I could see her fear written on her face. She was afraid, panicked, begging me to choose her and I fucking walked away from her.

My knee bobs up and down as I sit for what feels like hours and wait. Karma is a bitch. I think of the hours Reagan sat, alone, waiting to hear from me, and I was too wrapped up in my selfish world to think about how she must be feeling. My sergeant has been pacing the floor outside the room and I've been watching him walk back and forth past the window for the last hour or so. I've been frantically returning texts to Matt, who is just as anxious to find out what's going on—but hasn't been able to get to the hospital yet. I stand up and open the door. Stepping into the cool hallway, I walk in the opposite direction of the admitting desk, where I see Sergeant Daly leaning onto the counter, talking to the nurses.

The hallway is long, cold, and every door is closed. I don't know exactly what I'm doing, or what I'm looking for. I just know I couldn't sit for one more minute in that small room. I couldn't breathe. There is a flutter of activity down at the end of the hallway and I freeze as I see a gurney being rolled into a room. A large door opens and the medical staff are positioned on all sides of the bed.

I press my back against the cold wall and close my eyes. I take a deep breath, inhaling and exhaling, repeating that a couple of times. A sign catches my eye across the hall and I take two long strides and open the door. I step into the dimly lit room and shut the door behind me. The hospital chapel is quiet. There is a cross, a crucifix, and a Star of David all hanging on a wall behind a pulpit. I've never been religious—ever. But something called me to this room.

Taking a seat on the long wooden bench, I drop my head and pray. I pray for the first time in twenty years. I pray to God, begging him or her to spare Lindsay, Reagan, and my unborn baby. I make promises to be a better man, a better brother—and I promise to be a good father. The tears I've been holding back spill over and I choke back a sob.

Even though I'm stressed and I continue to wait, a sense of peace, of calm helps settle me down. I hear the door open and a quiet voice say, "There you are. We've been looking for you." It's the nurse who showed me to the waiting room earlier. I stand and offer a final silent prayer before stepping into the hallway. The nurse smiles at me. "Your sister is settled into a room, and you can see her now."

We walk briskly down the hall and she opens a door, holding it open for me as I step inside. Lindsay lies in a bed, her head propped on a pillow. Her eyes slowly open when she hears the door close as the nurse leaves. Another nurse stands next to the bed and jots notes into a chart as she checks the machines that Lindsay is hooked up to.

"Lan," she whispers.

"I'm here."

A tear slips from her eye as I approach.

"She's a little out of it," the nurse whispers as I get closer. "She's on some good pain meds."

"Morphine," Lindsay slurs and the nurse chuckles. "I love morphine."

"I'll leave you two alone for a minute, but I'll be back. Press the call button if you need anything." She shakes her head and smiles at Lindsay, who is clearly not feeling much at this point.

"Thanks," I say and wait for her to leave the room before I pull a chair from the corner up next to Lindsay's bed and sit down. "Are you okay?"

She nods her head. "Sore. How's Reagan?" she asks, as she seems to become a little more coherent.

"I don't know. I haven't heard anything yet. What happened, Linds? Where were you two going?"

She inhales a shaky breath and closes her eyes. I can't tell if she's thinking or the drugs are still keeping her groggy. "I was taking her to the airport," she mumbles.

"Why?" I cut her off.

"She was going home to Minnesota early. She thought you left her, like that other asshole did," she says quietly. "I offered to drive her so she wouldn't have to leave her car at the airport for two weeks." I grind my teeth in anger when I hear she was going to leave without telling me for two fucking weeks. However, the anger quickly dissipates when I remember I have no update on her or the baby.

"It was storming so bad, and I was driving so carefully." She pauses. "But there were tree limbs and branches all over the road. I was dodging them every half mile or so." Her voice is somber as she touches the IV that is stuck in her hand. "It all happened so quickly, Landon." I reach out and rest my hand on top of hers.

"I swerved to avoid hitting a giant tree that had fallen. I think I overcorrected, but I'm not sure. I remember the car rolling two, maybe three times. I couldn't see her, but I heard her before she quit talking." Her voice trails off.

"So she was talking?" I ask.

"For a minute. Then she stopped. I begged her to talk to me, Landon." Lindsay chokes up. "I'm so sorry. I'm just so sorry," she cries.

"It was an accident. Accidents happen, Linds," I reassure her. The door to Lindsay's room creaks open just a few inches and the nurse who's been keeping tabs on me sticks her head through the door.

"Mr. Christianson, the doctor is ready to speak with you out here." The door opens further and Matt pushes his way into the room.

"How is she?" he asks as he walks to the bed.

"Alive," I breathe. "Can you stay here while I go see about

Reagan and…" I pause. Matt eyes me suspiciously, but doesn't press me.

"Sure. Take your time. I won't leave her." He sits down in the chair I just left.

I squeeze Lindsay's hand and press a kiss to her forehead. "I'll be back in a few minutes; just get some rest, okay?"

"Okay. Landon?" she says. "I'm so sorry. Please tell Reagan I'm sorry."

"I know, and I will." I hurry to the door, anxious to speak to the doctor to get any news on Reagan. Stepping into the bright white hallway, a doctor and nurse stand outside a door just across the hall and catty corner from Lindsay's room.

"Mr. Christianson?" the young male doctor asks as I approach.

"Yes, how is she?"

The nurse looks me over, as does the doctor. "I understand you're the patient's…" He waits for me to fill in the blank on his sentence.

"Boyfriend…" I say slowly.

The doctor and nurse look at each other hesitantly before the young doctor gives me a brief run down. "I cannot legally give you information on her condition. HIPAA regulations. She is sleeping and heavily medicated. In fact, she'll be out for quite some time. Right now, that's all I can tell you." He flips through papers in the chart he's holding.

"She's pregnant and I'm the father." His hand stills, and he looks at me sympathetically. His face is conflicted, as if he wants to give me information, but he suddenly pulls the vibrating phone from his pocket and scrolls through the screen.

"I'm sorry. I have an emergency I have to attend to. I really wish I could give you more information. She should be awake tomorrow when the meds wear off. I will say this though… she's very lucky to be alive." He turns quickly and walks down the long corridor with the nurse on his tail. I rake my hands over my face in frustration. I peek through the long glass window on her door and the curtain is pulled near her bed so I can't see her face. A team of nurses is in the room with her and I crack the door and quietly enter.

My heart races as I near her bed and see her. Her face has a large bandage under her left eye and another across her forehead. Pillows are strategically placed under an arm and under one of her legs. Her face is swollen and her long dark hair is matted. I can see blood that has dried all along her hairline.

"Sir, she's not ready for visitors," the nurse says quietly as she stops writing in her chart.

"I'm… I'm…"

"Sir."

"I know. I just needed to see her," I whisper as I approach her bed.

"You have thirty seconds," the second nurse says as she looks at me sympathetically.

Machines beep and hiss all around me. She's got a blood pressure cuff on her arm and an oxygen monitor on her finger. She's got pads on her chest, monitoring her heart, and that's when I know this is much more serious than I thought it was.

I brush my finger across her bruised cheek and lean in to kiss her forehead. I need her to know I'm here.

"Doc, I'm here," I whisper in her ear. I rest my hand on top of hers and squeeze it gently. "I can't stay, but I want you to know I'm here. I'm not going anywhere—ever." My lips find their way to her temple and press a light kiss to her bruised head.

She doesn't react to my hand squeeze or the kiss. She

doesn't flinch, she doesn't moan—she just sleeps. The light purr of her breathing along with the sounds of the machines is all I hear.

"Sir, you have to leave now," the nurse says quietly. I nod at her and press one last kiss to Reagan's cheek.

"I love you." The words roll off my tongue like I've been telling her this for years. I should have been telling her for months, but I was too afraid. "I'll come back tomorrow." I run a finger over her dry lips. I quietly leave the room and walk back across the hall to Lindsay's room.

Matt is sitting on the side of her bed, holding a glass of ice water as she sips through a straw. "I need Mom's phone number," I announce. Matt and Lindsay look at me like I've lost my mind, and I'm damn close too.

"How's Reagan?" Matt asks.

"I don't fucking know. She's knocked out on meds, but nobody will tell me shit for privacy reasons." My tone is mocking.

"So why are you calling Mom?" Lindsay asks, confused.

"Just give me the number please," I plead with her.

"I don't know where my phone is. I lost it in the wreck."

"Goddammit," I mumble. "I'll be back. Matt, can you please stay with…"

"Of course, I'm not going anywhere," he interrupts me.

Three phone calls later and I pace in the hallway outside Reagan's room. After calling the office where Reagan works and speaking with their emergency dispatch, I was able to reach

Adam Gerard. Reagan's business partner, and my stepbrother—it's so weird, I don't even want to acknowledge that right now. What I do want is for him to get me information on Reagan—and stat.

I can hear the clicking of shoes in the barren hallway and I see Adam with my mom hot on his heels. "Where is she?" my mom asks loudly and frantically. I nod to the room across the hallway. She veers off track from Adam and flies past both of us as she rushes into Lindsay's room.

Adam stops in front of me. He's a hair taller than I am, with dark hair and features. He really hasn't changed since I saw him last, which was over fifteen years ago. I've got him by at least twenty to twenty-five pounds, though. We continue to size each other up before he finally breaks the silence. "What you're asking me to do is highly illegal," he says through gritted teeth.

"What I'm trying to do is get some fucking information on my girlfriend and baby." I take a step toward him. Our chests are damn near touching. He exhales loudly and drops his head as he takes in what I'm asking him to do. I take a step back and watch him—hoping that he will get me the information I'm so desperate for.

"I'll see what I can find out," he says as he pulls his white coat on. His hospital credentials hang from the pocket. "Give me a few minutes and meet me down in the cafeteria. If they see me talking to you here, they'll know I'm giving you information." I nod to acknowledge him and watch him disappear into Reagan's room.

I insert a dollar into the vending machine and pull the bottle of water out, finishing it in three swallows. I sit at a small table with a small vase of flowers in the center of it. There are a few people scattered throughout the large cafeteria, and two TVs blare, CNN loudly filling the quiet cafeteria with the voice of Anderson Cooper.

"Hey." His voice comes from behind me. He rounds the table and pulls out the chair directly across from me.

"That was fast."

"She's still out. She's on some heavy pain meds. I read her chart, checked her vitals, and left. I shouldn't have been there in the first place." He runs his hand through his hair as he looks around the cafeteria. Finally making eye contact with me, he leans into the table. "I could get in a lot of trouble…"

"Shut it, Gerard. I'm not going to tell anybody that you told me anything," I snap at him. I take a deep breath and exhale loudly. "Look, I'm tired, and irritable, and it's fucking killing me not to know anything."

"She's going to be fine," he cuts me off. "She has some facial lacerations, which the best plastic surgeon in Wilmington already stitched up. She has some bruised ribs, possibly broken, a pelvic fracture, and most likely a serious concussion. The CT scan showed that there is no bleeding on the brain, which is good; and she didn't break any other bones other than the pelvic fracture which will heal in time." His voice trails off.

"Thank God," I whisper and drop my head into my hands. My elbows rest on the table and I rub my tired eyes.

"But…" He pauses as he rubs the stubble on his chin as his eyes drop to the table.

"But what?" My hands fall from my face.

"There is no baby." His voice is quiet as he delivers the news.

"What do you mean there is no baby? She was never pregnant?"

He scratches the top of his head and closes his eyes. "She

256

lost the baby in the accident. There was noted vaginal bleeding and an ultrasound confirmed the pregnancy and then the loss." He pauses. "There was some pretty serious abdominal and pelvic trauma. I'm sorry," he says. "I don't mean to drop this on you and leave, but I need to go." I nod my head and try to swallow, but my throat is dry and I can't swallow against the lump that has formed. Pushing himself away from the table, he apologizes one last time and leaves.

I clench my fists in anger. This can't be happening to her again. She's lost one baby; she cannot possibly lose a second. If I hadn't walked out on her, she wouldn't have been trying to leave for her trip a week early. I curse at myself and drop my head into my hands, pulling at my short hair in frustration and anger.

"Landon." The quiet feminine voice of my mother comes from behind me.

"Now's not a good time, okay?" I don't even bother to look at her.

"There is never a good time for the news you got today," she says, sitting down in the chair Adam just exited. "I'm so sorry," she says quietly.

"He told you?"

She nods. "I just passed him as I got off the elevator. I came to get some coffee for Matt. Adam thought maybe you'd need me." I actually chuckle at those words.

"I've needed you so many times throughout my life and you weren't there. I think I can manage this alone as well." I push my chair back abruptly and stand up. "Go sit with Lindsay; she might *need* you."

"Sit down." Her voice is firm and loud. I look at the small-framed woman who is sitting across from me and I am at a loss for words. "I know you are angry, hurt, and upset... and I haven't been there for you when you needed me most, but I'm here now, goddammit."

"I'm sorry, but you haven't earned the right to scold me anymore. I'm no longer eight years old. I'm thirty, and I can handle this without you." I turn and walk away. I know I'm an asshole and right now, I don't fucking care. The only thing that matters to me is being there when Reagan wakes up.

After three verbal arguments, the threat of a lawsuit, and finally a visit and some sense talking from Mac and Gemma, the hospital staff allowed me to sit in Reagan's room. For the last three hours, I've sat, walked, stood, and paced in damn near every square inch of this room, never taking my eyes off of her.

I promised Mac and Gemma I would call them when she woke so they could return, but there was no sense in all of us staying here, waiting for her to wake up. I will do that. It's my job to take care of her now. I've wiped the remaining traces of dry blood from her face and hairline with a wet washcloth, and I've applied Chapstick to her dry lips. That's all I've been able to do without knowing if I'm causing her any pain. Within the last hour, she's slowly started moving. Her fingers twitch, or her head rolls to one side.

The nurses have been checking on her every thirty minutes, and I watch every move they make and every letter they write in her chart. I sit on the edge of the bed and run my fingers through her long hair, working to release some of the tangles as a nurse changes out her IV bag.

Warm fingers find my wrist and I am still waiting to see if

she's really awake. A gentle squeeze confirms my hope. "Hey, Doc," I whisper and rub her cheek. I turn to the nurse and she moves around to the other side of the bed. "There's a nurse here; are you able to talk?" Her eyelids flutter open and then close again for a few seconds before she's able to open them and squint.

"Thirsty," she manages to say. I reach across her to the rolling tray and pull off the small Styrofoam cup that holds ice water. I hold the straw and place the end of it against her lips. She tries to lean forward, but lays her head back down with a moan.

"Don't push yourself, Doc," I say and adjust the bed just a bit so she doesn't have to lean forward. The nurse begins running through a checklist of yes or no questions with Reagan as I hold her hand and rub her wrist. Reagan watches me intently while answering the questions. The nurse excuses herself to go find a doctor and leaves Reagan and me alone for the first time.

I run my knuckles up and down her cheek softly, careful not to apply pressure. She flinches as I near her bandage. "I'm sure the doctor will explain everything to you, but you've got some cuts on your face, some bruised ribs, and a fractured pelvis. You're so lucky, Reagan." She closes her eyes and gives a slight nod.

A small laugh escapes her lips. "No wonder it hurts to breathe. It feels like I was hit by a train." I give her hand a reassuring squeeze.

"Thank God it wasn't a train; it was just a tree," I say sarcastically. "I don't know what I would have done if..." Words fail me, and tears fill my eyes. We still and silence fills the air around us. "I'm just so thankful you're going to be okay," I finally finish. "I'm so sorry, Reagan."

She fakes a small smile. "We have a lot to talk about, but I'm kind of under the weather at the moment," she says dryly. The door opens and the room is suddenly immersed in medical staff, two doctors, three nurses, and me. There isn't enough room for all of us. I press a quick kiss to her lips. "I'm going to go grab a coffee while they check you out. I'll be back in five minutes, okay?"

"Okay," she whispers as I press another kiss to her lips. I want her to know I'm coming back. I'll always come back.

CHAPTER 24

Reagan

Everything hurts. Every muscle, every bone, every organ—hurts, aches. But it's my heart that is broken into a million little pieces. My eyes scan the empty room as my lungs struggle to find air. My bruised ribs are causing me from being able to inhale deeply, not that I could anyway at this moment. The doctors and nurses excuse themselves, promising me that this isn't how car accidents like the one I was involved in usually end up. I heard the phrase "you're very lucky" for the eightieth time in the last thirty seconds, but none of that matters. The one thing I cared about is gone—again.

The door opens and Landon steps into the room. I notice his normally bright blue eyes are dull, marked by dark circles under them. I didn't notice how exhausted he looked earlier. The look on his face when he sees me tells me he already knows—he knew before I did. In two long strides, he sets the cup of coffee he's carrying onto the tray table and takes a seat on the edge of my bed where he was seated before.

"Doc," he says quietly. I just shake my head from side to

side, my chin quivering. I'm not sure I can form any words.

"They told you?" he asks quietly as he rests his hand on my forearm. I can feel my lips begin to tremble and I drop my eyes to the hand that is holding onto me. "Fuck," he murmurs as he tries to lift my chin to make eye contact with me.

"Looks like you're off the hook," I manage to choke out before my throat closes up.

"What did you say?" he asks. His voice is quiet, but his tone is angry.

"I said you're off the hook. Everything always has a way of working itself out, doesn't it? Now there's really no reason for you to stick around. You have no obligations to anyone except yourself," I spit at him, my tone venomous. "Isn't that what you want? Your freedom?" I yank at my arm, trying to break free from his grasp, but he won't let go of me. "Now would be a really great time for you to leave, okay? You're great at running, so go." I lay back and rest my head on the pillow and the tears I've been holding finally spill from my eyes.

"You're hurting and I'm sorry," he whispers. He releases his grip on my arm, but pulls my hand into his and laces his fingers through mine. I don't try to pull away. "But I'm not running anymore—ever."

I choke out a sarcastic laugh, and he narrows his eyes at me. "I love you, Reagan. Baby or no baby." The words *I love you* fall from his lips naturally. They're not forced like I expected them to be the first time he says them. "I love you and I'm not going anywhere."

More tears break free from my eyes and roll down my face and into my hair. "Can you please call Gemma for me?" I ask him. I know I shouldn't be asking him for any favors right now, but I need Gemma.

"Of course," he says quietly.

"And please go. Leave me alone."

"That's not going to happen, Reagan." He stands up, dropping my hand. He hovers over me with the look of pure agony on his face. My head is throbbing in pain, my chest hurts, my abdomen hurts, but more importantly—I feel like my heart has been ripped from my chest. "I won't leave you alone, because it's you and me, babe. You. And. Me. We're undone." He points his finger at me and motions between us. "You know when we're done? When one of us is dead. Until then, we're undone. Do you understand? I'll leave you alone right now so that you have some time, and I'll call Gemma, but I'll be back tomorrow, and the day after, and the day after that."

A sob breaks free, and I gasp for air. "I love you, Reagan. And for the first time, I'm not afraid to admit it." His voice breaks. His breathing is rapid and his chest heaves with each breath he takes. "I love you," he says again, as if I didn't hear him the last two times.

"Go, please," I cry and I hide my face behind my hands, embarrassed of my behavior. I love him and I need him, yet I push him away. Minutes later, I pull myself together and lower my hands to find he's left me—just like I asked of him.

The bright morning sun creeps through the slats on the small metal blinds in the hospital room. "Shit," I mumble as the ray of sun hits me right in the eye. My hand fumbles around as I reach for the remote to adjust the bed, moving my head out of the direct line of sunlight that is determined to blind me.

I push the button and elevate myself to an almost sitting position, but the pressure on my pelvis is too much and I quickly lower myself again. I press the call button on and wait for a nurse to come. While I wait I focus on trying to take deep breaths without my ribs hurting—but everything from my chin down still courses with pain. The door opens quickly and a nurse enters quickly with a boisterous "Good morning!"

I offer her a quiet "Good morning" in return.

"How are you feeling?" she asks warmly.

"Can you adjust the blinds so the sun isn't hitting me in the eye?"

"Of course, and breakfast should be here soon. Are you able to sit up to eat?"

"I don't think so. I just tried to sit up, but the pressure on my pelvis and ribs is just too much yet."

"Okay, I'll help you," she says as she twists the blinds into a new position.

"No, I'll help her." His voice is strong and demanding. He didn't leave. He's here just like he said he would be. The nurse looks at me and I offer her a small smile.

"Well, then, you just call me if you need me," she says as she leaves the room. Landon stands just inside the door, watching me. His eyes are fixed on me and he is determined to get his way.

"I thought I told you to leave," I snarl at him.

"You did, and I told you last night. I'm not going anywhere."

"So it doesn't matter what I want, huh? You're just going to bully your way into my life even though I don't want you there?" His eyes fall when I say those hurtful words.

"I don't believe you don't want me here, Reagan. I think you're hurting—badly. In fact, I know you are. But trying to push me away when you need me isn't going to work," he hurls back at me.

"Stop it!" Gemma's voice is sharp and loud and she pushes her way into the room. Uncle Mac stops at the doorway.

"He's right," she scolds me. "You're hurting, Reagan—and you have every right to hurt, but what you don't have a right to do is push away someone who loves you because you're angry. I made that mistake. It's the biggest regret of my life. And when I finally realized that, it was too late." Her eyes shift sideways to Mac, who stands with his hands stuffed into his pockets. Landon backs away from the foot of my bed as Gemma approaches.

"Landon, I think maybe you should leave us alone for a little bit," Gemma says. She walks over to him and pulls him into a quick hug.

"Come on, boy, let's take a walk." Mac beckons him from the doorway. He looks tired, weak—and I know the cancer is breaking him down.

"I'll be back in a few minutes," Landon says, looking at me as he walks backwards toward the door. He turns and meets Mac, shaking his hand, and they disappear into the hallway. I close my eyes and wait for the verbal beating that Gemma is going to hand out.

"Don't push him away," she says quietly as she stands next to me. Taking my face into her hands, she leans in and presses a kiss to my forehead. "That boy…" She pauses and looks around the room before looking back to me. "You need each other."

"I need time," I say, barely audible.

"No. You need to let him love you. That's all. Reagan, you're a stubborn girl. You love him, and he just admitted he loves you. Lean on him. Let him lean on you. That's what a relationship is all about. There will be hard times—and this is one of those times, but stop pushing him away," she sighs loudly. "He hasn't left your side in three days. He hasn't slept, he's barely eaten, and he almost caused a goddamn riot trying to get to you. He loves you," she sighs. Although I feel like a child being scolded, I know Gemma is right.

"Why do you always have to be right?" I smirk at her.

"I'm not always right, Rea. I've learned a lot—I've made a lot of mistakes, mistakes I don't want you to make." She smiles softly at me.

For three days, my room has been a revolving door of visitors, doctors, nurses, and coworkers. Now that the swelling around my ribs has subsided a little, the doctor wants one more round of x-rays to ensure I've only got bruising before they send me home. I still feel like hell, I'm not going to lie. This morning, I walked for the first time in four days, if that's what you can call taking three steps. Breathing still hurts and to roll myself out of bed is pure hell.

Landon has been a permanent fixture here and has only left twice to shower and change. We still haven't really talked. I assume he's giving me the "time" I requested without actually leaving me alone. It's a bizarre situation—us. We haven't said a word to each other in four days, yet he knows what I need even before I do. He anticipates and is prepared for everything. He has water ready when I'm thirsty, a pillow ready to prop up my head when I sit up—yet I never have to ask him for anything.

"Today's the day," the doctor says as he sets down his chart on my tray table. "You've been cleared to go home, so long as you promise to take your pain meds and check back in with your primary care physician for regular check-ups to ensure you're healing."

"I think I can manage that." I smile back at him, excited to finally be free of these four white walls.

"I expect at least another four to six weeks of recovery time before you return to work, Reagan. Maybe even consider reducing your hours for a while after that," the doctor says as he checks the bruising on my ribs. "Stitches will come out next week." He points to my head. "Call Doctor Lombardi's office to schedule an appointment. Physically, you'll start feeling better soon." He pauses. "Emotionally, it will be much longer. Remember, this is just one chapter in your life. Turn the page and start a new one, Reagan."

"I will." The room is quiet as the weight of those words settles in. Landon never takes his eyes off of me and Gemma sits quietly with her hands folded in her lap. The silence is uncomfortable and the doctor finally wraps up his orders.

"No driving for a couple of more weeks and definitely not while on the pain meds," he instructs. "I know you're a doctor and you already know this, but I have to tell you anyway," he says with a laugh and I offer him a small smile. "What are your plans for care when you get home?" he looks back and forth between Gemma, who has been a fixture in the chair next to my bed, and Landon, who hasn't left my room for four days.

Gemma looks at Landon, then to the doctor before she quietly announces, "She'll be staying with me—for now," she sighs. Looking back at Landon, she says, "Lindsay will need your help for a couple of more days." He nods slowly in agreement.

"Well, then, it looks like you're all set to go. I'll send for a wheelchair and here are your discharge papers." He sets the stack of papers on the tray table to the side of my bed. "Take care of yourself and don't push it." He raises his eyebrows at me.

"Thank you, doctor."

"Landon, can you help her while I go get the car?"

"Of course," he says quietly and we both watch Gemma shuffle out the door. I glance at the stack of clothes Gemma brought for me to change into, and grab the white tank top. Pulling it over my head, I'm careful not to touch my ribs.

"Here, let me help," Landon offers, moving quickly to my side. He unfolds the black yoga pants and holds them low so that I can easily step into them. Pulling them up my legs, he's careful not to touch my hips. "Are you okay?" he asks. I realize these are the first words we've spoken in days and I can hear the exhaustion in his voice.

"Yeah. My pelvis is sore, but my ribs hurt more." He drops a pair of flip-flops onto the floor and I carefully step into them. He holds my arm to help balance me and the mere contact from his touch sends my aching body into overdrive. I've craved his touch. He senses my need and pulls me carefully into a sweet and caring embrace. No words are said as he holds me in his arms— the only place where I feel at peace.

Our moment is cut short by a light knock on the door. "Sorry to interrupt," a soft voice says. A young girl pushes in a wheelchair and her eyes widen when she sees Landon. For someone who hasn't slept in two days, he still looks like he stepped off the cover of a GQ magazine. His short hair is messy, but it looks like it was styled that way, and his two-day facial hair growth gives him a perfectly rugged look. His dark denim jeans are offset by a light grey t-shirt that make his eye color change from blue to grey and stand out against his tan skin.

"Here," he says as he pulls the soft black jacket over my

shoulders so that I can slip my arms into the sleeves.

"Thank you," I say quietly as I take two small steps toward the wheelchair. He moves quickly, helping me sit down as comfortably as possible.

"Ready?" the young girl asks, and I nod my head. She releases the brake on the wheelchair and begins pushing me toward the door. I look over my shoulder to see him with his back against the wall, his head hung.

"Stop," I say to the girl. "Can you give us just a minute?" I ask her. She looks confused, but steps around the front of the wheelchair.

"Yeah, I'll wait in the hallway. Just let me know when you're ready." She closes the door behind her.

"Lan..." I don't even finish saying his name before he's standing in front of me. I push myself up from the stupid wheelchair and our eyes meet. I haven't even begun to speak, but I'm overcome with emotions, making it hard to form the words I need to say.

"It's okay," he comforts me. He's holding onto my arms, his thumbs rubbing circles through my thin jacket.

"I just need some time, okay?"

His hands still and his eyes search mine for answers. "So what exactly are you asking of me?" he asks.

"Just... give me some time alone," I breathe.

"Why?" he says, looking confused as his hands fall from my arms slowly. "Don't run away from me, Doc."

"No one is running. I just need some time, okay? A lot has happened, and I just don't know..."

"That's all I needed too, Reagan. Some time to let things settle and you accused me of leaving you," he interrupts me. His voice is quiet, yet I can tell he's frustrated, maybe even angry.

"But I needed you."

"And I need you." His voice breaks. His eyes search mine, pleading with me—begging me to change my mind. I wrap my arms around my waist and drop my eyes to my feet. "You know where to find me when you're done needing *time*. I'm sorry I hurt you, Reagan, but two wrongs don't make a right." His voice is hushed as he backs away from me toward the door.

"I'm sorry too," I whisper, but never lift my head to look at him as he slips through the door and disappears.

CHAPTER 25

LANDON

Days.

Weeks.

Nervously, I wait in this warm church. North Carolina summers are hot and humid and this church and its rickety air conditioning are doing nothing to cut the heat. I fidget with the buttons on my suit jacket as the low sounds of an organ begin to play. One by one, the bridesmaids and groomsmen file down the aisle, arm in arm. Lindsay is last, the maid of honor and Reagan's best friend. She catches my eye and offers me a little wink as she mouths the words "love you," and takes her place up on the altar.

The entire church stands up and turns around when the familiar music plays. Bright light from the stained glass windows illuminates the aisle as she begins her walk. I've never seen a more beautiful woman. Her long dark hair is pulled up and a simple long veil trails behind her.

When her eyes meet mine, she offers a simple, stunning smile. Arm in arm with her father, her blue eyes twinkle with unshed tears—happy tears. Peaceful contentment is what I see in her face when her father sets her hand in his. *His* not mine.

I jolt awake, my heart racing and sweat trickling down my temples. I groan in frustration when I look at the clock taunting me. I wake up almost every hour on the hour. I haven't slept well in weeks—since Reagan walked away.

It's been three weeks, twenty-one of the fucking longest days of my life. I haven't seen her, or heard from her—but I think about her every goddamn second of the day. Every woman I see reminds me of her, except they're not her. No one will ever compare to her. Gemma provides me with brief updates on her progress: she can sit for longer periods of time, her walking is improving, her ribs are still tender—but her heart is irreparably broken. So is mine. I am lost without her.

It has taken every ounce of self-control to not call her, text her, or stop by Gemma's to check on her. The human mind's ability to fuck with you is simply amazing. I wake up to the scent of her, even though she's not here. I feel her soft hands run across my body as I try to sleep, and I feel her presence even though she's miles away.

I stumble from my bedroom down the hallway, toward the kitchen, to get myself a glass of water. The light from the TV is on in the living room and I find Lindsay on the couch under a blanket, watching infomercials.

"You couldn't sleep either?" she says quietly.

"Bad dreams," I grumble. She pushes the blanket off her legs and pats the soft leather cushion next to her. "Sit down." I sit next to her and she lowers the volume on the TV. "Still haven't heard from her?" she asks.

I shake my head.

"You know," she says, picking at the blanket. "It wasn't too long ago that I urged her to fight for you—to not give up on you."

"She gave up," I interrupt her.

"No, she didn't. She needs you to fight for her. You can tell her all day long how much you love her or care for her, Lan, but show her."

"Why do you always have all the answers?" I joke with her.

"Don't do anything stupid like hold a boom box blaring Peter Gabriel in front of her window, wearing a brown trench coat and green pants while standing in front of a 1975 Chevy Malibu, though." She laughs. "But *show* her."

"The fact that you just recalled an entire scene from a movie by memory, down to the make and model of a fucking car, scares me." We both laugh.

"I'm good for useless movie information, plus you love me."

"Always, Linds."

***

Gemma was right when she told me I could find her at the beach. She sits in the sand, almost at the water's edge, her long legs bent with her knees pulled up to her chest. The morning air is crisp, causing her cheeks and nose to pink slightly.

"Ready to do this, big guy? Let's go get our girl." I rub behind his long, soft ears. Ollie, who I adopted and is now mine, gives my hand a little lick and stands up, his tail wagging violently. She saw me watching her from the table that sits high up on the bluff, so I'm not surprised when she doesn't startle as the sand crunches beneath my feet as we near her.

She turns to make eye contact with me, but then looks away. Her dark, beautiful hair whips around in the breeze, and I can smell the light hints of her perfume as I get closer. She stands and hesitates as I approach, wiping sand from her bottom.

"Hi," I say cautiously.

"Hi," she whispers back, looking down to her feet, then to Ollie, who stands next to me. My stomach flips when she drops her eyes from mine. For me, that is a sign of mistrust—hurt. My greatest fear, aside from losing her, is that I hurt her beyond the point of being able to fix it.

I'm at a loss for words. Weeks of emotions and feelings sit on the tip of my tongue, waiting to roll off, but I'm frozen in fear that she will reject me. For once in my life, I have to break out of my comfort zone, or I may lose the only thing that I have ever loved more than myself. I clear my throat and take a deep breath,

"I love you." It rolls from my tongue quietly. "I love you more than anything in the world." I repeat it a second time so she knows she heard it correctly. She looks up at me cautiously. I told her in the hospital that I loved her, but for some reason, this time, it feels like she heard me—that maybe she believes me.

"Do you still trust me?" I ask her. She has every reason to say no. I have walked away from her, pushed her away too many times to count. She has chased me until now and I have done nothing but push her further away.

"I always have." Her voice is quiet. I nod and exhale loudly and take a step closer to her.

"I always thought I had the answers to everything. That I could never be wrong, but I was. I never thought I needed anyone, but I now know that's not true, Reagan. I need you. These last three weeks without you have been a living hell for me. Whoever said that time heals all wounds is a fucking liar, because time has done nothing but suck the life from me. When you're not with me, I can't think straight. I physically hurt without you by my side. You make me want to be someone better, someone you deserve." I reach out and pull her hands into mine.

"Please come home to us. You are everything I want and need. I will give you ten babies if that's what you want. I'd be fine with just two, but if you want ten—I'll give you ten." A small smile tugs at her full lips. "And I'll buy you a house with a white picket fence and a tire swing that hangs from a giant tree in the front yard. I will give you the whole fucking fairytale, just come back to me." I'm damn near begging her. My voice is shaking and full of emotion and for the first time in my life, I know. I know the path I want. I stand at those crossroads and I choose the road with her.

She pulls one of her hands from mine and wipes the tears that are falling from her striking blue eyes. My heart races as I watch her shaking hand wipe the tears, and I don't know if those are tears of sadness or happiness.

"I'm done running from you because I should have been running to you the entire time. You are where I need to be. You are my safe place and the only person who has ever loved me unconditionally. I was so afraid you would see the real me and leave, that I ran from you, but I'm done running, Reagan." Tears roll down her soft cheeks. I'm done making her cry. I'm done hurting her. "I can't promise it will always be easy, but it will always be perfect for *us*." I take her face in my hands and wipe her tears.

"I love you, Reagan. I choose you. I will always choose you—choose *me*."

275

"It's only ever been you," she whispers, and buries herself in my arms. She holds onto me, like I've never been held, and this time I'm never letting her go.

EPILOGUE

LANDON

"I said get her some wine and distract her, not get her fucking wasted," I hiss at Lindsay through closed teeth. Reagan sits on a stool at the kitchen island, giggling with Matt and a couple of girls from the doctor's office. I can't help but stare at her and think how lucky I am that she is mine.

"We're just waiting for Mom and Louis," she whispers back, snapping me out of my thoughts.

"Well, where the fuck are they? And figure out a way to cut her off. I want her to remember this."

"Really? You're asking me where they are? And what do you expect me to do, snatch the glass of wine out of her hand? Or should I just make an announcement that she's having far too good of a time and should really stop sipping the vino?" She rolls her eyes at me. I hate when she does that.

"Sorry we're late!" My mom bursts through the door with a bouquet of flowers. Reagan jumps up from the island to greet them and pulls my mom into a hug. She hands me her glass of wine, *thank God*, and takes the flowers from my mom. "Reagan, you look beautiful," my mom says, standing back to look at Reagan. She does. She's wearing a black strapless pantsuit that hugs her long curves.

"So do you, Josie. I love that necklace." Reagan returns the compliment and hands the bouquet of flowers to me. She gives me a little wink, which means go find a vase and put these in water. I know every thought she's thinking before she ever has to tell me. That's how it is with her—she is the other half of me.

"Louis," Reagan says as he reaches out and pulls her hand to his lips. He places a kiss to the top of her hand and she blushes.

"Reagan, you're simply stunning—and tall!" He laughs.

"Everyone, please, let's sit down to eat," I say as I stuff the flowers in a crystal vase and try to gather the small crowd of our closest friends and family to the dining room table, but everyone excitedly stands around in small groups talking, not hearing a word of what I've just said.

Setting the vase of flowers on the kitchen island, a sexy voice whispers in my ear from behind me, "Would anybody notice if we slipped away for a couple of minutes?" Her arms snake around my waist from behind. She trails her long fingers over my stomach muscles.

"There's no way we'd be gone for just a couple of minutes—because what I have planned will take hours," I whisper back at her. She squeezes me and giggles.

"Promise?"

I twist around in her arms and hold her. In her heels, she stands as tall as me, and her legs travel for miles. Her blue eyes are striking against the dark pantsuit and her long dark hair. "If you can help me gather these assholes so we can eat, I can get them out of here faster and then we can…" She presses a kiss to my lips, stopping me.

"Deal," she says. "All right, everyone—sit!" she says, taking over the room. Everyone follows her to the long table that is covered in more china than I've ever seen before, truly a touch of Reagan. Reagan prepared a delicious meal with the help of a local caterer—prime rib, grilled salmon, and enough side dishes to feed a small army. I sit back and look at the table of our friends and family eating, smiling, and laughing and wonder how, in just a year, my life is so seemingly different—better. Lindsay is whispering something to Matt and he laughs. She better not ruin this surprise. Louis sits with a protective arm around my mom's shoulders while sipping a glass of red wine.

To have my mom sitting at my dining room table is something I never imagined happening. With the help of Reagan and Lindsay, we've forged a new relationship. It has not been an easy road, but I'm finding that when I choose the roads that aren't guaranteed to be easy, I'm finding the best surprises along the way. I'm excited to have her back in my life and look forward to sharing many more years with her.

"So." I push my seat back and stand up. Reagan places her napkin on the table and joins me at my side. "Reagan and I have an announcement." The dining room quiets suddenly and everyone looks around. The girls all gasp and Lindsay reaches for Reagan's left hand. Reagan pulls it back quickly and shakes her head.

"So a year ago, I met this beautiful lady." I pull Reagan's hand into mine, lacing our fingers together. "We've had a crazy year—lots of ups and downs and new beginnings," I smile at her. My mom's eyes fill with tears and she leans into Louis as I continue.

"Reagan and I wanted to bring our closest friends and family together to say thank you for supporting us, but to share some exciting news with you." I step back from Reagan, dropping her hand before I pull out the large board that I stashed behind the large plant in the corner.

"Reagan and I are selling our homes and building a house—together." I hold up the sketch of the house that Reagan and I hired an architect to draw up. It's the perfect combination of classic and modern, Reagan and me.

"That's it?" Lindsay bursts out. "I thought you're going to get engaged." She sets her drink down animatedly. Everyone laughs, and Reagan is buying right into this.

"Pfft," Reagan snorts. "We love each other, Linds... but don't hold your breath on an engagement anytime soon. I mean the look of anxiety on his face when he had to sign for a mortgage loan with me, you should have seen it. He was sweating..." She pauses when she looks around at everyone's faces. The room is silent again and Lindsay has her hands covering her mouth. Matt is sitting next to her, smiling, and my mom is damn near hysterical, crying.

"Reagan," I say, getting her attention. She turns around slowly and looks down at me on bended knee.

"What are you doing?" she asks with a look of concern on her face. "Get up."

"Reagan, I know we invited everyone over here to tell them about our new house—but there's something else I want to do while they are all here." Her eyes open a little wider and her body stills. Sheer terror grips at me as I reach into my pocket and pull out the little black velvet box I've been hiding for weeks. Picking out a ring that is perfect enough for her was singlehandedly the hardest thing I've ever done. There is no diamond, no gold—no gem beautiful enough to describe my love for her.

"A year ago, I met a girl in a bar." Everyone laughs quietly.

"And she changed my life." She smiles down at me. "And while our path wasn't always smooth, it led us to here." Suddenly, Reagan drops to her knees in front of me. Her arms are shaking as she lifts her hands, clasping them in front of her chest.

"What are you saying?" she asks me, her voice breaking.

"I want more than just a house with you. I want a family, I want a future, and I want to be the last person you love. Will you marry me?"

"Yes," she says. "More than anything in the world, yes."

From Safehorizon.org

FACT:
Most domestic violence incidents are *never* reported.

- Help change the facts. Speak up, speak out, and make a difference for victims of domestic violence.
- Every year, more than three million children witness domestic violence in their homes.
- Children who live in homes where there is domestic violence also suffer abuse or neglect at high rates (30% to 60%).

Call for help (llámenos para ayuda) **1.800.621.HOPE (4673)**

Turn the page for a brief look into the companion novel,
Unforgiven
Lindsay and Matt's story

PROLOGUE

"Well, that went better than I expected." I breathe a sigh of relief as I slide into bed next to Matt.

"Because it's been obvious to everyone around us what's been going on for the last year. We clearly suck at being discreet, Lindsay."

"I'm just glad we don't have to lie anymore."

"We weren't lying; we just weren't being open about our relationship," he says, wrapping his naked, lean, yet muscular body around me.

"I guess, but it just didn't feel right, keeping us a secret."

"I like when you say *us*." He presses a kiss to my lips, then behind my ear.

"I like it when you do that," I whisper, "and I like it when you..." My work cell phone begins ringing, interrupting us.

"Leave it," Matt growls in my ear.

"I can't." He rolls off of me while I reach onto the nightstand and glance at my agent's name flashing on the screen.

"It's Jack," I mumble as I jump out of bed and pull on a robe.

"Jack," I answer curtly.

"Lindsay, I presume you've gotten my three voicemails, two emails, and endless text messages. Why the hell haven't you returned one of them?"

"We had an important family dinner. I'm sorry." I notice Matt slide out of bed and step into a pair of chambray-colored pajama pants. His tan skin is perfection against the light blue. He leaves the room while I talk in a hushed tone with Jack.

"Lindsay, this isn't an opportunity to pass up," he says, his voice becoming louder. Jack is my agent and one pushy motherfucker. "People kill to get into a market the size of Phoenix. The money is phenomenal, the exposure…"

"Phoenix," I whisper as I pace the bedroom. "I need a couple of days," I respond, a million thoughts swirling through my head.

"A couple of days, Lindsay?" Jack repeats me.

"Did I stutter, Jack? I need a couple of days. When we had lunch last week, you mentioned looking for other opportunities, but I didn't realize it would happen so fast and so fucking far away. Do you have any idea where Phoenix is, Jack?"

"It's in Arizona, Lindsay. Listen to me. If you don't take this job, it will be the biggest mistake of your career." His husky voice pulls me from thoughts of everything I'll miss if I leave Wilmington.

"Two days, Jack. I need two days. Give me that. Stall them."

There is a large sigh on the other end of the phone, and what sounds like a hand hitting a table. "You have until noon on Friday."

"Thank you, Jack." He disconnects the phone without saying goodbye. I know he's pissed. I catch a glimpse of Matt leaning against the doorframe of the bedroom. His head has fallen forward and he stares at the ground.

"Talk to me," I say as I walk over and wrap my arms around him.

"What do you want me to say, Lindsay? It sounds like you have a great opportunity—and I'll be damned if I'm going to be the person to hold you back from that." His dark brown eyes meet mine.

"What would you do if you were me?" I ask him.

"That's easy. I'd choose you because I love you and you mean more to me than any job or any opportunity. But Lindsay, I will not stop you from chasing this dream. You will live with your decisions for the rest of your life. I never want to be a decision you regret." He pulls away from me as he turns toward the hallway. "But promise me something, will you?" I nod at him as a lump forms in my throat. "Follow your heart. I know you better than you know yourself and I know how your brain works— listen to your heart." I hear him shuffle down the hall toward the kitchen.

I have no idea how long I've been standing, staring at that damn phone when I pick it up and hit Jack's name on the recent calls screen.

"Lindsay," his deep voice drawls.

"I'll do it." My voice shakes. "I'll take it." My heart sinks and tears fill my eyes.

"Welcome to Phoenix, Sweetheart."

My legs are weak and my hands shake as I second guess my decision to leave, knowing I very well may be making the biggest mistake of my life. Sliding down the wall I've been leaning against for support, I wrap my arms around my knees as I try to calm myself. Glancing back at the open door, I see Matt standing in defeat, broken. His brown eyes are grim, lost, while his face says everything my heart is feeling—shattered.

ACKNOWLEDGEMENTS

This is almost harder than writing a novel. There are always endless amounts of people to thank and I always worry I'm going to miss someone.

Thank you to my family for living with me when I'm excited, angry, sad, delusional, and insane. When you live with characters that talk inside your head, it always makes for an interesting environment. But mostly, thank you for your never-ending support, even when it means sacrificing the most precious thing we have together—time.

Thank you to my readers. There are not enough thank you's to go around. Thank you for loving *Unbreakable* and forcing me to write Landon's story. I loved that you all fell in love with a beautiful, dark, damaged man named Landon. I hope you will continue with this series and love Lindsay and Matt just as much.

Cisco: Thank you for answering every single stupid question I had about law enforcement, and for letting me crawl around in your head for a bit. Your stories, your advice, your opinions helped shape this book and I'm eternally grateful (and you're not off the hook yet—Matt's a cop too!)

Amy, Molly, and Kristen: I still love *us*.

Lauren: Thank you for loving *Unbreakable* and helping me brainstorm for *Undone*. It amazes me that friendship can blossom from a single message and grow into something beautiful. Thank you for your friendship and your help. I adore you.

Christine Estevez, thank you for being the biggest supporter, the biggest champion, the best blog tour host, and an amazing friend. I love you to the moon and back.

My beta readers: thank you for your input, advice, and guidance. You have no idea how much I appreciate you.

My street team girls: especially, Virginia and Kelly. Thank you for your endless support and keeping me sane when I have my "moments." Love you all!

Regina Wamba: I'm not sure there is a better cover for this story. You are amazing... but more importantly, you are the kindest person I've ever met. Caribou—soon! Love you.

Bloggers: Thank you for loving *Unbreakable* and promoting the hell out of me, and now *Undone*. Without you, I am nothing. Your support means the world. Thank you.

I'm sure I've missed a million of you. I'm so thankful to everyone for your support! I hope you loved *Undone* as much as I loved writing it and I can't wait to share *Unforgiven* with you.

CONNECT WITH REBECCA SHEA

Website: www.rebeccasheaauthor.com
Facebook: www.facebook.com/rebeccasheaauthor
Twitter: @beccasheaauthor
Goodreads: www.goodreads.com/goodreadscombeccashea
Email: rebeccasheaauthor@gmail.com